Every Sunday

Books by Peter Pezzelli

HOME TO ITALY

EVERY SUNDAY

Every Sunday

Peter Pezzelli

KENSINGTON BOOKS

KENSINGTON BOOKS are published by

Kensington Publishing Corp.
850 Third Avenue
New York, NY 10022

Kensington and the K logo Reg. U.S. Pat. & TM Off.

ISBN: 0-7394-5905-8

Printed in the United States of America

To my mother, Norma

Chapter 1

Sit down, let's talk. Relax. I've got a few things on my mind to tell you about, so pay attention. Who knows, you might learn something. For starters, the word around here, that nobody dares question by the way, at least not too loudly, is that God has some sort of master plan that He's using to keep things in order. Don't believe it. Between you and me, sometimes you can't help feeling that the Big Guy's just making it all up as He goes along, know what I mean? It's like He's one of those performers who's trying to keep all the plates spinning up in the air over his head. He keeps trying to put more and more of them up there, except in this case some of the plates fall and break now and then no matter how hard He concentrates. So He tries to do the reverse, to not think about it while He's doing it, to just go with the flow so to speak. This doesn't necessarily make things any better, but it doesn't seem to make them worse. The same number of plates, more or less, get broken. Anyway, it's hard to know for sure what God's up to, He never talks much about it, but that's the way I see it. How else can you explain life and the never-ending lunacy we all put ourselves through? You just do the best you can, I guess, and hope it all works out in the end. But hey, nobody ever said it was gonna be easy, right?

Whatever.

So, it's like this. I'm having this off-the-wall nightmare about a dinosaur. You know the kind of dream I'm talking about, the kind that leaves your skin crawling and your whole body feels like a wet rag. It's brutal. The dinosaur's this big son of a bitch of a thing. It's huge and hideous and snarling and it's stalking me through the city, tearing down telephone wires and tossing cars and buses out of its path as it stomps along. I mean, it's coming for me, you know?

So there I am, running down the sidewalks just ahead of it, and suddenly all these people are calling to me from the doors of the shops and offices. Friends and family members and people I'd done business with over the years, some who had died long ago and others I haven't seen in ages, they're all there shouting, "Yo, Nicky, you stupid bastard! Hide in here where you'll be safe!" But before I can make a move, the beast appears at the corner, looming over me, and now I know it's no use. My fate's sealed.

So I run and run and run, a hundred percent sure I'm going to be eaten alive at any moment. Last thing I remember is that my lungs and legs feel like they're burning up, like somebody's filled my body with a bottle of crushed red pepper. I can hardly run and the dinosaur is gaining on me fast and it's right at that instant when I feel the hot, steamy breath on the back of my neck—that gut-twisting realization that those terrible jaws with their daggerlike teeth are about to snap shut on me and snuff out my puny little life forever—that I wake, open my eyes, and look about the room.

No sign of the dinosaur, just my wife and daughters hovering over me.

"*Azzo,* what is this, a staring contest?" I grumble. "I'm not dead yet."

At that the four of them burst into sobs. A nurse comes in and helps my wife to the chair while the other three keep carry-

ing on. Teresa looks awful, worse than I feel. Eyes swollen and
bloodshot, her hair a tangled mess. I sigh and close my eyes once
more. The constant wailing's giving me *agita* and I'm thinking,
why couldn't I have just gotten run over by a bus or something?
At least then it would all have been over with quickly. And where
the hell's the priest? Would the whole thing ever end?

You have to understand that this scene of constant lamenta-
tion has been going on for the three days since the surgeon
opened me up, took one look at the sorry state of affairs inside
me, and decided there was no point in even trying. He sewed me
right back up and told the family it was only a matter of days.

Like the doctor was telling me something I didn't already
know. I'm no fool, I knew my number was up weeks ago. You
can just sense these things. But I went through the motions, the
endless tests and consultations, just to appease everyone. Otherwise they would have driven me crazy. But it was all for show, I
knew it was a waste of time. These things happen; you can't live
forever. And who'd want to? Besides, I've had a full life, watched
the kids grow up, seen my daughters married off, have children
of their own. I have no complaints.

The dream about the dinosaur, though—that still bothers
me. What the hell was all that supposed to be about anyway?
Thinking about it really pisses me off. You'd think that on my
deathbed, God might grant me a dream about Raquel Welch or
Gina Lollabrigida or any woman for that matter, just as a farewell
gift, if you know what I mean. Instead I have to get the crap
scared out of me by the Creature Double Feature.

So I keep turning it over and over in my head, trying to
figure out what it was that scared me so much about it. Tell you
the truth, it wasn't the fear of death. I never bothered to worry
about things over which I had absolutely no control. So maybe
it's something deeper, I'm thinking. Then my son comes to
mind, and like a beam of sunlight bursting through the clouds, it

all becomes clear to me. So I open my eyes and scan the room for him.

"Where's Johnny?" I grunt.

"Downstairs, Pop," says my daughter Nina. "He went for a smoke."

"Well, get him up here," I tell her. "We need to talk."

Chapter 2

Let me introduce you to Johnny. At the moment, the poor kid's a wreck. This I know because he's smoking a cigarette and the only time he does that is whenever he's really nervous. Calms him down. He's thinking, how could Pop be dying? What's to become of the family and how would he ever run the store all by himself? He crushes out the cigarette and blows a last puff of smoke into the air. He's sure it's gonna be a disaster.

Johnny's the youngest of the four kids, my long-awaited heir after three girls. It never mattered to me that he was the baby of the family; he's my only son. Fathers love their daughters to distraction, but there's something special between a father and his son. I can remember joking about it with people in the shop while Johnny, who was just learning to walk, used to toddle around like a little demon, tearing everything off the shelves. All I could do was laugh and pat his head. As far as I was concerned, God's sun rose and set on my son Johnny. He was the future. The business, I always figured, would need a man to run things one day after I was gone, and the only man in line was Johnny.

Of course, no one ever told him or me that I'd be checking out so soon. So Johnny starts thinking of his sisters, knowing full well that they're not going to be much help to him in the business. All of them are married with kids, except for Gina who,

God willing, will probably have some before long. Their husbands all have jobs of their own, so he can't rely on them either. Not that he would have in any case. I was very fond of my sons-in-law, still am, but I always taught Johnny not to trust them completely. How could he? They aren't part of his blood. Of course, you can never be sure even when somebody *is* part of your blood. Best thing to do is not trust anybody on a regular basis, I guess.

So, you see, it was ordained from the day of his birth that one day Johnny Catini would be running the show, that is, if he ever found time between shooting pool and chasing skirts. I mean, he was still going through that stage guys go through when it seems like there's nothing to life but booze and broads. Some guys go through it faster than others. Some guys never get all the way through it. So you can understand then why this whole thing is giving Johnny a pain in the gut. He figures he's just not ready for it, you know?

Johnny sighs and leans against the wall, watching the people hurrying in and out of the hospital. It's one of those weird days that late August sometimes gives you to remind everybody that summer's just about history and fall is coming. It's damp and chilly out and the dark clouds rolling through the afternoon sky are all twisted and gnarled like a loaf of Sicilian bread. A steady drizzle is falling. Shivering a little, Johnny digs his hands into his pockets and wonders why the hell they don't allow smoking inside anymore where he'd at least be warm.

Johnny's in a tough spot now. You know, I'd always did my best to take care of things for him, especially whenever he got himself into a little scrape. You know how it is. Little things, like I had a few friends downtown in the traffic court to take care of his speeding tickets; otherwise he'd be paying through the nose for his car insurance. And I was pretty friendly with most of the city police, so I smoothed things over for him whenever he and his friends got a little too rambunctious at the bars. I mean, routine stuff, nothing major. Johnny's always been a good kid.

But it's time for the kid to start acting like a man and it's sinking in that he doesn't know nobody except the bunch of coconuts he likes to pal around with. They're good at helping get him into trouble, but not so hot at helping him get out. Not like his old man who, Johnny figures, knew just about everybody in the state of Rhode Island. It's funny, but I can see how he would think that. I mean, Rhode Island's a pretty small place. You stick around long enough and pay attention, you get to know who's who and what they can do for you—and what you can do for them.

"Johnny!" someone calls from behind him. It's his sister Gina, waving for him to come inside.

"*Azzo*," he mutters. He shrugs himself away from the wall and trudges to the door. Gina takes him by the arm and leads him toward the elevators.

"What are you doing out there all by yourself?" she says tersely.

"I wanted to be alone for a few minutes so I could think. That a crime?"

"No," she says in a gentler voice. "I guess we all could use some quiet time to ourselves. Things have been pretty crazy, haven't they?"

"*Uff*," Johnny grunts. "What's goin' on up there now?"

"Pop wants to see you," she says, her eyes getting misty. "I don't think it's gonna be too much longer."

Johnny lets out a sigh and puts his arm around her shoulder. "Come on," he says as the elevator opens, "let's go up and see what the old man wants."

Chapter 3

So everyone—aunts, uncles, cousins, friends, relatives, and bene-factors—is milling around outside my room when the two of them come down the corridor. They all turn and look at Johnny.

"Where have you been?" his mother cries.

Johnny's got that look on his face—you know the one. It's like you see him thinking, here we go again. "I was out having a smoke," he answers.

"Mary mother of God!" she explodes. "Your father's dying of cancer and you're out smoking cigarettes!"

Teresa's probably got a point, but it's a tense situation, you've got to give the kid a break. As a matter of fact, he even says it.

"Gimme a break, Ma, will ya?" he says, rolling his eyes. Wrong thing to do.

"I'll give you a break," she screams. "I'll break your head for bein' so stupid!" She turns to the others. "He's just like his father, thick in the head!"

Teresa can be a force of nature when she's worked up, so Johnny knows better than to argue with her. Instead he just turns away and heads over to the door to my room, where his Uncle Victor is standing guard.

"What's goin' on, Uncle Vic?" he asks. "How come every-body's hangin' around out here?"

Victor lays a finger aside his lips. *"Shh,"* he whispers, "the priest just went in."

That's my cue. "Hey, Johnny, is that you out there?" I call.

Johnny sticks his head into the room. "Yeah, it's me, Pop."

"Come on in," I tell him.

Johnny comes in and sees the priest making preparations to perform the last rites on me. The priest gives him a kind smile then goes about his business, setting the vestments, prayer book, and a bottle of holy water onto the bedside table.

"Johnny, this is Father Giuliano," I tell him. "You'd know him if you ever showed your face at mass on Sunday."

Johnny gives this nervous little cough and shakes his hand. "Hi, Father," he says. "Thanks for comin'."

Father Giuliano nods and turns to me. "I thought you might want to make your confession, Nicholas," he says in that solemn voice that only priests can do. "I assume you will want some privacy."

"Yeah, you're right, Father," I tell him. "Would you mind waitin' outside while I talk to my son?"

Before the startled priest can even respond, Johnny's got him by the arm, ushering him to the door. "Don't go away," he tells him, "this shouldn't take long." With that he pushes Father Giuliano out into the corridor with the relatives. The poor guy doesn't know what to make of the situation, so he looks at the others and shrugs.

Back in the room, Johnny closes the door and comes over to my side. He sits on the edge of the bed and looks me straight in the eyes. Funny, but just then I get this flashback to when Johnny was just a little kid, maybe five or six. He used to come over to the side of my bed every morning at the crack of dawn and wake me up. I can still see him staring at me with those big eyes, trying to get me out of bed to play with him or make him breakfast or something. All of a sudden I get this big wave of guilt over me because I'm thinking about all the times I just rolled over and pulled the covers over my head when maybe I should have got up and spent some more time with my boy. But hey, you do the best you can do, right?

"What's the matter, Pop?" says Johnny.

Before I can talk, I get hit with one of these coughing fits. It's horrendous, like my whole body is going into convulsions or something. It makes Johnny wince just to watch, but it doesn't last too long.

"What's the matter?" I finally start wheezing. "Well, for starters, how about the fact that I'm about to roll a seven any minute?"

"Pop, why do you gotta say things like that?"

"Why? Because it's true."

"Believe me, I know that," says Johnny. "But you don't have to rub it in. So what is it you gotta talk about that you can't tell me in front of the others?"

One thing you can say for Johnny, he likes to get straight to the point. So I sit up and look past him to the door. "You sure that door is shut?" I ask.

"Yeah."

"*Eh,* what difference does it make," I sigh, settling back onto the pillow. "They probably all have their ears to the door anyway."

Johnny's also a little short on patience. "Pop, are you gonna tell me what this is all about or what?" he says.

"All right, sit," I tell him, pointing to the chair next to the bed. "What I've got to say is important."

Johnny gets off the bed and pulls up the chair. "Okay," he says, "now I'm sitting."

Now I'm just studying him for a time, and I can feel the furrows in my brow deepening. You've got to understand, I got things on my mind at this moment and I want to make sure it all comes out the right way. So I start rubbing my chin, which is an old habit of helping my mouth form the words I want to say when things get tight. Sounds strange, but it works. At last I take a deep breath and figure it's time to forge ahead.

"What the hell," I begin, "I'm about to die anyway, so what's to worry about?"

"You tell me," my son answers.

"Okay, here it is," I say. "There comes a time when a father has to talk to his son like a man, to teach him about the important things in life, to ask—"

Johnny holds up his hand. "Hold on, Pop. I think we already had this one about fifteen years ago when I turned thirteen."

I don't know what it is about this kid, but sometimes he makes me want to slap him in the head. Two seconds and he's got me all agitated. Know what I mean?

"This is something different!" I yell, throwing my hands up. "Why don't you just sit and listen for once?"

"All right, all right," he says, rolling his eyes. "Just get on with it."

"Okay," I say, starting over again, "let's make it easy. I got two things I wanna ask you before I croak."

"Will you stop talkin' like that!" he cries. Now it's my turn to roll my eyes.

"Look," I tell him, "the first thing is simple. I want you to find somebody, a good woman, and settle down."

"*Ayy*," sighs Johnny, turning away. Now I've got him squirming a little.

"I'm serious," I continue. "You can't go on forever chasing all these little *putannas* around like you do."

"Hey, they're not all *putannas*," says Johnny.

"You know what I mean. Now shut up and listen to what I say. It's time to start thinking about marriage and having a family and children to carry the name forward. You're my only son, the one who'll carry on the name. These things are important. If you wait too long, nobody's gonna want you. Before you know it, you'll be an old man all by yourself and then you end up ex-tinct like these dinosaurs you read about."

He looks at me. "What do you mean, stink?"

I can't help it, I slap myself in the forehead. "EX-tinct, *capo-dosso!*" I cry. "While you're at it, maybe you should go back to first grade for a while."

"Stink, stank, stunk, who cares?"

"I care. We're talking about your future here."

"I thought you were talkin' about dinosaurs."

The kid can be dense, no question about it. "Johnny, Johnny, Johnny," I say in exasperation. "Just try to understand what I'm telling you for a second. I want you to be happy, to have some-one to take care of you. I want you to have children because, otherwise, your life comes to nothing in the end. Just promise me you'll think about these things, that you'll at least try to settle down."

"Yeah, all right," he says with a sigh. "I'll think about it."

"Good," I say, a little bit relieved. If I can get him thinking, at least it's a start, I figure.

"So what's this other thing you wanted to talk about," says Johnny.

The heat's on now and I got a knot the size of an oil tanker in my gut. Who knows how Johnny's gonna take this. I glance at the door and gesture for him to come closer. "All right," I say in hushed tones, "what I'm about to tell you stays between you and me and you take it to the grave. *Capisc'?*"

Johnny just shrugs.

"Now what I have to tell you, I tell you as one man to another. And what I ask you, I ask as one man to another."

"Get to the point, Pop," says Johnny. "You're wastin' so much time here that I'm gonna be dead of old age myself before you tell me what's on your mind."

"Okay," I sigh. "Here it is. You know I've always loved your mother. I couldn't have asked for a more wonderful wife. I would have become nothing without her."

"Yeah, so?"

"Well, something happened a few years ago."

"What?"

"Something."

"What is this, Pop? You're like talkin' in code here. Spit it out!"

"There's been another woman," I finally blurt out.

You know, I really couldn't predict how Johnny'd react to this thing. Wasn't what I'd hoped. He just stares at me for a minute, and little by little his eyes start to pop out of his head. He cocks his head to one side, like maybe he hadn't heard me right.

"A *what?*" he says.

"A woman."

Now he's out of the chair with this astounded look on his face and he's just staring at me, shaking his head. "Are you tellin' me," he starts, "that for all these years while Mommy was cookin' and cleanin' and sewin' your socks that you were out scorin' some *putanna?*"

I have to offer some protest here. "She's not a *putanna,*" I yell. "She's a nice woman!"

"She's a *putanna!*"

"You don't even know her."

"I don't have to. All I know is that you're a married man and any woman who screws around with a married man is a *putanna* in my book."

"Ugh," I groan.

Johnny's beside himself now, pacing back and forth. "How could you do this to Mommy?" he's saying. "After all she's done for you."

"What do you want me to say?" I sigh wearily. "These things

just happen. Nobody plans them. I thought you of all people would understand."

"Yeah, right, Pop. And how long has this been goin' on?"

I squirrel up the corner of my mouth, which is another habit I have when I'm in a spot. "I dunno," I tell him. "Three, three-and-a-half years maybe."

"Whoa," is all he can say. He collapses back onto the chair and stares out the window. For a long time neither of us says anything. The silence is almost deafening. So I close my eyes for a minute and, I don't know, I guess I nod off for a second because all of a sudden Johnny's shaking my arm to wake me up.

"What's the matter!" I snap.

"Geez," says Johnny, breathing a sigh of relief. "I thought for a second that you were—you know . . ."

"Yeah, I know, but I'm not. Not yet anyway."

Johnny sits back down and rubs his eyes. The whole thing is blowing his mind; I can see it in his face. I can understand. I mean, hell, this kind of thing can turn your world upside down.

"Why did you even have to tell me about this?" he grouses.

"Because I need you to do something for me," I say. "Just one last favor."

"I don't even know what you're goin' to ask me and already I don't like the sound of it."

"Just listen," I tell him, "and try to understand. I love your mother, but these things are beyond people's control. They just happen. Blame God. He arranged it so that I met this other woman, the sparks flew between us, and that was that. But I don't want you to think it was something cheap, because I really care for this person and she cares for me. That's why I want you to do this favor."

"And that is?"

My back is starting to bother me, so I shift around uneasily in the bed and settle back down on the pillow. "Obviously," I begin, "she's a little upset about what's happening to me just like everybody else. The thing is, it all happened so fast that I haven't really had a chance to talk with her and say goodbye. She hasn't been able to come to the hospital because your mother and sisters have been here night and day, and once I'm gone, she'll probably be too scared to come to the wake. I haven't even had two seconds to myself to call her on the phone. So, you see, it's like I'm just disappearing from her life. You know what I mean? Now, I know how you feel and it's understandable. What I'm asking you to do is to set aside your feelings for just a while. Think of her as just a person with all the same human faults as you have. All I want you to do, just once after I'm gone, is to stop by, knock on her door, and check on her. See how's she's doing. See if she needs anything. Just tell her that I was thinking about her and that I wanted to make sure she was all right. Tell her I'm sorry that things worked out this way. We're talkin' five minutes here, Johnny. You're in, you're out. That's all. If you could do just that for me, at least I'll have a little peace of mind. What do you say?"

Johnny shakes his head. "I dunno, Pop," he says. "I don't even know this woman. I'd feel stupid."

"Please," I beg him. "You've got to do it for me."

"But who is she, what does she do?"

"She's a schoolteacher in the city," I tell him. "Her name's Victoria Sanders. Vicki, I call her. She lives on the East Side. You'll find her address in the phone book."

"But—" he starts to say. Before he can finish, I'm like in convulsions again, retching up my lungs. I reach out to him.

"Please, Johnny," I start pleading. "I'm on my deathbed here! Just say you'll do it. I haven't got much time and you're the only one I can trust."

Johnny throws up his hands. "All right, all right," he finally agrees. "If that's what you want, I'll take care of it—as soon as I think the time is right."

At those words, I can feel myself calm down once more. "Good," I say, breathing easier. "You're a good son, Johnny. I knew I could count on you."

"Sure, Pop," he says, forcing a smile. "I'd do anything for you. You know that."

I smile back at my son because I know he means it. "I do," I tell him.

"Just tell me one thing," Johnny says, leaning closer. "Was she the only one?"

I gotta hesitate now. "No," I finally admit, "there was one other, but that was before and I didn't care about her the way I care about this one. Satisfied?"

"Yeah, I guess," says Johnny.

"Good. Now go get Father Giuliano for me."

Johnny's eyebrows meet his hairline. "Don't tell me you still need to confess."

"It's a long story," I sigh with a shrug.

"I don't wanna hear it," says Johnny. So he bolts for the door and calls for the priest.

Chapter 4

Okay, so try to imagine this: You're at the show, watching this really intense movie. I mean, you're so deep into it that you forget about everything else and everything around you. You forget about yourself. Who you are. Where you came from. What you did. Who you did it with. Understand? Now, the main character on the screen is so believable that you think you can see what he's seeing, feel what he's feeling. His pain, his joys, his sorrows. It's so staggeringly real and manipulative in its effect, that you get drawn right into the whole make-believe world and for the entire time you're sitting there that's all you know about anything.

That's the movies—at least when they do it right. But life is not so different. It's like you're up there on the big screen, doing all these crazy, wonderful things for an entire lifetime, and then all of a sudden, the show ends, the lights come on, and you realize that you were never really up on the screen to begin with, you've been in this other place all along. What's more is that there are all these other people milling around, watching your show for a while then ducking into the theater next door to see what *they're* showing. Outside in the lobby, everybody's coming and going, talking about this show or that show. "How's it going in that one?" someone might ask. "Tell me when it gets to the good part." It's kind of weird, actually, but you get used to it.

So, your show's over. You get up and start walking to the exit because that seems like the thing to do. But sometimes you stop and turn around and look back at the screen, you know, like those people who like to watch the credits at the end of the movie. God knows why. Who cares who the key grip guy was? Anyway, you look back at the screen and you realize that there's still something going on up there; it's just very dim because of all the light you're walking into. So sometimes you go back and sit closer to the screen, and you discover that if you focus really, really hard, you can see that the movie is still going on—it's just going on without your character in it. So since everything is still fresh in your mind, and you figure you've got nothing better to do, you decide to stay and watch for a while, just to see how things turn out. It's sort of like watching a sequel. But of course, the powers that be don't like it when you hang around too long, watching the same show that you just got bounced out of, so sooner or later you get yanked out. Then later on there's this little question-and-answer session about the whole thing that you have to put up with, but I'm not supposed to talk about that.

Anyway, that's the way things are where I am now. If I want, I can know way more stuff than I ever did before. I get to peek in on what's happening and occasionally look back at what's already happened. The future is a little more tricky. Of course, whenever you're talking about, I'm not allowed to interfere, but I can still throw my two cents in from time to time.

You'll see what I mean.

Chapter 5

So, the wake, by any standard, is a big success. No question about it. Vito Bombarelli is looking out his office window and smiling with secret satisfaction at the line of cars he sees waiting to get into the funeral home parking lot. Traffic that evening is still backed up along Broadway in both directions. Been that way since they opened the doors for the afternoon viewing. With all due modesty, this is one of those big wakes that other funeral parlor owners just dream about, but Bombarelli's hosts with regularity. Anyone who's anyone gets waked at Bombarelli's Funeral Home; what can you say, he's the biggest and he's the best.

Bombarelli turns away from the window and checks himself out in the mirror. He's straightening his tie, thinking about how they're all in there gaping in wonder at how well Nicholas Catini looks. You'd never even know that he was dead. What a miracle worker is Vito Bombarelli!

But one thing's bothering him. It's the flowers. He can't figure out why I insisted there be none at the wake. The way he sees it, it ruins the look of the room. Caskets are supposed to be surrounded by piles of flowers from everybody under the sun, especially when someone so well known is laid out. If nothing else, it diverts attention from the deceased.

I had my own reasons for telling Teresa to nix the flowers, which was part of why I wanted the wake at Bombarelli's. Other undertakers might have pestered the family about it, but Bombarelli knew better. He and I went way back—not exactly as friends; it was more of a mutual respect thing. We were alike in a lot of ways, just simple men who took pride in what they did and shared what they had. We'd both gone into business at virtually the same time years ago when we were young and tough and just trying to establish ourselves in the community. It takes balls to hang your name out on the front door of your business, believe me. I admire anyone who does it. Once you do it, that name stands for something, so you gotta make sure it stands for something good. You stake your claim and slug it out through thick and thin to make things work. It might take years, but you dig in and stand tall. You serve your family and friends and neighbors, and if you're lucky, you earn a bit of quiet respect from all of them that's worth more than all the gold in King Solomon's mines. That's just the way it is.

Anyway, Bombarelli peeks out at the family and can see that they're all holding up pretty well. Draped in black from head to foot, Teresa and my daughters are sitting in line at the foot of the casket. Their job is to look suitably convulsed with grief while everyone and his brother files by and offers condolences. Johnny's the only one who stands throughout the proceedings. He dutifully shakes hands and thanks people for coming. If you watch him for a while, it almost looks mechanical. No matter what someone says to him, he simply smiles, shakes hands, and says, "Thanks for comin'." Knowing Johnny, if someone at that moment were to ask him if he wanted to go out for a pepperoni pizza, the response would probably be the same.

All in all, though, I have to admit that they've been putting on a dignified show. No one has made a scene by collapsing in a faint or throwing themselves on the casket. No surprise there. Teresa has a heart of gold, but a backbone of forged steel. She'd never stand for any nonsense from the kids or anyone else for that matter.

Bombarelli knows that, but like just about everyone else, he's watching Johnny, wondering if he's made of the same stuff as his old man. Can he step up to the plate and produce now? Can he build on the foundation I leave behind? Bombarelli thinks of his own sons and asks himself the same question. Life, he well knows, is built on nothing but uncertainties—save one.

So, he looks again at the flowerless casket and clicks his tongue. To each his own, he decides. If that's the way Catini wants it, that's the way he gets it. Flowers or not, the bill's gonna be the same. Bombarelli gives a satisfied sigh and strolls out to watch the multitudes as they pass in awe of his creation.

Undertakers, you gotta love 'em.

Anyhow, Johnny barely notices Bombarelli; he's too astounded at the endless line of people streaming into the place. How many friggin' people did his father know? he's asking himself. Watching them all traipse past the casket, he can't help thinking that I must have been friends with half of Rhode Island—and the other half was all my cousins. Johnny is seeing people that night he hasn't seen in a hundred years. We're talking second cousins here, third cousins, old friends of the family. The room is full of talk and laughter. It's more like a friggin' family reunion than a wake.

The best part for Johnny is the chicks. It seems like every broad he ever dated is coming out of the woodwork—and they all look good in black. Johnny casts his gaze over to the door and spies another familiar pair of legs waltzing in. They belong to Angela Antonelli, an old girlfriend from the neighborhood. I knew her family pretty well. Her father's a builder, one of my very first customers when we opened the store. Long time ago that. We were good friends. I can remember Teresa and I visiting the house when Angela was born. She was just this little thing, but she grew up very nicely.

Of course, Johnny hasn't seen Angela in ages, not since she gave him a backhander in the mouth after she'd caught him putting the moves on her sister who, by the way, has grown up quite nicely herself. But Johnny figures that was a long time ago and bygones can be bygones.

Wrapped in a short black leather skirt and tight knit blouse, Angela struts in on stiletto heels, her hair and face done up to the max. She kneels at the casket for a respectable time, makes the sign of the cross, and gives me a little pat on the hand. As she stands, Johnny lets his eyes roam from her blouse and skirt all the way down her legs to her shoes. It's always amazed him that she's able to prance around on those heels without going ass over teakettle. Nonetheless, he has to admit that she still looks good, damned good as a matter of fact. Angela, her eyes wet with forced tears, slides straight past him to his mother, bends down, and gives her a hug.

"Angela," his mother cries, "it's so nice of you to come." As if Angela wasn't going to come, but Teresa always liked her. I think she always figured Angela was the one Johnny would settle down with.

"I'm so sorry, Mrs. Catini," weeps Angela.

"I know, honey," says Teresa bravely. "Thank you so much." She lets Angela pull away, but holds tight to her hand. "We haven't seen you in so long," she sighs.

"I know," Angela replies, straightening her blouse with her free hand. "I've just been busy, but I promise to stop by soon." She gives Johnny one of those sideways glances.

"Good, good. Don't be a stranger," says Teresa, giving Johnny a nudge. "Look, Johnny, it's Angela."

"I can see that, Ma."

Without so much as a glance at his sisters, Angela turns to Johnny and throws her arms around his neck. "Johnny, I'm so sorry about your father," she sobs, pressing her body against his.

Johnny lets her squeeze him tight. He likes the scent of her perfume and the feel of her hips beneath the leather skirt. She pulls back just a little and looks up at him.

"Are you gonna be all right?" she says.

"Yeah, I think so, Ange," says Johnny. He was feeling better every second. Believe me, I know my son.

Her arms still draped around his neck, Angela starts running her fingers through the hair on the back of his neck. "If there's anything I can do," she says with this furtive look, "even if you just need somebody to talk to, you know you can call me."

Listen, I know Johnny feels bad about me, but I also know that he's thinking that if this is what grieving is all about, he figures he'll have an easy time adjusting. So he leans closer and whispers in her ear. "Maybe we could get together later on—for a drink," he suggests. "Why don't I give you a call when we're all done here?"

Angela, looking very pleased, smiles and kisses his cheek. "I'll be waiting," she assures him.

Johnny watches the gentle sway of her hips as she walks on through the line. He's happily musing over the prospects for the evening when his gaze meets that of his sister, Gina. Gina's giving him daggers. She stands and comes quickly to his side.

"This is a wake," she snips, "not a nightclub."

"You coulda fooled me," says Johnny.

Before Gina can get on his case anymore, someone else comes through the line from the casket. The face is familiar, but Johnny can't quite put a name with it. Probably some old friend of the family or maybe a long lost relative of mine, he's thinking. Doesn't matter. He stops in front of Johnny and says something about being very sorry. Johnny, his thoughts drifting back to Angela, just smiles and thanks him for coming.

Chapter 6

The next day people start arriving early for the funeral procession. A thin drizzle is falling from the gray morning sky as they file into the funeral home and sign the register. Bombarelli's there, orchestrating the entire show, announcing the order in which those in attendance would drive their cars and reminding everyone to please turn on their headlights. Bombarelli's got every detail planned down to the second. After thirty years in the business, the guy knows precisely how long it takes a funeral procession to get from his funeral home to every church within a twenty-mile radius. And why shouldn't he, he gets paid enough. The hearse pulls out of the parking lot at precisely nine-fifteen. The line of cars falls in behind and slowly winds its way through the streets of Federal Hill toward the cathedral in downtown Providence.

Johnny looks out the limousine window and smiles as they pass in front of Catini's Hardware Store. A nice touch, he's thinking, Pop would have liked that. I did actually.

"Look," sobs his mother from beneath her black veil, "we're going right by the store." His three sisters, who haven't stopped bawling since they closed the casket at the funeral home, look out the window. "Isn't that beautiful?" she goes on. "That Bombarelli, he thinks of everything."

"He should for all the money we're payin' him," says Johnny.

"Money, money!" Teresa screams. "You're just like your father, always worrying about how much money you're spending. If your father had spent less time worrying about money, he probably would never have gotten sick."

Johnny doesn't know when to just shut up. "All I'm sayin'," he says, "is that the guy's not cheap, that's all."

"Just drop it, Johnny," says Gina, giving him a gentle kick in the shins. Johnny rolls his eyes and goes back to looking out the window while his mother and sisters go back to crying.

When they arrive at the cathedral, Bombarelli directs the mourners in first before personally ushering the family to its pew in the front row. With the cathedral's enormous organ blaring away in majestic tones, they roll up the casket alongside and position it in the center of the aisle.

Johnny gawks at the church's soaring columns and spectacular artistry above. Gazing up at the angelic scenes painted on the ceiling, it looks like the very roof opens up to heaven. Now, Johnny doesn't go to mass much, but this place always knocks his socks off. Mine too, when I had socks. The money they must have spent to build it!

Johnny glances over his shoulder and sees Angela a few rows back. The sun had just been rising when he left her apartment earlier that morning. He'd barely made it home in time to start getting ready for the funeral. Teresa was having a bird by that time. When their eyes meet, Angela gives him this almost imperceptible smile, then nods toward the altar to make him pay attention. She's really a good girl; she knows how to behave in church.

But Johnny doesn't. As he turns back around, he catches sight of a woman slipping into the church through one of the side doors near the front pews. More precisely, he catches a glimpse of an intriguing pair of legs as they move through the folds of the dark raincoat she's wearing. A silk scarf shrouds her hair and face as she hurries down the side aisle to the back. From the distance, Johnny can't tell if he knows her. He lets his eyes follow her, straining to keep her in view without turning his head completely around like that little girl in *The Exorcist*. To his disappointment, the woman kneels somewhere in the back, disappearing behind the sea of faces. The voice of Father Giuliano reciting the opening prayers brings his attention back to the altar. Gina leans her head on his shoulder. He takes her hand and tries to listen up.

It's a nice service. Getting buried out of the cathedral isn't cheap either, so Father Giuliano makes sure that people get their money's worth. He lets Maria and Nina do a couple of readings. Then Gina does all the prayers of the faithful, you know the let-us-pray-to-the-Lord part. Later, Father Giuliano gets up there and says all these nice things about me in the sermon, recounting my years of service to the community, my sense of duty, my devotion to my family. All that crap. Johnny tries to pay attention, but after a while he finds it hard to keep his eyes open.

Before you know it, though, the mass is over. The family stands and follows Father Giuliano back down the aisle toward the doors as the congregation looks on. It strikes Johnny just then that this is how it works when you get married. The bride and groom are always the last ones in and the first ones out. As they near the back of the church, he scans the pews for the woman in the dark raincoat, but she's nowhere in sight. He gives one last quick look around before he steps outside into the open air, where the morning's light drizzle has turned into a steady rain.

Chapter 7

Johnny's happy when they finally make it to the cemetery; I can see that. It's like the light at the end of the tunnel for him. He's figuring the service at the burial site probably won't last long and then they're outta there. Huddled under umbrellas, everyone gathers around while Father Giuliano reads a bunch of prayers and throws holy water on the casket, like it's not wet enough already from the rain. I mean, it's pouring like a bastard. Johnny's not listening too closely to the priest. He thinks he hears him saying something about being in the mist of life or the mist of death or something like that when he sees her again, the woman in the dark raincoat from the cathedral. Though she keeps herself at a discreet distance from the rest of the gathering, she's close enough for Johnny to recognize her shapely legs and the slender figure beneath the raincoat. Maddeningly, her umbrella is tipped just enough so that all he can make out of her face is the sleek outline of her chin and jaw. Now and then he catches a glimpse of her lips and mouth, but nothing more. So now it's driving him nuts, trying to figure just who she is.

At long last, Father Giuliano finishes up with the dust to dust and ashes to ashes and they-could-all-go-in-peace routine. People begin to file past the grave, tossing flowers onto the casket. Johnny cranes his head to see over them, hoping to catch her attention so he can talk to her after. To his disappointment, the woman has disappeared again. When the last of the mourners passes, Johnny gives a disgruntled sigh and trudges off to the limousine with his mother and sisters.

Funerals are a pain, but me, I used to like the feast after everything was over. It always seemed to put everybody back on an even keel. Sometimes they were almost fun, but for Johnny, this one's a pain in the nuts. Back at the house, Uncle Victor has him cornered in the living room, lecturing him on something to do with the business. Johnny's pretending to listen even though he and I both know that his uncle doesn't know squat about the hardware business. The house is full of people smoking and drinking and eating. Johnny's aunts have been cooking for two days to make sure there's enough for everybody. On the table there's a nice roast, some sliced provolone and cold cuts, two big bowls of pasta, and a pan of lasagna along with an enormous salad, vegetables, Italian bread, rolls, and two jugs of wine. A big pot of coffee is brewing in the kitchen. Beside it on the counter are stacks of cups, two cakes Johnny's Auntie Louise baked, and a tray of assorted cookies.

"You've got to keep track of your inventory or people will rob you blind," Victor is telling him.

"Yeah, you're right," says Johnny, stifling a yawn. He looks about the room, hoping to find someone to get his uncle off his ear. Gina comes to the rescue.

"Johnny, what are you doing?" she says, taking him by the arm. "All the food is getting cold. Come on, let me get you something to eat. You guys can talk later."

"She's right," says their uncle. "Go have something to eat, Johnny. You look hungry."

Johnny lets himself be hauled away to the table. "Thanks," he says once they're out of earshot of Victor. "I love the guy, but sometimes he's a real *chiacchierone.*"

"I figured you needed a break," says Gina. She lets go of his arm and begins to fix him a plate of food.

Johnny smiles. Gina's the youngest of his three sisters. The two of them have always gotten along royally. As he watches her fill his plate, Johnny's remembering how Gina's always looked out for him, helping him when he was in a tight jam or covering for him whenever he pulled one of his stunts. Like the time when he was nine years old and he came home from school scared out of his wits because he'd gotten a zero on an arithmetic paper. He wasn't worried so much about the grade as the fact that his teacher made him bring it home to have his parents sign it. Johnny knew he'd be in for the usual tirade from his mother. Worse, if the old man found out, he'd definitely catch a wallop. Before showing the test to his mother, he went first to Gina. When he let her in on his predicament, she just laughed, snatched the test from his hand, and signed it herself. To his amazement, she had forged their mother's signature to near perfection. They'd been partners in crime ever since. Of course, kids always think their parents are stupider than they are, but Teresa and I were wise to them all along. It was fun to watch.

"Not so much lasagna," says Johnny as Gina piles on the food.

She turns and gives him the plate, then reaches for a knife and fork. "Here," she says, "just be quiet and eat."

"I don't feel like eatin'," says Johnny.

"Why not?"

"Because all these people are givin' me *agita*."

Gina takes his arm. "Come on," she says. She leads him to the front hall, which is relatively clear of traffic. They sit on the bottom of the staircase while Johnny goes to work on his lasagna.

Gina sits there for a time without speaking. Off in the kitchen, Teresa is carrying on to Auntie Louise about something to do with the way Father Giuliano gave the sermon. Uncle Victor has hooked up with Uncle Julio at the other end of the hallway. The two are debating the merits of moving to Florida for the winter every year. It's still bedlam in the living room. Finally Gina turns to her brother and pokes him in the ribs.

"So, are you going to tell me?" she says.

"Tell you what?" answers Johnny between mouthfuls of food.

"What Pop wanted to tell you at the hospital that nobody else was supposed to hear."

Johnny just about chokes. He grabs a napkin and covers his mouth to keep from coughing out a mouthful of pepperoncini. "What do you wanna know that for?" he says once he's composed himself.

"Because I want to, that's why. What's the big secret?"

"There's no big secret."

"Then why are you blushing?"

"I'm not blushing," he says, wiping his brow. "It's these pepperoncini, they're hotter than I thought."

"Nice try," says his sister. "Come on, you can trust me."

"It was nothin'," Johnny lies. "Pop just wanted to get some things straight about the business and stuff like that. It was no big deal."

"Then why don't you tell me."

"I just did. There's nothin' else to tell."

"I'd tell you," she persists.

Johnny puts his plate down and takes her by the shoulders. "Look," he says, "it was just guy-to-guy talk, nothin' you'd wanna hear about. Pop said he wanted me to settle down and get married and have kids and all that sort of crap. I'd tell you if it was something important that you needed to hear."

"Would you?"

"Sure I would."

"Really?"

"Yes, really!"

Gina eyes him skeptically. "All right," she says, getting up. "I'll let you off the hook—for now." She starts toward the kitchen. "You want a cup of coffee?" she says over her shoulder.

"Later," Johnny answers.

"Okay, I'll be back."

"I know you will."

Gina walks away, leaving him alone on the stairs. Johnny sits there for a moment, breathes a sigh of relief, and goes back to eating his lasagna.

Chapter 8

All right, a little time goes by and I've been in the ground now, what, maybe three weeks? Meantime Teresa's been sitting around the house every day doing nothing and she's starting to crawl the walls. I know how it is with her. It's not in her nature to just fritter away her time, even if she is supposed to be in mourning. Sure, she misses me, but she's figuring if she doesn't start doing something pretty soon, she'll end up joining me from the deadly boredom. It's time to start making herself useful again. That's why she says yes right away when Johnny asks her to watch the cash register at the shop for an hour or so while he runs a few errands that afternoon. The way she looks at it, it'll give him a break and her a chance to get out of the house for a while.

First thing Teresa does when she gets to the store is grab a broom and start pushing it along the aisle past the bins of bolts and pipe fittings. She rounds the corner and makes her way back up the next aisle in time to watch Johnny hurry out the door. She stops and smiles. Teresa knows it's been tough on Johnny, taking over the full responsibility of running the hardware store. There's a helluva lot more to it than he ever realized, but it's good to see him finally starting to act like a man, at least when it comes to business. Now if she could only get him to settle down and stop chasing women around all the time. Teresa lets out a big sigh because she knows it's not his fault; it's just in his blood.

So she ambles on through the aisles with the broom. Things are quiet in the store. That's the way it gets sometimes. For me, those times were the worst. A minute is like two years when you're in retail and you're waiting for customers to start coming in. You stand there at the counter, looking around at all the inventory, all that money that you have just sitting on the shelves going nowhere. An hour goes by and you start to get afraid that maybe you're going to see the tumbleweeds rolling past you through the aisles pretty soon. It can get to you, believe me.

But women are more patient than men, so Teresa doesn't worry. She's been at it long enough to know that things will get busy again after lunchtime. So for now she enjoys the temporary tranquility as she reminisces about the years she's spent there. Every aisle brings back a memory to her. To me too. You know, you learn pretty quickly here that there's no use in trying to make yourself heard to the people you leave behind, but sometimes you can't help trying. So I decide to stroll along with her.

Teresa stops at the tool section and smiles.

"Remember that day?" I ask her. "The one when you got so mad that you flung a monkey wrench at me, but I ducked and it missed and instead it hit the stack of paint cans and toppled them all over?" She's laughing softly now. "That's right," I tell her. "Remember the poor bastard on the opposite aisle who all the cans landed on?" I'm laughing myself now. "I had to give him everything at half price just so he wouldn't throw a case and sue us. How we cracked up after he ran out of the store!"

Teresa moves on and pauses near the row of lighting fixtures. "I remember that day too," I say, though I know she can't hear me. "That was when you told me you were pregnant again, this time with Johnny."

She looks around and sighs again. Every nook, every cranny, every speck of dust means something. And it all comes back, all those memories since we first opened the store. That was over thirty years ago, but it seems like yesterday. It goes by so quick that you don't see it happening until you stop one day and take a hard look. It's scary sometimes.

Anyway, the little bell tied to the front door jingles and poof! like that, the memories all disappear into thin air. Teresa leans around the corner and watches a customer step inside. She's like a leopard now, stalking its prey. She narrows her gaze and scrutinizes the man as he moves toward the skill saws. It's an old habit, one she developed way back to help her spot potential shoplifters. You'd be surprised at how many of them she chased out of the store over the years. Contractors are the worst; they'll steal from anyone. Just so you know—never leave your tools lying around at your worksite when you're not there because nine times out of ten they're bound to end up lying around at someone else's worksite, know what I mean?

This guy, though, he looks all right. Clean, slightly rumpled trousers, flannel shirt, baseball cap. Seems trustworthy enough. Just the same, Teresa circles back to the counter to guard the cash register while he looks around. She's sizing him up, figures he's about my age, a little older maybe, but fit-looking. She's never seen him in the store before, but then again she hasn't worked much the last few years.

"Can I help you find something?" she calls out to him.

The man peeks his head out from around the corner. "Thanks," he says, "but I think I should be able to find what I need."

"Don't be so sure of yourself," says Teresa, on the prowl now. She comes out from behind the cash register. Thirty years in the hardware business have taught her a thing or two. Rule number one is to never let customers, especially new ones, pick out equipment by themselves. Nine times out of ten they pick the wrong item and end up bringing it back. Teresa knows full well that it drives the male customers crazy to have a woman telling them what kind of hardware to buy. It hurts their egos. Business aside, of course, that's half the reason she does it.

"Here," she says, "let me help you. What are you looking for?"

"A skill saw," he answers.

Teresa furrows her brow. "What do you want with a skill saw?" she says ominously. "Have you ever used one?"

"Well—no—actually, I haven't," the man admits.

"Then what makes you think you can use one?"

"Well, I don't know," he says, sounding unsure of himself. "I just thought that—"

"Look," says Teresa, "if you don't know what you're doing with one of these things, you could take a finger off. Believe me, I've seen it happen. These aren't toys, you know, they're tools."

She's right, of course. I mean, I've seen all sorts of guys who thought they knew what they were doing with equipment like skill saws. They don't listen, no matter how many times you try to show them how to work the things safely. Out they go to do battle and a month later they show up at the store minus a digit or two, their piano careers ruined for good. Guys can be like that.

Teresa folds her arms and taps her foot. She's got this guy on the hook now, so she decides to make him squirm a little. "What sort of project are you doing that you need a saw?" she says.

"I wanted to build a toolshed in my backyard."

"So, why do you need a skill saw?"

To her satisfaction, the guy's utterly confused now. I know just how he feels, been there many times myself. "I just thought I'd need to cut the wood, that's all," he offers.

"For what, four little walls and a roof? No, you don't need a skill saw. Follow me."

Off they march to the back of the store, where all the hand-saws are displayed on the wall. Teresa studies them for a moment before taking down a sturdy-looking model, same one I proba-bly would have picked out. She looks it over carefully and hands it to him.

"Here," she says, "use this instead. It has a good sharp blade and a lifetime warranty. And it's safer than those skill saws you were looking at. Forget those things, you'll just hurt yourself." The bell on the front door jingles again and two more cus-tomers walk in. "Why don't you look that over while I tend to these other customers," she says, walking away.

"Thanks," says the man, whatever ego he walked in with now mashed into pulp.

Things get busy all of a sudden and Teresa's in her element, directing the show. Customers are coming and going, keeping the cash register and the doorbell ringing. Even now, it's like music to my hears, that ringing and singing of the cash register. Believe me, when you see all that product finally flying off those shelves, the cash and the credit card receipts piling up, it's like winning the Super Bowl, only better because it can happen just about any day of the week, any week of the year. It's what I call the juice. And when the juice is flowing, life is good.

So the juice keeps flowing for a good solid hour or so, but Teresa's not showing any sign of wearing down. Just the same, she's happy when the front doorbell jingles once more and she sees Nina and Gina come in with Nina's little boy and girl in tow. A little help right now wouldn't hurt, she figures. Besides, she's always thrilled to see the grandkids. "Nonnie!" little Tommy and Joanna call out when they see their grandmother. They scamper over to her and wrap their little arms around her legs.

"What, are you here to work or to play?" Teresa playfully scolds them.

"To play!" they cry gleefully.

"Play?" huffs their grandmother. "First you work, then you

play." She takes their hands, leads them behind the counter, and gives each of them a broom. "Here," she tells them, "sweep up back here, it's a mess from when your uncle was working this morning."

Giggling nonstop, Tommy and Joanna immediately set to work swatting each other's brooms like hockey players fighting for the puck. Teresa just shakes her head and chuckles. At least they're occupied for the time being.

"Not so loud," she warns them. "And be careful not to bang into Papa Nick's new computer over there that he never bothered to learn how to use. Talk about wasting money."

Joanna stops for a moment and looks up with those big brown eyes of hers. "Where *is* Papa Nick?" she asks. "I miss him."

Teresa looks down at her and pats her head. "Papa Nick's up in heaven, honey," she tells her.

"But when's he coming back?" my granddaughter wants to know.

"I don't know, sweetie, but don't worry, he's watching over us all the time."

"Well, I hope he comes back soon. I have something to tell him."

"I have a few things to tell him myself," says Teresa.

Fortunately, Nina and Gina are still up front, having immediately started to help customers when they walked in. It's just as well that they missed this little exchange. Had they been there, the two would now be bawling their eyes out and of no use to anyone. It's like the littlest thing still sets them off right now. Same with Maria. What are you gonna do?

But anyways, things gradually wind down, so Gina takes the chance to duck out for some coffee. She returns a few minutes later and sets the coffees and a bag of cookies from the bakery around the corner on the counter. Teresa opens the cookies and dispenses two to the kids to keep them quiet. Meanwhile, Nina is still helping a customer. Turns out it's the same guy who came in earlier that wanted the skill saw. In addition to the handsaw, Nina's now got him carrying a level, a hammer, a bag of nails, and a few other odds and ends.

"I really came in just to buy a skill saw," he's saying as they make their way toward the cash register.

"You're better off with the saw you picked out," Nina assures him. "You can take a finger off with those other things if you're not careful."

"What, have they got all of you trained or something?" the guy mutters.

While Nina rings him up on the register, the man starts poking around the rack of books on do-it-yourself building projects. He settles on one, *How to Build a Deck*, and tosses it up on the counter. Teresa looks over from nearby and shakes her head. Tell you the truth, I'm doing the same thing. I mean this guy obviously doesn't know which end is up.

"Don't tell me," the man says, seeing the look on her face. "Wrong book, right?"

"You don't even have the tools to build a shed and now you want to build a deck where people are going to be walking? And then what, the thing collapses and somebody gets maimed?"

Nina and Gina are practically busting a gut now because Teresa's making the guy start to blush. They're laughing because they've seen their mother cut guys down to size like this a million times. "What would you suggest?" he asks, scratching the back of his neck.

Teresa points to the bottom of the bookshelf. "The one with the red cover. That's the one you need."

He reaches over and picks up the book. *"Basic Carpentry Skills,"* he reads aloud, *"A Guide Book for the Beginning Carpenter."* Now he's smiling. "What makes you so sure I'm a beginner?"

"Lucky guess," says Teresa. "You taking the book?"

"Absolutely. How much is it, by the way?"

Teresa hands the book to Nina. "No charge."

"No charge?" he says. "But—"

"That's for being a good sport," Teresa tells him. "We want to keep you coming back. You should open an account here. We'll have you up to speed in no time."

"Maybe I will," says the man, smiling. Tell you the truth, though, I figure the guy's gotta be dying to get out of there before his ears get singed again. After he pays, he collects his gear and scrams.

As soon as the door closes behind him, Gina and Nina are laughing out loud. Things are quiet in the store otherwise, and they're all at the counter sipping their coffee.

"You know," says Nina to her mother, "it always amazes me that you and Pop ever managed to keep any customers with you working here. The way you boss guys around!"

"*Ayyyy,* don't kid yourself," laughs Teresa. "I know what I'm doing. Believe me, men like it when women tell them what to do, it's that much less they have to think about."

They all laugh, but then Teresa sighs and gets this sad, wistful look on her face. Joanna and Tommy come over to her and she reaches down and squeezes them tight.

"What is it, Mom?" says Gina. "You okay? You thinking about Pop?"

"How can I not think about him?" Teresa answers, straightening up. "He's in you, he's in these kids, he's in the air we're breathing in this store. He's in me. I can't help but think of him. But something else came to me just now. I don't know why, but it occurred to me how full everything in life is because we were together. You kids, the grandkids, our house, this store, the people we've met and come to know through the years. Everything. It's all here because your father and I loved each other, and that's where it all starts. I mean, I look at some of these other women I see sometimes who have these fancy jobs and wear fancy clothes and ride around in fancy cars. Career girls. They're building up everything in their lives, but they're not building families. Like this one I see at the salon all the time. She's young and pretty, but I know she's not married. And I never hear her talk about children. I mean, what's she and all the others like her waiting for? Life's too short. I feel sorry for them all."

"Everybody does things in their own time, Mom," says Nina. "Not everybody wants the same things."

"They do in the end," says Teresa. She lets Joanna and Tommy go, and picks up one of the brooms. "But don't ask me why I'm thinking about all that right now," she says with a sigh. "Best thing for me right now is to keep busy."

So with that, Teresa turns away and starts to push the broom around again. She looks up as she passes the clock and wonders how long it's gonna be before Johnny returns.

It's gonna be a while, trust me.

Chapter 9

You know, you wake up one morning, see the sun shining through your window, hear the birds chirping. You stretch your arms over your head, shake the cobwebs out, and drag yourself from beneath the covers. Just the start of any ordinary day. But as you're standing there, checking yourself out in the bathroom mirror while you brush your teeth, you really have no way of knowing that this particular day could turn out to be anything but ordinary. For all you know, your life is about to be turned inside out, but at the moment the only thing on your mind might be wondering about stuff like whether you should switch brands of toothpaste or should you get a bagel instead of a cruller for breakfast at the drive-up on the way to work. But in a moment, everything can change, for good or bad. That's just the way life is; it can sneak up on you. For better or worse, the life you thought you were leading can end in the blink of an eye and then a whole new one starts. It's funny, we all think we're born and die just once, but the way I see it, we're always living and dying and being reborn all the time. We live moment to moment.

Anyways, this particular moment, Johnny's on his back with his head under the sink, looking up at the water oozing from a crack in the drainpipe. Slowly it burgeons into a sizable drop that rolls down the pipe and dangles for a time above his head. It hangs there like it's waiting for Johnny to make the first move. Before he can raise his hand to shield his face, the drop falls from the pipe and plops in his eye.

Johnny says something unmentionable, wipes his face against his shirt sleeve, and pushes himself out from beneath the sink. He sits upright on the kitchen floor and looks up at Maria. She's standing there, holding back her youngest son, Michael, who's straining to get a hand on Johnny's tool belt.

"Come here, Mikey," says Johnny, handing him a screwdriver. "You can help Uncle Johnny."

The two-year-old squirms free from his mother's grasp and happily goes to work banging the screwdriver against the kitchen cabinets.

"Don't let him play with that stuff," snips Maria. "He'll take an eye out—and he's going to ruin my kitchen!"

"Lighten up," teases Johnny.

Maria shakes her head. "So," she says, "what do you think, can you fix it?"

Johnny glances back under the sink to where a puddle is beginning to form beneath the drainpipe. "I dunno," he answers. "I don't think so."

"What do you mean, you don't think so?" says his sister peevishly.

"Maria, whatta ya want, the thing's got a crack in it the size of the Rio Grande. You gotta get somebody who knows what he's doing to cut it out and put in a new section of pipe."

"Pop used to fix things like that for us all the time."

"Pop used to do a lot of things. Besides, he was a plumber before he opened the store, remember? I'm not. I don't know what I'm doin' with this kinda stuff."

"Come on," she persists. "You can figure it out."

"What's the big deal? Just call somebody and have them fix it. It's probably only a thirty- or forty-dollar job."

"I don't want to call anybody," she pouts.

"What's the matter, you too cheap?"

"No, I'm not too cheap, smart aleck. It's just that . . ."

"What?"

"I don't know," Maria says gloomily. "It's just that Pop used to take care of all of this stuff for everybody. It doesn't seem right to have somebody outside the family do it now."

"Then ask your husband to do it."

"Don't be a jerk, Johnny. You know David's no good with tools. He'd end up hurting himself."

At that they both laugh and Johnny starts thinking about the afternoon he spent helping David put the crib together just before Michael was born. Thank God he was there; otherwise little Mikey would still be sleeping on the floor. Johnny likes his brother-in-law, me too, but the guy doesn't know which end of a hammer to hold.

Johnny picks himself up and goes to the refrigerator. He opens the door and peers in. "Whatta ya got to eat around here anyways?" he says. "I'm supposed to be on my lunch break, ya know."

"Sit down," Maria orders. "I've got some leftover eggplant from last night. I'll make you a sandwich. Just let me throw Michael in for his nap."

Upon hearing the word *nap*, Michael lets out a yap of protest, drops the screwdriver, and bolts for the living room. Maria catches him from behind in midstride and scoops him up into the air. Though going nowhere, Michael's little legs keep right on running, but he quickly tires and rests his head on his mother's shoulder. He's already sucking his thumb by the time Maria reaches the staircase.

"*Va nanon'*, Mikey," Johnny calls to his nephew as Maria carries him upstairs.

While he waits for his sister to return, Johnny leafs through the morning newspaper. He pays scant attention to the headlines, but studies the advertisements for the other hardware stores in the city. It's Friday and things have been slow in the shop all week. Now he knows why. From what he can see, just about everybody else in town has some kind of fall sale going on. He lets out a grunt, folds the paper, and tosses it onto the table.

Johnny glances up at the ceiling; he can hear Maria singing softly to Michael while she changes his diaper before putting him down for a nap. That, he figures, gives him just enough time to take a quick second look at the letter he received that morning. He reaches for his jacket and tugs the envelope from the inside pocket. The letter it contains is addressed to me, as most of the mail that comes to the shop still is. That sort of thing will go on for a long time yet. Salesmen I talked to months ago and told to come back another time will show up at the shop, looking for me. I won't be there, obviously, so they'll talk to Johnny instead. Mail with my name on it will keep coming to the shop for months, years probably, until my name is finally purged from every mailing list. It'll all go to Johnny. Life goes on. I know that, for Johnny, opening his father's mail gives him an eerie feeling, as if he's doing something wrong, even though he knows that it's now his duty to do so. But he'll get over it.

In any case, nine times out of ten, the mail that comes in is bills or junk, but this particular letter caught his eye that morning. He opens it and skims down to the paragraph that most interests him.

> *As you know from our previous communications*—it reads—*American Hardware Stores is seeking to expand its presence in the Northeast through the acquisition of small to midsized hardware stores such as your own that serve a well-defined demographic area. We are prepared to negotiate a variety of purchase options that would give you the fairest possible return on your investment in the store and, possibly, even continued control of*

its management. The final sales price would, of course, be based on current market conditions . . .

Before he can read further, Johnny hears Maria descending the stairs. He folds the letter in the envelope, tucks it back into his jacket pocket, and picks the newspaper back up. He tries to read, but the words *previous communications* keep bothering him. He's asking himself, what previous communications? Then he starts to wonder if his pop had really been talking to those people.

I'll never tell.

"What's the matter?" says Maria, coming back into the kitchen. "You seem kind of mopey today."

"Nothin'," says Johnny. "I just got a lot of things on my mind, stuff to do with the store."

Maria goes to the refrigerator, takes out a plate of fried eggplant and a package of provolone cheese. The cheese she sets on the counter next to a basket of Italian bread rolls; the eggplant she places in the microwave oven. She sets the timer and sits down at the table. Johnny's fidgeting with the newspaper, tearing bits off of the top of the front page and crumpling them into pea-sized balls that he flicks across the table.

"Do you mind," says Maria, pulling the newspaper away. "Somebody else might want to read the paper, you know."

"Sorry."

Maria gazes at her brother for a moment. "So what is it?" she asks once more. "What's going on at the store?"

"Nothin'," says Johnny. "I've just been doin' a little thinkin'."

"I thought I smelled something burning."

"Very funny."

"Sorry," says Maria, smiling. "Tell me, what have you been doing all this thinking about?"

"I dunno," Johnny answers, slouching back in the chair. "Things were pretty easy when Pop was around, but now I don't know if I'm runnin' things the way I should. Maybe I wasn't meant to do this job, know what I mean?"

Just then the timer on the microwave oven starts to beep. Without answering him, Maria gets up, opens the door, and removes the steaming plate of fried eggplant. She sets the plate on the counter and takes one of the rolls from the basket. She slices it open, lines it with provolone and then a thick layer of eggplant. For good measure she throws in a few roasted peppers, a splash of olive oil, and a pinch of salt and pepper. Her masterpiece completed, Maria places the sandwich on a paper plate and puts it in front of Johnny.

Johnny sits up and, wasting no time, takes a healthy chomp. He loves his sister's eggplant; it's definitely her specialty. I have to agree. I used to love Maria's eggplant myself; she made it even better than her mother's.

So Johnny happily munches away while Maria pours him a cup of coffee. Before long he's already devoured half the sandwich. I mean, the kid can eat.

"I think you're doing fine," Maria says at last. "We're all proud of the way you've been handling the store."

Johnny figures he's being put on. "Come on," he mumbles between mouthfuls.

"I mean it," she says. "We all know how hard it's been for you having to run things without Pop. It's been hard for all of us just getting through each day." Her eyes suddenly begin to well up. Like I said earlier, the littlest thing still sets her and her sisters off.

"*Ayyyy,* don't start that stuff," Johnny pleads as the tears begin to flow from his sister's eyes. "You're gonna give me *agita* here."

"I know," Maria sniffs, "but I can't help it. I miss him."

"You and everybody else."

Johnny reaches into his pocket, pulls out a handkerchief, and slides it across the table. It seems like he's been handing the things out like candy lately.

"Here," he says gently. "Come on, you're the oldest, remember? You're supposed to be keepin' the rest of us from fallin' apart, right?"

Maria takes the handkerchief, dabs her eyes dry, and blows her nose. She takes a deep breath to compose herself.

"Thanks," she says, pushing the handkerchief back to him.

"Keep it," says Johnny, glancing up at the clock. It's well past noon. He gobbles down the rest of his sandwich and pushes away from the table. As he collects his tools, Maria cleans off the table.

"You going back to the store now?" she asks.

"Nah, I've got some errands to do, so I left Mommy to watch things."

"That's good," said Maria. "Mommy needs to start doing something to keep active. It's no good for her to stay cooped up in the house forever and ever. Sooner or later she has to start getting out."

"I agree," says Johnny, though he's barely paying attention. He looks around, trying to find the screwdriver he gave to Mikey.

"Of course, don't let her do too much," Maria warns him.

"Heh?"

"You know what I mean. You're the one that's supposed to run things now. Sure Mommy owns the store now, but someday it's going to be yours. Everybody knows that, it's the way it should be. Nobody else wants to run it."

"Yeah," says Johnny, "but nobody ever asked me if *I* wanted to run the thing in the first place."

"Who else is going to do it and where else are you going to go?"

"Who knows," muses Johnny, "maybe I'll sell it someday if I got the right price."

"*Sell it?*" cries Maria. "What, are you crazy? You could never sell the store."

"Why not?"

"Because Pop would turn over in his grave, that's why."

Johnny's learning, so he knows enough to say no more on the subject, but he lets out a sigh of relief when he spies his screwdriver on the floor beneath the stove. He grabs it and slides it back into his tool belt. Maria follows him out to the front door.

"So, what are you going to do?" she asks before he leaves.

"I told you, I've got some errands to run before I go back to the store."

"Not that," says Maria. "I'm talking about the sink."

"Maria—"

"Come on, Johnny, just say you'll do it."

"But Maria—"

"*Pllleeeaaasssse,*" she begs, giving him a heart-wrenching look.

Johnny throws up his hands. "All right, all right," he relents. "I'll do it tomorrow, but I can't guarantee how it's gonna come out."

Maria beams a smile at him and gives him a kiss on the cheek. "Thanks," she says, pushing him out the door. "Now go, I've got to go watch my soap."

"Your what?" says Johnny, but by then the door has closed and he's standing alone on the front step. He turns and trudges off to the car, wondering all the way why his father had ever bothered to get involved with another woman when he already had a wife and three daughters to drive him crazy.

Good question.

Chapter 10

After he leaves Maria's, Johnny drives through downtown Providence and heads up College Hill past Brown University. It's one of those perfect warm days you get sometimes in September and the student body is out in force on the Green, the university's enormous front yard. You only get so many days like this, especially with fall and winter right around the corner, so it seems like just about everyone is out making the most of the sunshine. Students are tossing Frisbees around while others careen about on Rollerblades. Many just relax on the grass, reading books and soaking up the sun's warmth.

Johnny slows the car as he passes to survey the scene, noting with pleasure the legs of the young women strolling along in their T-shirts and shorts. He's thinking about how nice it would be to be out there strolling along with them. He sighs at the thought and wonders why he hadn't gone to college way back like Pop wanted him to. I can answer that one for you. It's because the kid has squash for brains. Wouldn't listen to anybody, let alone me. But that's the way it goes.

So Johnny reluctantly drives on. It's been ages since he last cruised around the East Side. He's never been all that familiar with the area, but he knows most of the main roads. He weaves his way through the maze of side streets, stopping now and then to consult his book of street maps. At last he pulls the car over to the side of the road and stops in front of a row of neatly kept town houses. He reaches into his shirt pocket and tugs out the address he scribbled on the back of a paper napkin. The telephone book had only one *V. Sanders* listed in Providence. This has to be it, he figures. He takes a deep breath and opens the car door.

Johnny's been dreading this day for three weeks, putting it off for as long as he could before the guilt of not honoring his father's last wishes became too much for him. I can't say that I blame him. Visiting *my* dead father's mistress probably wouldn't be all that high on my list of things to do either. But I know Johnny, and I can tell you that as uneasy as he is about the whole thing, he can't help being a little curious too. He's got a mischievous side of him that's dying to get a look at her. Still, his slightly more sensible side prevails. All along he's been thinking that there's no way he wants to do a face-to-face with the old broad. So, earlier that morning, he hit on the solution. He remembers that I told him she was a schoolteacher. Chances are that she won't be home on a weekday. So he figures all he has to do is stop by, she won't be home, and at least he can always say that he made the effort to go. Of course, no one will ever know but him, but that's okay.

Ambling up the walkway to the front door, Johnny tries to imagine his father dating a schoolteacher. The image of Mrs. Henderson, his silver-haired fourth-grade teacher, comes to mind. Mrs. Henderson seemed ancient to him at the time. Tell you the truth, back then she seemed ancient to me too. Always prim and proper, but with a lightning-bolt temper, she would let him have it with the ruler whenever the occasion called for it, which was fairly often with Johnny. Just the same, Mrs. Henderson was always one of Johnny's favorite teachers, and believe it or not, he was one of her favorite students, despite his classroom antics. Thinking back about his schoolboy days brings a smile to his face, but at the same time he has to shake his head. To think that someone like Mrs. Henderson could be carrying on with his father, it just doesn't seem right to him. He figures people that age aren't supposed to have affairs, but what does he know?

So Johnny rings the doorbell and waits. He's got a knot the size of a bowling ball in his gut and he's making buttons because what if she's home, what the hell's he going to say? Be in and out in five minutes, he tells himself. Just ask how she's doing, make sure she's not about to jump off any bridges, see that she's got enough Geritol, and then get out of there.

He waits a few moments before ringing the bell again. Satisfied that he's given it his best shot, he starts down the steps toward the car. To his dismay, though, he hears the metallic scratch of the door being unlocked. He stands on the bottom step and watches the door open.

Much to his relief, a woman far too young to be a dowdy old schoolteacher appears. Dressed in jeans and a Brown sweatshirt, she steps up to the screen door and looks out at him. She's wearing a kerchief around her neck and a pair of yellow latex gloves. Clutching a bucket in one hand, she uses the other to push a strand of long, light brown hair away from her face. She seems timid, and glances nervously behind her to where a mop leans against the wall.

"Yes?" she says cautiously.

Thank God, Johnny's thinking, it's only the housekeeper. Perfect, right? He'll just leave a message that he stopped by and then be on his way. Strange, though, the housekeeper seemed startled to see him when she opened the door. He steps closer to the door to get a better look at her and she almost drops the bucket.

"Can I help you?" she says, setting the bucket on the floor.

"Yeah," Johnny answers. "I was just lookin' for Mrs. Sanders."

"*Miss* Sanders?"

"Yes, Victoria Sanders," says Johnny. "This is where she lives, isn't it?"

"Well—yes, it is," she says in an odd tone. She purses her lips and gazes at him. "What did you want to see her about?"

Johnny scratches his chin. He's thinking this chick is nosy, even for a housekeeper. Of course, most women are; they can't help it. Wanting to know other people's business is just part of what makes them tick. Don't ask me why.

But this woman is about Johnny's age, he guesses, maybe a year or two older and not half bad looking. As a matter of fact, she has a very nice face, but it's the big bright eyes that strike him most. Johnny's always been a sucker for blue eyes. Hers are a liquidy blue shade, sort of like the windshield wiper fluid we sell in the store. Johnny's thinking, she can come and clean *my* room anytime she wants.

"It's just a—uh—personal matter," he says. "Nothin' major. Actually, I was just deliverin' a message to her. She's not around, is she?"

The housekeeper starts to fidget with one of her gloves. "Well—you see—she teaches at the university," she tells him.

Johnny breaks out in a smile. "At *Brown?*" he laughs. "My father told me she was a schoolteacher. I figured she taught second grade or somethin' like that."

The first hint of a smile breaks across the housekeeper's face. "Comparative literature," she says. "Who is the message from that you wanted to deliver?"

"My father."

The smile, slight as it was, fades from her face like the sun behind a cloud. "Why doesn't he contact her himself?" she says.

"That would be a little hard," says Johnny. "Pop bought the farm 'bout three weeks ago."

"He what?"

"Died."

"Oh, I see," she says, not sounding all that surprised. "I'm sorry."

"Yeah—well, to tell you the truth, I don't know this Mrs. Sanders myself, but she and my father were—let's say—good friends. I guess he never managed to get by here to see her before things happened and he felt a little bad about it. Anyway, he just wanted me to stop by and check up on her once the funeral and everything was over. You know, make sure she's all right, see if she needs anything."

"That certainly was nice of him," says the housekeeper, for some reason sounding slightly annoyed. "I guess he must have been too sick to pick up the phone and call her himself."

Johnny rubs the back of his neck. "Well, it wasn't so much that," he tells her. He leans closer and, in a lowered voice, says, "To be honest with you, it would have been a problem for him. You see, I think he and this Mrs. Sanders—"

"*Miss* Sanders," she corrects him.

"Whatever. But he and Miss Sanders had a little thing goin' on, see, and with my mother and everybody hangin' around the hospital day and night, it would have been a little bit of an awkward situation for him. Know what I mean?"

The housekeeper is bristling now. "And I suppose your father told you all this," she says.

Johnny's a little puzzled over why she should seem so annoyed about the whole thing. "It's no big deal," he says with a shrug. "It's just the way things worked out, that's all."

The housekeeper takes a deep breath and picks up the bucket. "Well," she fumes, "I'll deliver your message, Mr. Catini. Thank you and have a good day." With that she steps back and slams the door.

Johnny's just standing there, scratching his head. Now what the hell was that all about? he wonders. And how did she know his name is Catini? He shakes his head. Cute, but what a weird chick. He's mostly ticked because she didn't even give him a chance to get her name and number. But at least he tried. So he turns and starts back to the car. He's barely off the bottom step when he hears the door open once more. He stops and looks over his shoulder. The housekeeper is standing there, looking all downcast and depressed.

"I'm sorry," she says glumly. "I didn't mean to be so rude. It was wrong of me."

Johnny steps back up to the door. "That's okay," he says kindly. "I should've known better than to talk about these things with the wrong people. You know, especially with stuff like this, you don't know who it's gonna upset."

The woman gives him a smile, even though a tear is glistening in the corner of her eye. "It's not your fault," she says, her voice quavering. "Things have been a little topsy-turvy around here the past few weeks."

"Tell me about it," sighs Johnny. "Sometimes I feel like the whole world is goin' nuts all around me, know what I mean?"

The housekeeper just smiles and nods her head.

"That's better," he says. "You're a lot prettier when you smile." Johnny's one of those people whose brain is hot-wired to his mouth. He really hadn't meant to say it, but only think it. Regardless, the compliment elicits no response from the woman, and for a moment, neither speaks.

Johnny feels a little awkward so he decides that now might be a good time to scoot. "Well, I should probably get rollin'," he tells her.

"Wait," she says. "Why don't you come in? We could talk— that is—while you wait for Miss Sanders."

"I dunno," says Johnny. "Maybe this wasn't such a good idea. I mean, look how upset I got you. Who knows what's gonna happen when this Mrs.—I mean—*Miss* Sanders gets back. I don't wanna give her a stroke or somethin'. Besides, you'll probably just get yourself in trouble for lettin' a stranger in."

"Please, don't worry about that," she says, pushing the door open. "We have lots of time. Come in and I'll make us some coffee."

"You sure?"

"I'm sure."

Johnny shrugs and steps inside. What could be the harm? he figures. "My name's Johnny, by the way. What's yours?"

The housekeeper nervously runs her hand back through the long strands of her hair. "Actually," she says, "my friends like to call me Sandy."

"Nice to meet you, Sandy. You sure your boss won't mind me bein' here?"

"Don't worry," she answers. "Why don't you just go into the living room while I make some coffee."

Johnny pauses for a few moments in the hallway, just checking things out before moving into the living room. To him it looks pretty much like what he might have expected from a teacher. The walls are lined with shelves of books, making the room seem more like a small library than anything else. In the corner, beneath the picture of a statue of some naked guy with a slingshot over his shoulder, stands a small desk with a personal computer on top. The computer's monitor glows with a display of bright dots that look like stars whizzing across the screen's dark background. Johnny's chuckling because it looks like something you'd see on the *Starship Enterprise*. He walks across the hardwood floor to get a closer look. Out of curiosity, he taps the keyboard to see what happens. To his chagrin, the star display instantly vanishes, leaving behind nothing but a bunch of words. Certain that he's broken something, Johnny moves quickly to the other side of the room, where a comfortable-looking couch flanked by two upholstered chairs stands guard in front of a small fireplace. He decides to sit down before he has a chance to break anything else.

The windows are wide open, letting the warm breeze and

the chirping of the birds drift in. Gazing about, he has to admit that it's a nice place—not his style, but nice enough. Now he's trying to imagine his father sitting in that same room, but try as he might, he just can't picture it. He's wondering, what did they do here, have tea and crumpets while they discussed Shakespeare? He glances at the staircase leading upstairs and wonders what else went on. You can understand how he feels. It's weird for him to be there, no question about it.

A few minutes later, Sandy comes into the room. She's brought with her a tray on which rest a pot of coffee, cups, silverware, and a plate of cookies. "I hope you don't mind instant coffee," she says, setting the tray down on the coffee table.

"No problem."

Sandy sits down on the opposite end of the couch. Johnny watches intently as she pours the coffee. There's something sophisticated and graceful in the way she moves that intrigues him. Now, he knows nothing about her, but he can't help feeling that somehow she could do way better than being a housekeeper.

"Cream and sugar?" she asks.

"No, I take it black."

She hands him the cup. "Just like your father," she says with a smile.

"Like my father?"

"Why, yes," she says, suddenly very flustered. "I—uh—used to serve him coffee sometimes when he came to visit."

"Oh, so you knew my father?"

"Miss Sanders doesn't get many visitors," she says uneasily. "That's why I remembered. Besides you look a great deal like him."

"Yeah, you're right," says Johnny, "people tell me that all the time." He takes a sip of coffee and glances over at the computer. To his relief, the stars are back whizzing across the screen.

Sandy curls her legs up onto the couch and takes a sip from

her own cup. For somebody who's just a housekeeper, she certainly makes herself right at home, Johnny's thinking. Isn't she worried that her boss could come home and catch her entertaining company when she's supposed to be working? But, he decides, when the cat's away, the mice can play. Except from what Johnny can see, she's no mouse, she's a cat herself. Sandy stretches out her slender arm and reaches to the plate for a cookie. Oh yeah, Johnny's thinking as she dunks the cookie in her cup and begins to nibble on it, you're definitely a cat—but a nice cat.

"Was your father sick for very long?" she says after a time.

"I guess so," Johnny answers. "Problem was that nobody knew until he was almost ready to roll. It happened fast."

"That's sad," says Sandy, her blue eyes growing misty.

"Yeah, well, that's just the way it goes sometimes. Nobody plans on these things."

"I guess not," she says, looking down at her hands.

"Hey, but you can't let yourself get too down about these things," says Johnny, trying to keep things light. "You know, my father would be the first one to tell you that he lived a good life. Sure, he checked out a little earlier than he shoulda, but hey, I think he went without havin' too many regrets. Can't ask for too much more than that, right?"

Sandy nods even though she appears to be on the verge of tears—why, he can't imagine. After all, he asks himself, what was Pop to her?

"So what's the deal with you," he asks. "How long have you been workin' for this Miss Sanders?"

It's a pretty straightforward question, but Sandy seems a little thrown by it. She takes a sip from her cup and mumbles something about having always done the housework there. "So, what do *you* do for a living?" she says before he has a chance to ask her to repeat herself.

"I run a hardware store on the other side of town."

"I remember now," she says cautiously. "Your father ran the store before he passed away, isn't that right?"

"Yeah, so I guess I'm the guy in charge now," Johnny chuckles. "Not that I wanted it that way."

"It must be hard for you," says Sandy. "I mean, I'm sure your father had a lot of people to deal with."

"You have no idea," huffs Johnny. "Now I'm the one who has to deal with them. I wasn't ready for that to happen."

"Life works in strange ways sometimes."

"You got that right."

Sandy reaches over and takes his cup. "Tell me," she says as she refills it, "that is if you don't mind, what did your father say to you about Miss Sanders?"

"Eh, the usual," Johnny replies. "You know, that he really cared about her and that's why he wanted me to check up on her. That kind of stuff."

"Was that all?" she says, barely above a whisper.

"Well, he said I shouldn't hold it against her because of what happened between them. You know, that it was beyond their control and it was all God's fault for making them fall in love and that I should try to be nice to this Miss Sanders because she's just another human bein' and all sorts of baloney like that. He went on and on. Believe me, my father could be a real *chiacchierone*, even when he was dyin'. But I shouldn't even be tellin' you any of this."

"No, I'm glad you told me," she says, a teardrop rolling down her cheek.

"Oh no, don't do that," Johnny groans. "Please don't start cryin' on me. I can't take it anymore."

"I'm sorry," Sandy sighs. "It's just that he was such a nice man."

"My father was a great guy," Johnny agrees. He reaches into his pocket and pulls out a handkerchief. "Here," he says, handing it to her, "it's my last one."

"Thanks," she says, dabbing her eyes. "But don't you miss him?"

"Of course I miss him. Just because I don't have two fountains attached to my eyes like the rest of my family doesn't mean I don't feel things. But it's my job to be strong here for everybody. I've got a business to run now. I can't let people see me bawlin' my eyes out no matter how much it hurts. They'll all think I'm some kind of *mammalucc'*."

"It's all right for you to cry," says Sandy.

"Yeah, right."

Johnny sighs and gazes out the window. The sky has suddenly darkened and the air has grown heavy. Just as suddenly, for some reason Johnny can't understand, he begins to feel just as heavy inside. It's like some big weight is pulling him down into the couch. It's then that he realizes that he feels absolutely exhausted and has for many days. I saw it happening to him myself, but there wasn't much I could do about it. Sue me. Anyway, Johnny closes his eyes for a moment, wanting with all his might to just sleep for a while and not have to deal with anything or anyone anymore, to just forget about everything. We all go through that every now and then. There are those times when we'd trade all the treasures in the world just to be able to put our heads on the pillow and get one peaceful night's sleep, just to recharge the batteries. Seems you can never get it when you need it most.

Johnny opens his eyes and sees Sandy gazing at him. Just then from the distance comes the low rumble of thunder, and a gust of wind puffs up the curtains like sails on a ship. A storm is definitely getting ready to roll through.

"Sorry," says Johnny.

"That's okay," Sandy replies, moving closer to him. "I think you need to relax and let all those feelings out. It's not healthy to keep them all bottled up inside you. That's why it's all right for you to cry, to let them all go."

"I don't need to cry," says Johnny, yawning. "I just need a few nights of solid shut-eye to get my head back on straight." He begins to stand. "Anyway, I should probably get goin' before it starts to rain."

Sandy reaches out and touches his arm. "Please don't go," she says suddenly. "Not yet. I mean—I don't want to be alone if it's going to storm. Thunderstorms have always frightened me, ever since I was a little girl. Stay here and rest for a while. It's okay."

Outside, the dark clouds suddenly burst open with a brilliant flash of lightning and a crack of thunder. The wind whips up and beats the rain against the windows.

"Please stay," she says again.

"Well," sighs Johnny, easing back onto the couch, "for the moment it looks like I ain't got any choice." He gazes out at the storm as it roars in like a freight train, loud and fast and unstoppable in its fury. He figures he'll stay till it passes and then be on his way.

Doesn't work out that way, though.

Chapter 11

Who can explain why these things happen? Don't ask me, and forget about asking Johnny. If the truth be told, at the moment when it's finally over, the kid's at a complete loss. Of course, that's more or less a standard state of being for my son. But anyway, he tries to think back, to retrace his steps, so to speak, to where it all started. But where it all started isn't at all clear to him. He's thinking, there must have been some logical sequence of events, like the links of a chain, one leading to another, but this chain is a tangled mess. Everything seemed to happen at once.

Now he's putting it together in his head. The two of them were sitting on the couch, talking about me. Sandy starts to cry again, and before he knows it, Johnny finds himself brushing away her tears, trying to comfort her. Then, somehow, it seems like she's trying to comfort him. Why, Johnny can't figure out because at that particular moment he's not feeling particularly sad about anything.

Or was he?

Maybe Sandy's right, he remembers thinking now. Maybe he really has bottled up his feelings inside. In any case, he suddenly realizes that she's holding his hand. Or is he holding hers? Whatever, they're holding each other's hands. And then, somehow, they end up hugging each other and that's when things really start to happen. All at once it's like a blur and the two of them are doing a lot more than just comforting each other. Their lips are pressed together and their hands are all over each other. In a flash the clothes get torn off and the fireworks really start while all the while outside the wind and the rain are pounding against the house and the thunder's booming and the lightning crackling.

And then it's over.

The storm passes as quickly as it came. The downpour ends and the dark clouds rumble away across the horizon. Johnny sits up and looks out at the sun breaking through the clouds. Droplets of sparkling rainwater drip off the tree branches and onto the drenched earth. The birds take up their chirping once more and from somewhere nearby comes the sound of children playing. Off in the distance, a lawn mower growls to life. Cars splash by along the street. Everything is returning to the way it was.

Despite appearances to the contrary, Johnny's no dope. Things definitely are not the way they were anymore, and he knows it. All of a sudden he's gripped by this feeling of dread, of some kind of impending doom. It's a feeling he knows well for it's the one he experiences just about every time he spends the night with a woman. When the morning comes, he's always overwhelmed by the fear that somehow he's being lured into some terrible trap from which he might never escape. It's at that moment, when it comes time to snuggle closer, to let himself be drawn further in, to whisper a few tender words and perhaps even to say I love you, that the fear takes over and chokes the words in his throat. That's when he comes up with an excuse, anything at all, as to why he can't stay. Then he cuts and runs in a panic, like an animal fleeing the flames of a burning forest, and he stays away for a day or a week or a month or whatever it takes until the fear subsides or he finds someone new.

This time's a little different, though. The fear's not quite so overwhelming. It strikes Johnny that, despite the suspicion that danger lies in wait just around the corner, perhaps in the form of Miss Sanders, who would probably walk through the door at any second, he feels anxious, but not panicked. If he leaves now, he tells himself, it's because he has responsibilities, duties to attend to at the store and people who depend on him. There's no need for panic.

Still, Johnny knows he has to leave, so it's an awkward situation for him. Glancing down at the floor to where their rumpled clothes still lay, he wonders anew about how it all happened. It's not like he's never made love before on the first date, but he's never done it with someone he's known less than two hours. Not that he's complaining, for it wasn't an unpleasant experience, but for some reason he feels a little confused. No question, there's definitely something here worth coming back for, he's thinking. Problem is, he doesn't know what to say or do next.

Johnny turns and looks at Sandy. By now she's sitting up beside him, her slender legs pulled up to her chest. She doesn't speak, but rests her head against her knees and gazes past him out the window for a time.

"What time does the old lady get home?" Johnny says at last.

"Soon," she says softly. "You should probably go now."

"Yeah, I gotta get back to the shop anyway. I got my mother watchin' things for me. Hey, maybe we could get together for a little dinner after, I don't know, talk about things."

"I don't know if that would be such a good idea," says Sandy.

"Look, Sandy," Johnny starts to say. "I don't want you to think—"

"Wait, Johnny," she interrupts him. "There's something you need to know."

"About what?"

"About me."

Johnny looks at her. "You're not gonna tell me you got herpes or somethin', are you?"

"No," says Sandy with a nervous laugh, "it's nothing so simple."

"All right," he replies. "Go ahead, tell me anything. I can handle it."

She takes a deep breath. "Okay," she begins, very tentatively, "my name is not Sandy. Not really."

Johnny shrugs. "Okay, so what? We barely know each other anyway. Just tell me your real name."

She purses her lips as he'd seen her do when she first came to the front door. Then, barely above a whisper, she says, "Vicki."

Johnny cocks his head to one side. "Say that again," he says.

"Vicki," she repeats.

Now the dark clouds that had disappeared outside all suddenly seem to be gathering about my son's head. "Vicki?" he says anxiously. "You mean Vicki, like in Victoria?"

"Like in Victoria Sanders," she says, cringing.

Johnny bolts upright and sits for a moment in stunned silence. Then he leaps to his feet.

"Oh . . . my . . . God!" he screams. Now he's pacing about the room, squeezing his head between his hands. "My God," he screams again, "what did you make me do?"

"*I* didn't make you do anything," Vicki cries. "So don't blame me. *I* didn't plan for this to happen."

"But you should have told me who you were when I first got here. You lied to me!"

"I did not," she huffs. "Lots of people call me Sandy. It's my nickname." Vicki uncoils her legs and begins to gather her clothes together. "What was I supposed to do?" she goes on. "You just show up at my front door. How was I to know that you weren't some kind of psychotic son out to avenge the family honor?"

"Oh," scoffs Johnny, pulling his shirt on, "I guess you think that makes everything all right. You were just tellin' a little white lie." Johnny hops around, trying to pull his trousers back on. He stops and catches a glimpse of himself in the mirror on the wall. "Oh no," he gasps. "Does this make me have like—what do they call it—an edible complex?"

"A *what?*" Vicki exclaims.

"You know, like the guy I read about in high school. Edible rex or whatever the hell his name was."

"Oedipus!" cries Vicki. "Not edible!"

"Edible, Oedipus, what the hell's the difference?"

Vicki begins pulling her own clothes back on. "Well, for starters," she growls, "Oedipus killed his father and slept with his mother. I don't think what we did quite falls into the same category."

"Well, it's close enough," cries Johnny. "You'd think you would have known better, a schoolteacher like you."

"I'm a professor, not a kindergarten teacher," she says icily.

"All the more reason!"

Johnny stuffs his shirt into his trousers and frantically looks about the floor while he buckles his belt. "Where are my socks?" he says.

"They're right here," answers Vicki, flinging them at him. They hit Johnny in the face and fall to the floor. "So, now what are you going to do?" she says, glowering over him as he picks them up.

Johnny pulls on the socks and shoves his feet into his shoes. "I'm gettin' outta here, that's what I'm doin'," he tells her. "Far as I'm concerned, this never happened. Where's the phone?"

"What do you need the phone for?"

"Because I'm late and I don't know what's happenin' back at the shop. I do have a business to run, ya know."

Vicki clenches her teeth. "You're just like your father," she seethes. "Always running out on me because of the business."

"Yeah, well, don't knock it," says Johnny, gesturing about at the room. "It kept you livin' in style, didn't it?"

The moment the words leave his lips, Johnny regrets saying them, if for no other reason than the startling look of outrage he sees in her eyes. Now he knows he's in trouble.

"Just one minute, Buster," says Vicki, backing him into the wall. She starts poking him in the chest for emphasis. "What you see in this house is mine, bought and paid for with my own money. I don't know what your father told you, but I was not some kept mistress living in the lap of luxury. Everything I have I've earned on my own, *before* I knew your father—and he never gave me so much as a handful of flowers, not that it's any of your business."

Johnny squirms away from the wall and backs away toward the front door. "You're right," he says, "it's not any of my business. I never wanted to come here in the first place. I was just tryin' to be nice."

"And I never should have let you in the door. The first time I laid eyes on you at the funeral, I knew what type you were."

Johnny stops. "You came to the funeral?" he says.

"Of course I came to the funeral!"

"But I didn't see you," says Johnny, scratching his head. Then it dawns on him. "Wait a minute, I remember now. That was you in the dark raincoat with the scarf over your head?"

"How very observant," says Vicki, shoving him toward the door. "Now just leave."

"Don't worry. I'm outta here."

With that, Johnny flings open the door and hurries down the front steps.

"And stay out!" he hears her yell as she slams the door shut behind him.

Everything outdoors is still soaked from the storm. In his rush to get to the car, Johnny runs through a puddle and splashes muddy water all over the bottom of his trousers. Cursing the rest of the way, he climbs into the car and closes the door. He goes to start the car, but then drops his head onto the steering wheel in dismay. He climbs back out, trudges back to the front door of the house, and reluctantly rings the doorbell. The door opens just wide enough for Vicki's arm to slip out. From her hand dangles a set of keys.

"Thanks," says Johnny, taking them quickly before the door slams shut on his hand.

Chapter 12

Okay, fast-forward to the next morning. Johnny walks into the kitchen, yawns, and plops himself down at the table. It's only seven o'clock in the morning, but already the sweet aroma of sautéing garlic and onions fills the air. For as long as he can remember, that wonderful smell has greeted him every Saturday morning when his mother starts the daylong process of cooking her sauce for Sunday's pasta. I used to love that smell myself. The ritual's always the same. Once the garlic and onions are tender, his mother adds a little fresh sausage to the big cast-iron frying pan and lets it cook until browned. Later, this all goes into a big pot with the tomatoes, tomato paste, basil, and oregano. A pinch of salt, a little pepper, maybe a splash of red wine, a couple of nice thick pork chops, and then it will sit on the stove to simmer for hours and hours. A fresh loaf of bread for dunking is always nearby. How better to test the sauce than to break off a nice big hunk and plunge it into the pot to soak up a mouthwatering sampling? What I wouldn't give for that right now.

Of course, this particular morning, the pleasant smell of the kitchen does little to cheer up Johnny. He puts his elbow on the table and props his chin up on his hand. His mother comes over from the stove and places a steaming cup of coffee in front of him.

"What's with the sad face today?" she says.

Johnny just shrugs and takes a sip of coffee. Teresa goes back to the counter and begins to slice some carrots. She likes to add them to her gravy sometimes to sweeten it up and make it a little thicker. I liked the carrots in the gravy myself, but Johnny's never really cared for them.

"You're not puttin' those in the gravy, are you?" he says at last.

"You wanna cook this yourself?" says Teresa.

That answer brings a smile to his face because he knows that nobody meddles with his mother's cooking. He's thinking about when he was a boy and how many times he caught a slap across the top of the head for interfering with the preparation of supper.

"Good," says his mother, glancing at his still-grinning face, "I was beginning to think you were planning to go around looking like a mope all day. What's the matter, problems with one of your girlfriends?"

"Nah," he answers. "I've just got a lot of stuff to do today."

"I'll say you do. There's a pile of inventory at the store that needs to be shelved. I would have done it myself for you yesterday, but I was too busy minding the cash register while you were out all afternoon running your so-called errands."

"I got tied up. I didn't mean for it to happen."

"Well it did happen, so you'd better get over to the store and get things straightened up before you open. People will think you're running a junk shop."

"Yeah, sure," Johnny mutters, but he knows she's right. He'd been expecting a big shipment of stock to come in that afternoon while he was out, and he'd planned to be there to put everything away when he got back. But how was he to know that things were going to work out the way they did? The way he looks at it, it wasn't his fault that the sparks just flew between Vicki and him. Of course, the more he tells himself he wasn't to blame, the guiltier he feels about the whole thing. All night long he tossed in bed, tormented by the knowledge that he had made love to his father's—his *dead* father's—mistress. How do you explain *that* to your mother? Good luck. The worst part about it is that, in thinking back on it, Johnny realizes that he actually enjoyed it. To his dismay, some dark force within himself is urging him to go back there, to see her again. Johnny buries his face in his hands. He figures this is what he gets for trying to obey his father. What a friggin' mess.

"So, are you going to tell me about it?" says Teresa, tossing the carrots into the frying pan. She pours herself a cup of coffee and sits down at the table with him.

Johnny takes his hands away from his face and sits back. Just like I used to do whenever I was thinking over something, especially when something was troubling me, he starts squirreling up the side of his mouth. Teresa notices him doing it all the time. She always lets him know how much it reminds her of me. Naturally, being a typical son, every time Johnny hears that, he tries to break himself of the habit because he figures he wants to be his own man, not his old man. But he never can. Some things are inescapable. So he sighs and stares at his coffee cup for a few moments, listening to the ticking of the clock on the wall and the sizzling of the frying pan on the stove.

"Do you miss Pop?" he says at last.

"Johnny," she says with a wistful smile, "I was married to your father for almost forty years. Do you know what that is? That's forty years of sharing the same bed, sitting at the same dinner table, holding the same hands, talking about things, shouting about things, joking, crying, watching our children grow up, making plans for the future. Half of everything I've become was wrapped up in your father. That's what marriage is like. From the day you meet, your lives get so tangled up with each other that you can't remember what was yours or what was his. And the beautiful part is that, after a while, you realize that it belongs to you equally. It's like you've created your own little world for yourselves."

"So what are you sayin'?" says Johnny.

His mother throws up her hands. "Of course I miss your father! That's what I'm trying to say!"

"Oh."

"You think a minute goes by when I don't think of him? Sometimes when I'm alone, I even find myself talking to him."

Actually, it's usually more like yelling at me. Johnny's thinking the same thing, but he knows enough to keep it to himself. He's heard her more than once, still needling me about not taking out the trash or spending too much time with my cronies. What can you expect after so many years of marriage? It's a tough habit to break. In any case, Johnny decides to choose his next words carefully.

"Yeah, I know what you mean," he says. "Sometimes I catch myself doin' the same thing when somethin' comes up at the shop that I haven't handled before. It's weird."

Teresa shakes her head. "It's natural," she tells him. "When you lose somebody like your father, it takes a big chunk out of your life. You can't expect to just forget about him overnight or ever for that matter. Besides, I feel like he's still with us, watching over us all the time. Sometimes I swear I can feel him next to me."

Johnny starts to squirm in his seat. "Come on, Ma," he says, looking anxiously about, "you're startin' to give me the creeps."

Tell you the truth, now she's giving me the creeps too—and I'm the one that's dead. I mean, how do women know these things? Sometimes I wonder if God didn't take the rib from Adam and turn it into some kind of invisible antenna that He only gave to Eve and all the other women to come down the pike after her. It would explain a lot.

"What's so creepy?" says Teresa. "Wouldn't it make you feel good to know that your father was watching you, making sure that everything goes all right for you?"

"Wonderful," says Johnny.

"I think it is. You see, I don't believe people just leave this world behind when they die. Not completely anyway. I think they stay near the people they loved or at least within earshot. Maybe we can't see them or hear them, but they're there and they can see and hear us. Which is kind of nice because I still have one or two things left to tell your father."

"Like what?" says Johnny.

Teresa stands and goes back to the stove. With a big wooden spoon in hand, she lifts the cover off the pan. A great hiss and a puff of steam greet her as she plunges the spoon in to stir up its sizzling contents. She places the cover back on the pan and lowers the heat.

"Your father was a good man," she says, sitting back down at the table, "but he had his faults."

"Such as?"

"Oh, mostly just little things," she says with a smile. "When you're together with someone for so long, you can't help but get on each other's nerves every now and then." Teresa pauses and the smile fades from her face. "There was one thing, though, that wasn't so little."

Johnny sits up straight. "What was that?" he says.

Teresa lets out a long sigh. "When your father started getting on in years, he began to go a little crazy, not the senile kind, but crazy just the same. It will probably happen to you someday; it does to most men, I think. One day they wake up and they suddenly realize that they're not twenty-one anymore. Trouble is, they want to act like they're still twenty-one even when they're closer to *sixty-one.*"

Johnny just shrugs. He figures he knows what his mother is leading up to, but he's not about to get himself into any more hot water than he's already in by saying so. He gulps down the rest of his coffee and waits to hear what she says next.

"What was the problem?" he says.

"You," says Teresa with an ironic laugh.

"Me?" exclaims Johnny.

"That's right, you. You and all your girlfriends," she tells him. "You see, your father and I got married when we were very young. That's what you did in those days. You didn't wait around until you were in your thirties like people do today. You found somebody you loved, or at least you thought you could learn to love, you got married, settled down, and raised a family. And all that was fine while you kids were growing up. Then, one by one, your sisters got married and started families of their own. But you—you go into convulsions anytime you hear the word *marriage,* even though you're chasing around a different girl every day of the week."

"That's not true," says Johnny, trying to offer some bit of defense for himself. "I've gone steady with a couple of girls."

"Sure," laughs Teresa. "And you've cheated on every one of them."

"Hey, it's not like I was married to any of them."

"That's exactly my point!" cries Teresa, slapping her hand down on the table. "Your father would see you running around, living it up with these young girls all the time like you didn't have a care in the world. Like any man, after a while he begins to think that maybe that's the way it's supposed to be. And that's when he starts to get in trouble, when he starts to think that maybe *he* should do a little running around himself while he still can."

Now, of course, the skin's starting to crawl on the back of Johnny's neck. He shifts uneasily in the chair and holds up his hands.

"Whoa," he says. "Maybe you better not tell me any more."

"No," says his mother, standing up. "You should know about your father. It's important. Maybe you'll learn something and won't make the same mistakes he made."

Teresa goes back to the stove, lifts the lid off the frying pan, and gives it one last stir before pushing everything into the big pot on the back burner. She covers the pot and sets the heat low before coming back to the table.

"What kinda mistakes are you talkin' about?" says Johnny.

Teresa sighs. "Can't you guess? Your father had a girlfriend."

"*Pop?*" says Johnny, doing his best to act surprised even though beads of sweat are forming on his forehead. "No way."

"Yes, it's true," she says sadly. "It was going on for a long time, but I never said anything about it. I thought it was just a little phase he was going through and that it would end soon enough. But it didn't."

"*Aaayyy,*" says Johnny, waving his hand. "You probably imagined the whole thing. How do you know he had a girl-friend?"

"Because I saw them together."

"You did?" Johnny gulps.

"Just once," says Teresa, a faraway look coming across her eyes. "It was a while back. I'd gone up to the East Side to do some shopping with Maria. I wanted to buy her some new clothes for the baby. We were hungry and had just decided to stop someplace for lunch when I happened to look across the street. That's when I saw them, your father and his girlfriend, going into a restaurant."

"Come on, Mom," says Johnny. "Just because Pop had lunch with someone doesn't mean he was cheating on you. It proba-bly had something to do with business."

His mother chuckles. "They sat down at a table by the win-dow," she says, "so I got a good look at the two of them to-gether. Believe me, they weren't talking about business."

"Well, it was probably somethin' completely innocent," says Johnny unconvincingly. Actually, I'm proud of him just for try-ing. Anyway, he suddenly thinks of his sister. "Hey, did Maria see them?"

"No," says Teresa, her expression darkening even further. "I steered her away down the sidewalk before she had the chance to see her father making a spectacle of himself. But I made sure I took a good long look before I left. I'll never forget that face for as long as I live."

"So, what did you do?" says Johnny, not at all anxious to hear the answer.

Teresa's face brightens a bit. "Strange as it sounds, I decided that it really wasn't his fault," she tells him. "Like I said, men just lose their minds sometimes. I think it must have something to do with their genes. As much as it hurt, I knew that in his heart your father loved me and that one day I would forgive him."

Johnny lets out an audible sigh of relief. "That's good, Mom. You've got to put these things behind you. Things like this just happen to people. It's good that you forgive them."

"Not *them,*" says Teresa, menacingly, "I said *him.* I managed to forgive your father, but that little tramp? Never. I stood on that sidewalk, watching her, and I swore in that moment that if I ever laid eyes on her again, I'd kill her with my own two hands."

Johnny feels the color drain out of his face. I mean, the kid looks like a ghost himself. He watches his mother get back up and return to the counter, where she takes out a big knife. With unabashed zeal, she plunges it into the loaf of bread and lops a good-sized piece off the end. She lifts the cover off the pot and dunks it into the rich, red gravy.

"Here," she says pleasantly, as if she's suddenly forgotten about the whole thing, "have a taste. You look like you need to eat something."

Johnny swallows the savory treat and forces a smile even though he barely tastes it going down. His mother, still holding the knife, smiles back at him. As he watches her return to her cooking, Johnny thinks back to his high school English class and tries to remember how everything turned out in *Edible Rex.*

Chapter 13

We should probably get one or two things straightened out here before I go on any further. First of all, speaking on behalf of the male species, I resent Teresa's insinuation that men go a little crazy sometimes just because of some genetic defect we've got. I will grant that some of us do occasionally lose our marbles for a while and do things that—well, that we really don't plan to, but it's for reasons that have nothing to do with our chromosomes. There's way more to it than just that. My own theory is that it's all part of some kind of conspiracy God cooked up with the women to enable them to drive us nuts whenever they feel like it, but I haven't been able to prove that yet. I'm working on it.

Second of all, Teresa was telling a little fib when she told Johnny that she decided to just forgive me that afternoon up the East Side. Okay, maybe she did, eventually, decide to just forgive me, but she left out a few key elements of the rest of the story. For starters, there's the part about that night, after I'd gone to bed, when I awoke from a sound sleep because of this peculiar sensation between my legs. I open my eyes and there's Teresa hovering over me. She's got this very sinister look on her face that I've only ever seen maybe once or twice before and I know she's up to no good. So I lift my head off the pillow just enough to look down and I can see that the peculiar sensation that woke me up is being caused by the big carving knife Teresa has pressed against a part of my anatomy I consider very precious.

"How was your lunch today, *cara mia?*" she asks, giving me a smile that's way too sweet to be wholesome.

"Lunch?" I gulp, trying real hard not to stare at the knife. I'm finding that a little difficult to do. Keep in mind that Teresa's father was a butcher, so you can understand why I'm a little apprehensive here.

"Yes, lunch," she says, pressing the blade ever so slightly harder. "You know, that little meal between breakfast and supper. How was yours today?"

You know, women are like lawyers sometimes. They almost never ask their husbands a question without already knowing the answer. The guy is always at a distinct disadvantage in these situations because he never sees it coming. It's like getting cross-examined by Perry Mason. You come home, sit down at the kitchen table, relax, maybe read the paper, and your wife just starts to chat about nothing in particular while she's frying up the zucchini in the pan. Everything's hunky-dory. Then all of a sudden she'll ask you what you think is just this innocent little question about nothing. Turns out, though, that it's just the opening of a very carefully plotted interrogation, and before you know it, she's sucked you right into it. Suddenly you're up there on the witness stand, babbling like an idiot because you realize that the prosecution has acquired incriminating evidence against you about a crime you may or may not know you've committed. It can be pretty scary, believe me.

So now I'm lying there, sweating bullets, and it's not because I turned up the thermostat before I went to bed. Teresa definitely knows something that I'd rather she didn't, but there's no way of telling how much. One thing I *am* sure of is that my choice of words here is very important. That being the case, I decide to say nothing. Seems like the safest bet.

"Let me tell you what *I* was doing today at lunchtime," says Teresa, chillingly calm. "I was up the East Side with Maria, looking for clothes for the baby."

"R–really?" I stammer.

"Mm-hmm," she coos, running the fingers of her free hand across the top of the knife. "Maria and I were just about to stop for lunch when I happened to look across the street. Imagine my surprise when I saw *you* on your way to lunch."

"Imagine," I say, clearing my throat. "What a coincidence."

"Wasn't it?" is all she says, and then we're both quiet for a time. To tell you the truth, there's really not too much else left to be said. Both of us know that I'm trapped like a bug on flypaper. The only thing that remains to be seen is just what sort of justice Teresa is planning to mete out here. I mean, right now she's judge, jury, and prosecutor. Judging by the look in her eyes, I can see there's no point in trying to throw myself on the mercy of the court. So I wait.

"I'm going to cut you some slack, Mister Midlife Crisis," she says at last.

"I'd rather you didn't cut anything," I say nervously, my eyes glued to the knife now.

Teresa chuckles menacingly. "I'm going to pretend that today was the first time you've been with this person. Understand?"

I just nod my head, relieved that there's a glimmer of hope now that I might emerge from this snare with all of my bodily appendages still intact.

"In that case, I'm going to give you an option," she continues, glancing over to the corner of the room, where there's a suitcase she's obviously packed for me. "You want to see what you've been missing all your life? Then you're all packed. Take the bag and go live with your friend—but don't ever come back."

"Or?" I ask—very meekly.

"You stay," Teresa answers. "But if I even suspect, for one

second, that you're seeing her again, I'm not going to be so for-giving. And then I wouldn't advise you to ever go to sleep in this house again so long as there's a single sharp object I can lay my hands on. *Capisc'?*"

"Absolutely," I assure her.

"So which is it going to be?"

Like I have to think about it. "I'll stay," I tell her.

"Good," says Teresa in that terrifyingly soothing voice that torturers sometimes use. "Now why don't you just go back to sleep and we'll pretend that this little incident was nothing but a bad dream, okay?"

"Okay," I answer, duly humbled. So we shut off the light and I close my eyes, but I don't fall asleep again for a very long time.

Chapter 14

So life goes on.

Anyways, it's Sunday morning and Teresa's on her way to the bakery. It's a beautiful morning. Blue sky, crisp air, the whole nine yards. Everything's a little damp because it rained the night before, but now the sun's glistening on the leaves of the trees and across the rooftops of the houses along the street.

I'm glad to see Teresa out and about. Her little walk to Nocelli's bakery has always been part of her Sunday ritual. Eight o'clock mass, the bakery, then home to make Sunday dinner. Never failed. But up till now she hasn't done any of those things since I threw a seven. Tell you the truth, I was beginning to get a little worried, so I take this as a good sign that she's getting back into her old routines.

At any rate, Teresa's planning on picking up some wine biscuits for her coffee and some nice fresh bread to go with the big pot of gravy she made the day before. The whole gang, kids and all, is coming to dinner that afternoon, so she's figuring on buying an extra loaf and some pastries for dessert.

Teresa's looking forward to having everybody over again, but she's feeling a little blue. I can tell. See, strolling along the street kind of reminds her of the old days. Since the beginning, Catini's Hardware always opened on Sunday mornings just long enough for customers to come in for whatever they needed, and then closed in time for me to be back home in time for dinner. How many times did we open up the store together? Don't even ask. But the thought of it makes her smile, all those years, all those Sunday dinners together. All the family coming to visit, gathering around the table, the talk, the laughter. That's what Sundays are for.

Of course, it's Johnny's job now to open the store on Sunday mornings, and Teresa's wondering, just like me, whether he's up to doing it week in and week out. I mean, the kid's going through a major lifestyle change here. You can't expect too much from him all at once. That's why Teresa let him off the hook so easy after he pulled his little disappearing act on Friday afternoon. She figures she can't keep the leash too tight on him. It's all right if he knows that he still has his family there to catch him when he trips up now and then. Of course, if he knows what's good for him, Johnny will watch his step so that he doesn't trip up too often.

But you know, when you're feeling a little down, it's the small things in life that usually pull you through, all those everyday things that we mostly take for granted. That's just what happens when Teresa rounds the corner and catches a whiff of the bread baking in the ovens at Nocelli's. I loved that smell; show me someone who doesn't. I don't care who you are or where you go in the world, but the smell of bread baking makes you believe in life. Even now I can almost taste it, that nice crispy crust and the steaming white bread inside. I can tell just looking at Teresa that the warm, delicious scent of it lifts her spirits.

Funny thing is, stuff like that happens a thousand times a day, but most of us never notice or at least we don't pay it much attention. For instance, ever notice how one of your all-time favorite songs just about always comes over the radio when you're driving home after a really horrendous day at the office and you're feeling like a piece of overcooked cappellini? All of a sudden you're singing along, not a care in the world. It's no coincidence. Or how about that sweet scent of flowers in spring that greets you when you roll out of bed in the morning even though you feel like pulling the covers over your head? Or that cool passing breeze that comes from out of nowhere on a blistering hot day in the summer? Or the color of the leaves in the fall that turns you on even when you're feeling bad that the summer's over. And snowflakes. I mean, have you ever stopped and thought about snowflakes? You look out the window in the dead of winter when everything's barren and frozen and lifeless. Just when you're sure that you're gonna start crawling the walls any second from being cooped up inside, a single little snowflake drifts down and sticks to the window. And you look at it. And the closer you look, you start to see that it's not just some cold white speck of nothing. No, it's really this beautiful little work of art that just fell out of God's hand and right through that gray, dead sky to land on your window right in front of your nose so that you alone in the world could see and appreciate it. And then you look outside at your snow-covered front yard and you realize that everything out there is just buried in all these little works of art that are just waiting to be discovered. And suddenly you're in a better mood. Say what you want, but sometimes I think God thought up all those little things as a way of tiding us over when we're going through a rough patch and really need a lift. You just have to pay attention, that's all.

Anyway, feeling better about things, Teresa gives a little contented sigh and pushes open the door to the bakery. The baker's wife smiles when she sees her come in. She hurries over to the counter. "Mrs. Catini, how are you?" she says. "We haven't seen you since before your poor husband died. We were so sorry to hear the news."

"Thank you, Anna," says Teresa.

"It was such a shock to us all," Anna goes on. "We were so disappointed that we couldn't get someone to watch the shop so we could go to the funeral. I heard that Father Giuliano gave a beautiful eulogy."

"Wonderful," Teresa agrees.

Anna leans over to the kitchen door. "Hey, Vito," she calls inside. "Come out and say hello to Mrs. Catini. We haven't seen her for weeks."

Vito's a thin little man with bright blue eyes and snow white hair. He and his wife have been in the bakery business for as long as I can remember. Funny, but in all that time I can't ever once remember seeing either of them outside the bakery. I'd probably never recognize them, especially Vito, even if I did. He emerges from the kitchen, just like always, his forearms and apron covered in flour. I can't picture him any other way.

"Well, good morning, Mrs. Catini," he says kindly. "It's good to see you out. How have you been since your husband passed away?"

"Pretty good," says Teresa with a shrug. "You know how it is."

"You look wonderful," says Anna, patting Teresa's hand. "Vito's right, it's good to see you out and about. Now don't be foolish. Go right out and find yourself another man before it's too late."

"Anna!" exclaims Vito.

Anna gives Teresa a conspiratorial wink. "Well, what's she supposed to do, sit around all by herself for the rest of her life? You men are all the same, you always think we can't live without you once you're gone." She turns and gives her husband a shove. "Now go back into the kitchen and get back to work."

Vito rolls his eyes and lets himself be pushed back to the ovens. "So long, Mrs. Catini, have a nice day," he calls over his shoulder.

Teresa laughs for what, to her, feels like the first time in ages. Anna turns back around and laughs with her. After a moment, though, she pats Teresa's hand and looks at her with true concern.

"How are you doing?" she says sincerely. "I mean, really."

"Eh," Teresa shrugs. "I'm trying to keep busy, Anna. It keeps my mind off of it."

"That's the spirit," says Anna. "Now, what can I get for you today? Some biscotti or maybe some nice fresh pizzelle Vito just made?"

Teresa picks out some wine biscuits, a bag of the pizzelle, two nice big loaves of bread, and a boxful of pastries. Anna puts everything into a bag for her and Teresa's soon on her way.

Instead of walking home, though, she finds herself walking toward the store. She's thinking maybe she'll pop in on Johnny, just to see how he's doing. Before she gets there, she stops and buys a couple of coffees to bring with her. When she finally walks through the door, the place is empty, save for Johnny sitting at the counter, staring at the Sunday paper. The kid's a sight. His hair's all tousled and his eyes are barely open.

"Slow morning?" says Teresa.

Johnny just shrugs and yawns.

"Here," she says, handing him one of the coffees.

Johnny perks up. *"Ooh,"* he says happily. "How did you know that's just what I needed?"

"A little bird told me," says Teresa, opening her bag. "Here, have a biscuit with it."

Johnny grabs a wine biscuit and starts munching away. Soon he's looking reasonably revived. Just in the nick of time because right then the door swings open and two customers walk in. Johnny jumps up to help them. Teresa takes that as her cue to go home. She collects her things and heads for the door.

"Don't be late for dinner," she tells Johnny.

"Right," Johnny answers, but he's too busy to notice her leaving.

Teresa smiles as she watches our son go to work. Then she turns and heads home to start dinner.

Like I said, life goes on.

Chapter 15

So now pandemonium reigns at the dinner table, just like always, but Teresa's all smiles when she walks in with the big bowl of ziti. How can she not smile, now that the dining room's crammed full of people again? Everybody's talking or shouting at the same time while the kids are chasing each other around the table. It's the first time she's cooked Sunday dinner for everyone since the funeral, so it's good to hear the voices and the laughter and the carrying on. It's the first sign that things are getting back to normal.

Teresa sets the bowl at the end of the table and orders everyone to sit and pass their plates up. They've got a portrait of me already hanging on the wall behind her. So with me staring over her shoulder, she begins to serve the family dinner.

"Mom, let me do that," Maria offers.

"Sit down," she tells her daughter in that kind, but firm voice she gets when she wants to make a point. "You're in my house and I'll do the serving."

They all smile because they know, with that simple remark, Teresa just dismissed any notion that she might turn into one of those pathetic old widows that can never lift a finger to help themselves. How many times have you seen it happen? Like Teresa's Aunt Clara after Uncle Jack died. Suddenly, this woman who once did everything on her own couldn't drive anymore. Somebody had to take her to the market or the hairdresser or the doctor or wherever else in creation she had to go. What a pain in the ass she turned into!

Well, it goes without saying that Teresa's not about to let that happen to *her*. Just the same, it's good that she let everybody know where she stands on the subject. Sure, their world's been turned upside down for a while, but everything's going to be all right. Teresa would see to that.

When the plates are all filled, Teresa goes back to the kitchen and returns a few moments later with a steaming platter of pork chops and sausage. This she sets at the center of the table next to the basket of bread and instructs everyone to help themselves. Satisfied that everything's in order, she finally takes her seat at the head of the table and raises her wineglass.

"Salute," she toasts them. "Now shut up and eat."

"Salute!" they all reply happily before digging into their plates.

For a few moments the dining room is quiet save for the sound of everyone munching their food. It's not long, though, before they're all talking again.

"Hey, Johnny," says Uncle Victor, who just conveniently decided to drop by for a visit just before dinner that afternoon, "what's with you? You look like you're half-asleep over there."

"Yeah," says Gina, nudging him in the ribs, "and what's this I hear about you leaving Mommy stranded at the store all day Friday? What are you doing, taking Friday afternoons off now?"

"I was busy," Johnny mutters.

"What is it, a new girlfriend?" she teases. "Come on, tell us."

"There's nothin' to tell," he answers, but his face is reddening. "Now let me eat."

Johnny's brothers-in-law all look at each other and begin to chuckle. Uncle Victor joins in.

"And you guys shut up," Johnny adds. By now, though, it's

too late, for his face is betraying him. He grabs a piece of bread from the basket and bites off a big chunk.

Teresa gives him one of her looks. "Come on," she chides him, "tell us who this person is that keeps you from taking care of your responsibilities. I was the one stuck working all day at the store. I think I have a right to know, don't you?"

Johnny looks about at everyone and rolls his eyes. Then he takes a bite of his bread. He looks around the table again to see if the heat's off, but he sees that they're all still waiting for a reply. He lets out an unintelligible grunt.

"*Shmph z nmbdee,*" he finally replies.

"What did he say?" says Nina.

"Swallow your food and speak like a human being!" cries Teresa.

Johnny swallows the piece of bread with an audible gulp. "She's nobody," he finally admits. "Okay? It's no big deal. Just somebody I met. It was nothing, I just lost track of the time, that's all. Now, can I eat my dinner in peace here?"

"Come on," Nina persists. "You can tell us."

"That's right," Gina chimes in. "We'll all keep it a secret, if that's what you want."

"Yeah, sure," Johnny mutters before shoveling a fork full of ziti into his mouth.

Everyone chuckles again. Teresa lets Johnny squirm for a little while longer before she finally decides to intervene. She knows there's not much use in pressing him on the subject even though his sisters love doing it. There's no way to ever get a straight answer out of Johnny when it comes to women. That's just the way it is with him.

"Let him alone," says Teresa, and with a nod of her head, she orders the rest of them to go back to eating their dinner.

Afterward, the men and children go into the parlor to watch the football games while Teresa and the girls clear the table for dessert. After so many years of cleaning up after Sunday meals together, the four women have practically got the whole thing down to a science, each of them moving about the kitchen and dining room with more precision than a Marine Corps silent drill team. The difference, of course, with this team is that they're not silent for more than two seconds at a time. While Teresa spoons the leftovers, what little there is of them, into bowls and covers them with plastic wrap, the others collect the dinner plates and silverware and stack them on the counter by the kitchen sink. Yacking nonstop all the while, the three girls set up an assembly line to wash, rinse, and dry them all.

Teresa gives a contented sigh as she puts on a big pot of coffee. It's good to hear the girls talking and laughing among themselves again. Watching them as they happily toil away gives her this renewed sense of the continuity of things, you know, the feeling that life really is going to go on for them all. It's important for all of them to feel that. But you know, for Teresa, just being in the kitchen is sometimes all it takes to put things right.

Don't get me wrong, Teresa's never had her leg chained to the stove, but the kitchen's always been a special place for her. Besides being the place where she's cooked all the meals, the kitchen's been the center of just about every waking moment in the house. Think about it yourself, where's the first place you go when you get home? To the kitchen, right? You check out the refrigerator to see what's there to nibble on before supper. You check the little notepad near the phone to see if anybody called for you. Maybe you sit at the table and look over the newspaper while the kids do their homework. Then while you're checking out the headlines, you talk about the weather or what happened at school or about what you're going to do on that vacation you've been planning. You talk and you listen to each other and you spend time just being around each other, and that's how you grow stronger as a family. It's no joke. A lot of the really good stuff in life happens in the kitchen.

That's the way it is for Teresa anyway, especially during the cleanup after a big dinner. That's when the kitchen turns into this secret little world that belongs exclusively to the women. There, with the men off on their own someplace, they can talk freely about all those things, great and small, that women like to talk about. They share their most intimate thoughts or their juiciest tidbits of gossip, something that's impossible to do with men hanging around. Men always think they're getting away with something by not taking part in this after-dinner ritual, but as far as Teresa's concerned, they don't understand what they're missing. Then again, as far as *I'm* concerned, flopping on the couch to watch the ball games when you're stuffed to the gills has its virtues too. To each his own.

The sound of her three daughters giggling brings Teresa back from her reverie. "What a bunch of *chiacchieressas!*" she kids them. "How can you three get any work done when all you do is talk? What's so funny anyway?"

"Oh, nothing," says Gina. "We were just talking about something."

"Or some-*one*, more likely," Teresa replies. She eyes the three of them. "Come on, let me in on it."

"It's nothing, Mom," says Gina. "We were just laughing about something Nina said."

"*I* didn't say it!" exclaims Nina. "It was Maria."

"*Me?*" cries Maria. "It was Gina."

Inside, Teresa's ready to bust a gut laughing because she's thinking about how many times this little scene has been played out since they were all little kids. So, with her arms folded and foot tapping, Teresa glares at them with that somebody-had-better-tell-me-what's-going-on-or-else look. They all shut up for a second so that all you can hear is the coffeepot percolating on the counter and the racket coming from the living room where Johnny and the others are horsing around with the kids.

"Okay," says Gina, trying to keep a straight face, "we were just laughing because *one* of us was wondering if you would ever get—you know—someone."

"Someone?"

"You know, someone."

"Someone who?"

"Someone to be with!"

Teresa gives them her best scowl. "Oh, I see, you mean a boyfriend," she says, putting on the indignant act. "So that's what you were all laughing about."

"Well—yes," says Gina, unable to suppress a devilish grin.

"Hmm," grunts Teresa. "And why is that so funny? How do you know that I haven't already got a boyfriend?"

"Ahh!" shrieks Maria, covering her ears. "I told you, I don't want to hear this."

"Why not?" says Nina, laughing. "What's Mommy supposed to do, not talk to another man for the rest of her life?"

"I think it would be wonderful," says Gina, then cautiously, "I mean, when the time is right, Mom *should* find someone to be with. Why should she be alone all the time?"

"So what are you saying," says Maria, "that Mommy should go out and marry some guy?"

"Will the three of you listen to yourselves!" exclaims Teresa. *"Dio mio,* I was only joking!"

There's a pause, then they all break out in laughter.

"Uff, thank God," says Maria. "I couldn't deal with that right now."

"Actually," Gina admits, "neither could I."

"Me either," Nina adds.

"Well, I guess that makes it unanimous," says Teresa, nodding in agreement, "because neither could I."

And neither could I, for the record, but nobody else needs to know that. Keep it to yourself.

"Seriously, though," says Gina, "do you think it could ever happen?"

"*Ayyy,*" sighs Teresa, picking up a dishcloth, "who knows what God has in mind? It's like you said, when the time is right, maybe I'll think about it. But for now I have enough men left around for me to worry about and they're all in the living room waiting for their dessert. So what do you say we get these dishes done and get the pastries on the table?"

With that, they all get back to work, washing the dishes and wiping the counters, but their endless gabbing goes on unabated. Mercifully, though, the topic of Teresa finding someone new finally gets dropped. Hey, I'm glad that life goes on just like everybody else; it's just that I don't want it to go on too quickly. Know what I mean?

Chapter 16

So where was I? Checking in on Johnny, right? It's October now, a nice time of year in New England. I always loved the fall. Everything changes all of a sudden. The air starts to get that dry bite to it, and the leaves on the trees turn on the colors. The days, of course, are getting shorter, but the sunlight looks and feels brighter. It's like suddenly everything comes into sharp focus and you can see what the world is truly like. Nature looks its best, if you ask me, even though it's all getting ready to die.

Anyway, Johnny's at the shop. He stoops over, hoists up a case of assorted nuts and bolts, and rips off the cover. One by one, he opens the little boxes inside and deposits the varying sizes into the appropriate labeled bins that run almost the entire length of the aisle. It's been a quiet morning, unusual for a Saturday, but the weather's been lousy outside, kind of dark and damp and chilly. Weather-wise, that's the flip side of what October can give you in New England, but you take what you get.

At any rate, Johnny's thinking it will probably be slow all day. Just as well, he figures, glancing out the storefront window at the steady drizzle that's started to fall. He's not in the mood for dealing with the mob. Besides that, he hates stocking inventory; it makes him grouchy. All things considered, he decides that he'd just as soon be grouchy by himself all day. So he lets out a grunt and tries to concentrate on his work.

But it's not easy. Johnny's head hasn't been screwed on just right ever since his little escapade with Vicki. Try as he might to forget the whole thing, he hasn't been able to stop thinking about it. It's been driving him nuts. Worst part about it is the way he's been behaving in the store. The kid's been so distracted that sometimes he just zones out in the middle of a conversation or while he's ringing up someone's purchases. At times he forgets to charge customers for items that are right on the counter in front of him. Other times he rings up a ridiculously high price for a small item.

"Forty bucks sounds a little steep for a bag of grass seed," I can remember one of them saying.

"Two hundred dollars—for a shovel?" exclaimed someone else.

"Are you sure you want to give me this electric sander for free?" another hopeful customer asked him.

"*Mannagia,*" Johnny groaned each time. "Sorry, I'm havin' a bad day."

People are generally pretty understanding, though. They figure Johnny's a little out of it on account of his having just lost his father not too long ago. Nice that they might think that, but it doesn't help. Johnny still feels like a dope every time it happens.

So Johnny muddles through the day, wondering all the while if his old man's mind got bent out of shape in just the same way. He tries to think back over the years to see if he can ever recall me acting as strange as he has been acting. I won't lie, there were plenty of days when I myself didn't know which end was up. Women can do that to you. Thing is, you've got to learn how to keep things to yourself without letting it show. You have to look like you're in control, even when inside it feels like the wheels are all coming off. Johnny, though, still tends to fly off the handle when things get crazy. That's something that he probably inherited from his mother—not that either of us would ever tell her that.

But anyway, the day drags by and customers come and go. Finally it's almost closing time. Johnny pulls the stool up to the counter and starts to write up the day's receipts. It turns out to be a pretty good day after all despite the dreary weather. He grabs a handful of cash for spending money, folds it, and tucks it into his pocket. The rest he shoves into the leather deposit pouch with the credit card receipts. He tosses in a deposit slip and zips it shut. Just then the door to the street opens.

"Yo, Johnny C!" calls a familiar voice. In walk a trio of Johnny's friends from the neighborhood. All of them have been buddies since before high school. With their hair slicked back, shirt collars open, and gold chains glistening, they're all decked out for Saturday night. I've known the lot of them since they were peewees. They're all decent kids, but when the bunch of them get together, it usually amounts to no good.

Johnny lets out a good-natured groan. "Oh no," he says, holding his hands up. "Don't tell me it's Vinny the Bum and the rest of the crew!"

"Who were ya expectin', the pope?" says Vinny, flashing that Cheshire cat smile of his from behind his dark sunglasses. He ambles up to the counter with his cohorts in tow.

"How's it goin', Johnny?" says one of them.

"Not bad, Al," says Johnny. "I'm keepin' busy. You still knockin' around with this Bozo?" he says with a nod at Vinny.

"Whatta you mean, Bozo?" laughs Vinny.

"You're all Bozos, the three of ya!"

They all laugh like a pack of hyenas. Johnny gives a nod to the third of the bunch. "What's your excuse, Tony?"

Tony's the shortest of the three, but he's dressed to the nines. I used to know his father; we went way back. *"Eh,* long time no see, Johnny," Tony says with a shrug.

"Not long enough," says Johnny. "Every time I see you guys, it's bad news."

"Who, us?" says Vinny, leaning on the counter.

"Yeah, you. So what do you guys want now?"

"We just wanted to stop by and see if we can't get you out for the night," says Vinny.

"*Ayyyy,* don't you guys ever do anything besides boozin' it up at the nightclubs every weekend?"

"What else am I supposed to do with my hard-earned money?" Vinny answers. "And besides, since when are you of all people on the wagon?"

"Since they dropped this friggin' business on my lap," groans Johnny. "Believe me, it's a pain in the nuts. I'm like wiped out here."

"All the more reason that you need to get out and blow off some steam," says Vinny, patting him on the shoulder.

"*Ooof!* Don't stand so close!" exclaims Johnny, waving his hand. "The three of you smell like a bottle of Aqua Velva."

"Yeah, but it drives the chicks wild," says Al.

"Oh yeah, I always see the women just fallin' at your feet."

"So, what's the deal?" Vinny says. "You comin' out with us tonight or what?"

"Please," Johnny replies. "I still have brain damage from the last time you hooligans took me out. I puked for a week."

"*Commmmmmme on,*" Vinny prods him. "Al here just landed a job at the Registry, so we gotta celebrate because none of us is ever gonna pay a parking or speeding ticket again."

"That true, Al?" says Johnny, most impressed. I'm impressed myself; those jobs are hard to come by.

"You got it."

"So come on out," says Vinny. "I promise, we'll go easy on ya tonight."

"Yeah, right. Whatta you guys got lined up?"

"We're goin' to the Columbus Day feast down at Saint

Rocco's," Tony chimes. "Come on, it'll be fun. We'll get some sausage-and-pepper sangawiches and then we'll hit the town."

Johnny hesitates for a moment before shaking his head. "No thanks," he says, "you guys go ahead without me tonight. I've got some things on my mind that I've got to take care of."

Vinny throws his hands up. "Oh no," he groans, "don't tell me. It's gotta be a broad."

"That's it!" laughs Al. "Look at his face. He can't hide it."

"Let's have it," says Tony. "Who is she?"

"Gimme a break," says Johnny, trying to stifle a smile. He reaches down behind the counter and comes up with a handful of the cheap key holders we sell at the register. He lobs them in their direction, making them duck for cover. "Get outta my store, you pack of lowlifes!"

"*Ayyy!* All right, we're goin'!" laughs Vinny. "Just don't forget who your friends are after this chick dumps you like all the others."

"Beat it!" shouts Johnny.

Laughing all the way, the three march down the aisle and out of the store. Johnny follows them to the door and hangs up the CLOSED sign. Before he can lock the door, though, Tony opens it and sticks his head back inside.

"Hey, Johnny," he says, "I forgot to ask you. Any chance of you scorin' me some tickets for the Pazienza fight that's comin' up in a coupla weeks?"

"Why you askin' me?" says Johnny. "I hear they got plenty of tickets still on sale down at the Civic Center."

"Yeah, but all the good ringside seats are already gone, know what I mean? I figured maybe you might know somebody like your father used to. I mean, your father could get tickets to anything. I remember the time he scored me tickets to see Sinatra when the whole friggin' thing had been sold out for weeks. And that other time when he got us all in to see the NCAAs for the bubble. Unbelievable."

"Wish I could help, Tony, but I'm not my father."

"Eh, don't sweat it," says Tony. "I just figured it was worth askin'."

"Sorry."

"No problem," says Tony as he starts to go. He pauses for a moment. "But your father," he says wistfully, "he was the best."

"No question about it."

Tony nods and slips back out the door. Johnny sighs and starts back to the counter to finish closing up. He whirls around at the sound of the door opening once more.

Tony sticks his head back inside. "You sure you don't wanna come with us?" he says.

"Get outta here!" shouts Johnny.

"All right, all right!" laughs Tony. He quickly closes the door and heads off to catch up with Vinny and Al.

Later, when Johnny has finished sweeping the floors and making sure that everything's in order, he pulls on his jacket, turns the lights out, and heads for the door. It's still damp and chilly even though the drizzle has finally let up. Johnny locks the door and steps out onto the sidewalk. With the deposit pouch tucked under his arm, he stands there for a time, wondering what to do next.

Along the sidewalk, one by one the street lamps begin to snap on, their soft glow making the wet pavement glisten. It's kind of neat, actually. Standing on the curb, the street looks almost like a river of light flowing past Johnny's feet. He gazes over it to Bento's, the flower shop across the street. They've been there for years. Nice people. Anyway, Mrs. Bento, the shop's owner, is also getting ready to close up for the night. Johnny can see her through the window, packing the flowers away into the refrigerator. That's when an idea suddenly occurs to him. His heart's racing now and he starts to step off the curb. Then he catches himself and stops.

"What am I, sick in the head?" he mutters, pulling himself together. "I'm not buyin' flowers for anybody tonight."

Johnny turns and heads to the back of the building, where his car is waiting. He hops in and gives himself a quick look in the mirror before revving up the engine. He's figuring that if he hurries, he might be able to drop the deposit pouch in the overnight drawer at the bank and still catch up with Vinny and the others in time to get a sausage-and-pepper sandwich at the feast. It'll be just another ordinary Saturday night out on the town.

If he hurries.

Johnny puts the car in gear, pulls out of the parking lot, and begins to drive down the street. He only gets a little ways beyond the store when he screeches the car to a halt. Actually, to Johnny, it seems as if the car brings itself to a halt. Whichever the case, Johnny hits the brakes when he sees an old man selling flowers from the back of this ramshackle pickup truck. The sight of the old man stooping over the buckets of flowers strikes an eerie chord somewhere deep inside him. It's like an inspiration to him. So, forgetting about the feast and the sausage and peppers and the deposit for the bank, he jumps out of the car and hurries over to the man.

Johnny's dead sure that he has never seen this old man before, but as he draws nearer, he can't help feeling there's something familiar about him. There's a twinkle in the old guy's eyes that reminds Johnny of someone, but he can't quite remember who.

"Don't tell me," says the man before Johnny can open his mouth. "I know exactly what you need." He turns and begins to carefully sift through the buckets of flowers, plucking out the best for the bunch he's making.

"How do you know what I need?" says Johnny with a laugh.

"Ayyy," says the old man, waving his hand, "a young fellah hurrying along on his way somewhere on a Saturday night, it's not hard to guess."

Johnny chuckles. "It's not like you think," he says.

The old man straightens up and begins to wrap the flowers. "Only five bucks a bunch," he sighs, "but these are really gonna make some lucky girl very happy."

"Yeah, sure," says Johnny, handing him a ten-dollar bill. "Keep the change."

"Well, at least they make me happy," says the old man, gleefully tucking the bill into his pocket.

Johnny starts back to the car. He pauses suddenly and turns to face the old man. "Do I know you?" he says.

The old man smiles. "Maybe," he says. "I've been selling my flowers here for a long time."

"But I never saw anyone selling flowers here before."

The old man smiles again. "Maybe you just never looked."

Johnny shrugs and heads back to the car. He hops in, bangs a U-turn in the middle of the street, and speeds off. You know, the kid's always in a hurry, always on the move, never really thinking about what he's doing at the moment. That's just the way it is sometimes when you're young—even sometimes when you're old. I guess it's like I said before, all of us live moment to moment.

Chapter 17

When he rings the doorbell the first time, Johnny feels a chill run up his spine, understandable because he's standing in the cold drizzle. He shakes it off and turns up the collar on his jacket. He waits for a few moments before ringing the bell again. Still no answer. He reaches once more to press the button, but then thinks better of it.

"This was a bad idea," he mutters to himself. Before he can turn to walk away, though, the door swings open.

Vicki's standing there, clutching a jacket and an umbrella. When she sees the flowers in his hand, she seems to wilt a little and lets out an exasperated sigh. Johnny just hands her the flowers and steps back away from the door.

"Johnny—" Vicki starts to say.

"Don't get the wrong idea," Johnny interrupts her. "These are just a peace offerin', so don't get rattled. I didn't come here to bother you or anythin' like that. I've just been feelin' bad, you know, about what happened that day I came here. It's been botherin' me ever since about the way I left and the things I said and, I don't know, I guess I just wanted to say I'm sorry, and that's all. If you want to talk about it, then so do I. But if you don't, that's okay too. I just had to do this to get it off my mind."

Vicki says nothing, but gazes at him with this questioning

look she gets sometimes. Johnny figures the jig's up, so he shrugs and starts to turn away.

"He never brought me flowers," she suddenly says.

Johnny turns back around. "How's that?"

"Your father. He never brought me flowers."

"What can I say?" he tells her. "I'm not my father."

"And I'm not your mother."

Johnny relaxes a little and smiles. "I guess that means I'm off the hook with that Oedipus Rex character, huh?"

"Yes, I think so," says Vicki, returning his smile. She lifts the flowers and breathes in their aroma. I have to admit, the old man picked out a nice bunch for him. "They're very nice," she says. "Thank you."

"You're welcome."

Now they stand there for a time, neither one speaking.

"So what now?" says Vicki.

"I don't know," Johnny replies. "I was hopin' that maybe we could have a cup of coffee someplace, maybe talk a little bit. But it's no big deal. I mean, it looks like you're already on your way out, so don't worry about it. Maybe we can do it some other time."

Vicki hesitates. "I do have someplace to go," she says at last, "but I still have time for a cup of coffee. It would be good if we talked."

"It can't hurt, right?" says Johnny.

"I suppose not."

"Good," says Johnny. He digs his hands down into his pockets and looks down at the ground. A brief silence ensues for now it occurs to him that he hasn't thoroughly planned out the whole thing. That's about par for the course for my son. "Um," he says at last, "you have any place in particular in mind where we could go?"

"Sure," she answers to his relief, "I know a nice place."

"Great," says Johnny. He nods toward his car. "We can ride, if you feel like it."

"Okay. Just let me put these in some water," she says, holding up the flowers. She turns and goes back inside. A few moments later she comes back, locks the door behind her, and the two walk together down the walkway to the street.

As they near the car, Johnny hurries ahead and opens the door for her. Watching her climb in, he can't help but notice the slender curve of her figure and the scent of her perfume. Right then he realizes that this is going to be a little more complicated than he thought. He swallows hard and hurries around to the other side of the car.

"You know, Johnny," says Vicki as he climbs in beside her, "we don't have to do this right now if you're not ready."

Johnny starts the engine.

"No," he says, shaking his head. "Now's as good a time as any. I'm ready if you are."

Easy to say, but truth be known, he doesn't feel ready at all. Can't say that I blame him.

Chapter 18

All right, so Johnny and Vicki end up at this little coffee shop up the East Side on Thayer Street. It's one of those new places they have just about everywhere now. You know the kind I'm talking about. They crack me up. They've got about two hundred and fifty different types of coffee. Time was when you went into a coffee shop and ordered a cup of coffee, that's what you got—a cup of coffee. Plain old coffee, in just about the same size cup, no matter where on the planet you went. Nowadays, though, you can't just order a cup of coffee. First you've got to decide if you want mocha or hazelnut or French vanilla bean or God knows what. Then do you want small, medium, large, mucho large? Do you want that with steamed milk? Nutmeg? Cinnamon? Oregano? And of course, don't forget you have to decide whether you want regular or decaf. It's enough to give you a headache.

Anyway, Johnny and Vicki walk in and settle into their seats at a table by the window. It's warm inside and the smell of freshly brewed coffee is everywhere. Outside, a thin mist hangs in the air like a veil over the people bustling along the sidewalks. Despite the damp chill, a crowd waits patiently on the sidewalk to be let into the movie theater across the street. University students stroll along in small groups, pausing now and then to peek into the shop windows. Couples amble by arm in arm. Pretty much a typical Saturday night on the East Side.

"I feel like I'm going to confession," says Vicki.

"Tell you what," says Johnny. "Say three Hail Marys for the two of us while I try to flag down the waitress."

"Deal."

It takes a minute, but Johnny finally manages to catch the waitress's eye. When he turns back to Vicki, he sees that she's gazing out the window to the sidewalk where a young couple is mugging it up beneath the glow of the street lamp. People are coming and going, jostling past them, but neither of them notices. They're in a world of their own.

"Nice to have a clear head, huh?" says Johnny.

"I can't remember a time when I felt that carefree," Vicki replies wistfully.

Before long the waitress shows up and takes their orders. When she returns with their coffee, Johnny raises his cup with mock reverence. *"Nome di padre e spirito santo,"* he intones, "and however the rest of that goes. It's been about a zillion years since I last went to confession. How 'bout you?"

"Oh God, not since I was a teenager," laughs Vicki. "My mother used to make me go at least once a week."

"Same with my mother," says Johnny. "Of course, I never really went. There was this little basketball court in back of the church. I used to take my ball with me and just shoot hoop until I figured it was time to go home. My mother never caught on."

"Don't bet on it," says Vicki. "Mothers always know a lot more than they let you think."

"You might have a point there," says Johnny. No doubt he's remembering that morning his mother told him about the day she saw me having lunch up the East Side. For a moment he considers telling Vicki about it, but then decides against it. What's the point when it would probably just upset her? Besides, the way Johnny figures it, chances are they'd never see each other again after they finished their coffees. At the same time, he realizes that he's having trouble not staring at her. So he takes a sip from his cup, turns his head, and gazes out the window. "Where are you from anyways?" he asks, not knowing how else to continue.

"Maine," says Vicki. "I grew up near Portland, but my mother lives in Kennebunkport now."

"What about your father?" asks Johnny. He tries alternating his gaze back and forth from the window to her face so as not to appear rude. It's kind of funny to watch, actually.

Vicki looks down at her cup. "He's not alive anymore," she answers after a time.

"Oh, I'm sorry to hear that," says Johnny. "When did he die?"

"Oh, a long time ago," says Vicki, "when I was a little girl." She takes a sip of coffee and looks up at Johnny. "It's funny how much you remember sometimes from your childhood, but I can still recall him almost as vividly as if I'd just seen him yesterday."

"What kinda guy was he?" says Johnny.

Vicki gazes past him with this faraway look in her eyes. "He had this big warm smile and bright twinkly eyes," she says, smiling. "What I remember most, though, is his arms when he carried me up to bed every night and tucked me in. He had these big strong arms. When I snuggled up against his shoulder and he wrapped them around me, there was no place on earth where I could have felt more safe and protected. You know?"

"That's what fathers are for, I guess," says Johnny.

"I guess," says Vicki, bowing her head. "You know, every day I would sit in my room, playing with my dolls while I waited for him to come home from work. The second I heard his car coming up the driveway, I would run as fast as I could down the stairs and right out the door. Then, without stopping, I would run straight across the porch and just jump off the top step without even looking because I knew my father would always run from the car so that he'd be there to catch me. Then one day after he had died, I was sitting in my room and I thought I heard a car coming up the drive. I was so sure it was him that I ran downstairs and out the door and without a thought I just jumped straight off the step like always—but of course this time there was no one there to catch me. That's when I finally understood that my father wasn't coming home anymore."

"How many stitches?" says Johnny.

"Oh God, it seemed like dozens!" says Vicki, laughing and crying at the same time. "My knees and elbows were practically skinned to the bone." She takes a deep breath and wipes the tears from her eyes. "I don't think I've ever told anyone that story. Don't ask why I thought of it just now."

"I didn't mind listenin'."

Vicki smiles. "You might think it's strange, but after all this time, I still find myself talking to him, asking him for help, asking him to keep me safe. It sounds weird, doesn't it?"

"Hey, it's not so strange," says Johnny, looking directly at her at last. "You know, you lose a father and it blows a major-league hole in your world. Know what I mean? You don't just forget about him overnight or ever for that matter. Just talk to my mother, she'll tell ya.

"On second thought," he hastily adds, "don't talk to my mother. It's probably not a good idea . . . I mean, given the circumstances."

"Don't worry, I understand," she tells him. "But what about you? I lost my father years ago, but it's only been a few weeks since your father died. With your business and family and everything else, I can only imagine how hard it must be for you. Your father knew so many people."

"You got that right," says Johnny. "My father made friends the way Rockefeller made money. He just had this knack for meeting people that was unbelievable."

"I think he was able to do it because he liked helping them," says Vicki.

"*Uff*, did he ever," laughs Johnny. "We're talkin' friends here, relatives, priests, local politicians who want money, people who want tickets to ball games, others who want to get a parking ticket fixed. It was like everybody and their brother was tapped into my father for somethin'. The thing is, I used to be one of those people myself, I can see that now. But now all of a sudden everyone's startin' to come to me. I can see it happenin'. It's like this big friggin' hole opened up when my father died, and like a vacuum, it's just suckin' me right in."

"I think you're strong enough to handle it," says Vicki. Now she's looking directly at him with those baby blues of hers.

"Yeah, maybe," says Johnny. "But things have changed. You see, the store, as much as I can't stand workin' in it, was like the base that my father was built on. It's given us everything we have, or at least what I have, if you know what I mean. Not to be cynical, but most of those people I was talkin' about came to my father because he was a soft touch. The business churned out the money so he could give it away whenever he wanted. But the money's not there anymore."

"Why not?"

"You gotta first understand, the store isn't all that big, but my father made some real good money back during the real estate boom. You see, he'd done a favor for one of the big contractors, so after that they all bought their supplies from us."

"What kind of favor?" says Vicki, a little cautiously.

"Don't worry," chuckles Johnny, "this wasn't like a Don Corleone–type favor. It was really nothin' special when you think about it. What happened was my father was drivin' down the highway one night when he sees this pickup truck with a flat tire pulled over in the breakdown lane. My father stops to see if he can help. The guy doesn't have a spare, so my father gives him a lift to a gas station. It was no big deal, but along the way, of course, my father introduces himself, and it turns out that the other guy is this bigwig construction executive. So the two of them talk, have a couple of laughs while the guy's tire's getting fixed. Then my father says goodbye, good luck, and he goes home. The next day, everyone, and I mean everyone, is buyin' their supplies from us. We made a killin'. Of course, my father always kept the store small. He could have expanded, no problem, bought a new house, a car, whatever. But he didn't. He liked to keep things simple, you know, never flaunt his money around."

"I admired that about your father."

"Yeah, but people find out you have it just the same. Anyways, after the real estate market in Rhode Island hit the skids, people stopped buildin' and business started to dry up for us. Don't get me wrong, we still do okay, but nothin' like the old days. So, now it's my turn to duke it out every day to make the place run. Not that I plan on doin' that forever. But that's my tale of woe."

Johnny takes a gulp of coffee and settles back in his chair. "So, what's your story? I mean, it's none of my business really, but what did you and my father . . . you know. What I mean to say is, how did you . . ."

"Meet?" Vicki finishes for him.

"Yeah."

Vicki takes a deep breath. "Actually," she begins, "the first time I saw him was at the bookstore down the street. I was going into a book-signing event where a friend of mine on the faculty was autographing copies of the book of poetry she had just published. As a matter of fact, tonight on campus she'll be reading from her newest collection of poems. That's where I'm planning to go later. Anyway, I bumped into your father while he was coming out and I dropped the copy of the book I had brought for my friend to sign. He was so nervous and apologetic when he picked it up for me."

"Yeah, I guess I can see my father bein' like that. I mean, I can't picture him in a bookstore, buyin' poetry."

"Well," Vicki continues, "that's why I remembered his face when we met again a few weeks later when we happened to get picked for jury duty together."

"Wait a minute," says Johnny. "I remember when my father had to do that. It was about three years ago. I remember the case, some kind of bank fraud or somethin', wasn't it?"

"That's the one," says Vicki, nodding her head. "When it came time to decide the case, your father and I had a big argument in the jury chambers."

"Let me guess," says Johnny. "You thought he was innocent and Pop thought he was guilty."

"No, just the opposite," she says. "The guy was a real slime. He deserved to go to jail, but your father wasn't convinced. We argued for nearly six hours."

"He was probably a friend of my father's, the guy knew everybody," Johnny chuckles. "So what happened after that?"

"Well, as it turned out, we ended up with a hung jury because one of the other jurors ended up siding with your father. I was really mad—but then, after it was over, your father asked me if I wanted to get a cup of coffee so we could talk about it. At first I said no, but he was so sweet about it, I changed my mind. So we went for a cup of coffee and started talking. Coffee led to dinner and dinner led to a drink afterwards and—well—"

"One thing led to another," says Johnny.

"Right."

Johnny looks back out the window. The kissing couple are gone, replaced now by some youngsters rolling about on skateboards. Across the street the last few people at the end of the line are making their way into the theater. He turns back and takes a sip of coffee. The cup, he realizes, is nearly empty. He squirrels up the side of his mouth in consternation. It's then that he notices that Vicki is staring at him.

"What is it?" he says.

"I'm sorry," says Vicki, shaking her head. "I didn't mean to stare, but it's just that your father used to make that same exact face that you were just making. It was kind of eerie."

"People have told me that before," says Johnny ruefully. "Some things you can't escape."

"That's life, Johnny."

"Now you sound like my father," he chuckles.

Vicki sighs and lowers her eyes. For a time the two sit in silence until she finally looks back up at him.

"Johnny, about that day you came to see me," she says in a halting voice, "I don't know how to explain what happened. I don't know if it was grief or anger or lust or whatever. But all these feelings had been bottled up inside of me since your father died and there was no one for me to talk to about him and suddenly it all just came out at once. It was like an explosion."

"Hey, don't sweat it," Johnny tells her. "It wasn't your fault. These things just happen sometimes, you know? Besides, it wasn't like I could do anythin' about it either. Like you said, it was like an explosion. It just happened. There was no stoppin' it, so why waste your time tryin' to explain it?"

"But I want to explain it," she says. "I need to."

"Hey," Johnny says with a shrug, "look at it this way. It was like the Big Bang."

Vicki, as you can imagine, has already guessed that Johnny's no Albert Einstein, so she doesn't quite see the analogy. "I beg your pardon," she says.

"You know, this big explosion thing that the scientists are always talkin' about that supposedly created everything, but nobody can figure out how or when it happened. Once the fuse got lit, though, forget it. Bang! It was done. But we're all here, right? We survived."

"Yes," says Vicki, smiling but blushing slightly. "I think I see what you mean, but I just don't know what this particular explosion might have created."

"With my luck, it's a monster," laughs Johnny.

Vicki laughs too and for a time their eyes meet and neither looks away. Suddenly, Johnny finds himself leaning closer to her over the table. Vicki, in turn, leans closer to him, her gaze never straying from his. As he reaches for his coffee cup, his hand brushes against hers, but she doesn't pull it back. Though the moment passes quickly, it seems as though they stay that way for a very long time.

"You want another cup of coffee?" says Johnny, finally breaking the spell.

Coming back to herself, Vicki looks at her watch and frowns. "I'd love to have another cup so we could talk longer," she says to his disappointment, "but I do have to be somewhere."

"Oh, right," says Johnny. "The poetry reading, I forgot." He's thinking maybe he'll say something about getting together again some other time, but he doesn't.

They both stand. Johnny reaches over and helps her put on her jacket. He tosses a few dollars onto the table and the two walk out the door. Outside on the sidewalk, they pause for a time, both looking up at the black sky. The drizzle is starting to turn into a steady rain.

"It's not that far," says Vicki, opening her umbrella. "I can walk from here."

"Don't walk," says Johnny, shaking the raindrops off his brow. "Come on, I'll give you a lift. You can tell me what a poetry reading's all about before I drop you off."

Vicki hesitates. Johnny figures it's because she doesn't want to get back in the car with him, but then she steps closer to him.

"You can come to the reading and find out for yourself," she says unexpectedly.

Johnny does a double take. *"Me?"* he laughs. "At a *poetry reading?* I don't think so."

"Come on," says Vicki with a twinkle in her eye, "it might be fun for you. It's a chance to do something I bet you've never done before."

"I've already done something I've never done before with you," he answers.

"This is a little different," she assures him. "Why don't you come? This way we can talk for a while longer. If you don't like it, you can always leave."

Johnny mulls it over for a few moments. "Okay," he says at last. "I'll go, but on one condition. You come with me to get something to eat after. I'm startin' to get hungry. Deal?"

"You're on."

"All right," says Johnny, a bit apprehensive about the whole thing. "But just tell me, who's gonna be at this thing? I mean, poetry has never been my thing. I don't want to embarrass myself."

"Oh, all the august personages of the Brown literary scene will be there," she says jokingly. "They're a very intimidating lot. Think you can handle them?"

"Hey, I'm not intimidated by anybody," huffs Johnny. "I don't care what month it is."

Vicki gives him an odd sort of look, then starts to walk away.

"Hey, where you goin'?" he calls after her.

"Come on," she tells him, holding up the umbrella, "we can still walk from here."

The rain starts coming down harder, and Johnny hurries to join her beneath the umbrella. "You sure you don't wanna take the car?" he asks as they walk away side by side.

"I like walking in the rain," she says. "Don't you?"

Johnny presses closer to her so as to stay dry beneath the umbrella.

"Eh," he says with a shrug. "I'm startin' to."

Chapter 19

By the time Vicki and Johnny make it to the poetry reading, things are already under way, so the two slip quietly into the back and stand against the wall. Johnny looks about the room. It's an enormous study, its walls lined with bookcases and the floor covered in a heavy, but worn rug. There's a mustiness in the air, the smell of all the old dust-covered books that have sat undisturbed on their shelves since God knows when. The center of the room is filled with several dozen folding chairs. These seats are all filled, their occupants all squeezed in knee to knee. Around the perimeter of the room, everyone else who came too late to get a seat is pressed up against the wall, listening intently to the speaker, who's standing at a little podium in front of the window at the far end of the room.

The speaker is this small, fragile-looking woman with jet black hair and milky white skin. She's holding a sheet of paper before her, but she's staring upward at the ceiling as she speaks. To Johnny, it looks likes she's reading aloud whatever it is that she sees written above her, so he strains to get a view of just what it might be. All he can make out, though, are the cracks he sees in the water-stained ceiling. As the woman rambles on, it occurs to Johnny that they'd better call a plasterman pretty soon. It looks like the whole thing is getting ready to come down.

Johnny turns his attention back to the speaker. It now appears that her eyes are rolling in the back of her head. It looks like she's gone into some kind of trance. That's when it finally dawns on Johnny that she's probably memorized whatever it is that's written on the paper and all this is some kind of performance. Performance or not, though, just about everyone else in the room is staring up at the ceiling with *their* eyes rolling in the backs of their heads. This being my son's first exposure to this sort of cultural event, it's all he can do to stifle a giggle.

The reading goes on for some time, hours it seems to Johnny. Now and then the woman picks up a new sheet of paper, but always her eyes are glued to the ceiling. It's not long before Johnny becomes aware of the gnawing hunger in his stomach. It's getting late and he hasn't eaten all day. To make matters worse, his stomach is beginning to growl. Luckily, the woman's voice suddenly grows louder and louder. It's like she's working herself up into a final, maddening crescendo.

"I see within the pools of light," she calls out eerily, "shimmering, swirling, incandescent. I reach out to a star and grasp its soul; it draws me in and I am reborn."

There she stops. The piece of paper flutters to the floor and she opens her eyes. As if on cue, everyone else pulls their eyes back into place and bursts into applause. Vicki claps enthusiastically along with them.

"She has such a gift," she says to Johnny. "Did you enjoy it?"

"It was definitely different," says Johnny, diplomatically enough.

People are standing now, still applauding. Soon they all gather about the woman. Vicki gives Johnny a tug on the elbow.

"Come on," she says. "Let's go congratulate her."

They squeeze through the crowd until they reach the besieged woman who, by now, looks completely overwhelmed by all the attention. Up close, Johnny can see that, with her eyes looking straight ahead, she's a reasonably attractive woman, older but definitely not old. But she's as skinny as a strand of linguine! Johnny can't help wincing when Vicki reaches out and gives her a gentle hug. From what he can see, anything harder and the poor little woman might get snapped in two.

"That was brilliant, Emily," says Vicki. "Not that I'm surprised."

"Thank you, Vicki," Emily replies. "I'm so glad you came."

"Me too."

"Emily, come along!" someone suddenly calls from across the room. A thin, balding man is beckoning to her. "We're all going to the café," he calls.

Emily sighs and turns back to Vicki. "Time to go," she says apologetically. "You know how it is. Once wasn't enough. I have to rehash the whole thing for them." She looks at Johnny and smiles. "Have we met?" she asks.

"I don't think so," he answers.

"This is Johnny—a friend of mine," says Vicki.

"You look so familiar," says Emily. "I could swear that we've met before. I almost never forget a face." She turns back to Vicki. "Why don't the two of you come along with us, Vicki. Perhaps later I'll remember."

The women turn and look at him. By now, of course, Johnny's had just about as much as he can stand of poetry for one evening, but he can tell that Vicki wants to go. What he can't tell is if Vicki wants *him* to go.

"Go ahead," he decides to tell her. "You go on with your friends, I should probably just head home."

"Nonsense," says Emily. "I insist you come."

"Me too," says Vicki.

So Johnny goes. Later at the café, he just sits there quietly while the others at the table babble on and on about rhyming couplets and iambic pentameter and rhyming schemes and rising rhythms. For all Johnny knows, they might just as well be speaking in tongues. So he barely pays attention to the conversation, but he keeps his eye on Vicki, who seems completely at ease exchanging all this mysterious blather. Even though he has no idea of what she's talking about, he can tell by the way the others pay attention whenever she speaks that they think highly of her. He's not sure why, but he can't help being impressed, even a little proud.

At the same time, Johnny's picked up on how closely Horace, the thin balding man from the poetry reading, has been eyeing Vicki. From what he can see, Emily is the star of the show, but Horace seems to be the ringleader of the bunch, at least judging by the way everyone seems to let him direct the conversation. Johnny finds it a little annoying because Horace has this strange voice, sort of like he's got a bad case of postnasal drip. Gets on your nerves. I ran into this guy myself once or twice when I was still aboveground. Tell you the truth, I thought he was annoying too, but that's another story.

Anyway, the conversation finally turns from the literary to the more mundane when Horace suddenly starts yapping about the parking situation in Providence.

"What is it about this city that you can never find a free parking space where you can leave your car without worrying about getting a ticket?" he grouses. "Downtown is the worst. Last month I got a ticket on my car that I forgot to pay right away. Now they're telling me that if I don't pay it by next week, it will cost me seventy-five dollars. Imagine!"

Everybody just kind of shakes their heads in sympathy. Finally, though, they're on a subject that Johnny can say something about, so he decides to open his mouth.

"You just gotta know somebody," he tells Horace.

Johnny regrets saying anything because suddenly all eyes are focused on him. He clears his throat and straightens up.

"What do you mean, know someone?" says Horace.

"I mean you can't go parkin' in places where people don't know you," explains Johnny. "I never do that. See, I know a guy with a lot downtown that lets me park for the bubble."

Horace squints his eyes as if he hasn't understood. "The bubble?" he says in that same nasally voice, only worse. The others lean forward as if this is the most fascinating thing they have ever heard.

"For nothin'," says Johnny. "Of course, I still duke the guy a coupla bucks for watchin' the car, but it's worth it."

"Duke?" says Horace.

Johnny can't help smiling. He's enjoying the fact that now *they* can't understand what *he's* talking about.

"Don't worry," Johnny tells him. "Next time you gotta go downtown, just give me a call first and I'll let you know where to go."

"Well," says Horace expansively, pretending to be impressed for the benefit of the others, "I finally know someone downtown who can help me. At last I feel like a true Rhode Islander."

The others, except for Vicki and Emily, laugh. Johnny just smiles. "Welcome to the club," he says. I know Johnny, and what he's really thinking inside is that what he'd like to do is take a club to Horace and that stupid irritating voice of his. My son's generally not too subtle, but sometimes you have to read between the lines.

"Where downtown do you work, Johnny?" one of the others asks.

"Johnny runs his own business," Vicki interjects.

"But on the Hill, not downtown," Johnny adds. "I sell hardware."

"Really?" says Horace, feigning great interest. "Tell me, I have a Macintosh, but everybody tells me I should get rid of it and buy an IBM. What do you think?"

The others lean closer, seeming as anxious as Horace to hear the answer. Vicki opens her mouth to answer for him, but Johnny beats her to the punch.

"I think we're talkin' about the wrong kind of hardware, Horace," says Johnny. "I sell hammers and nails, know what I mean?"

"Hammers and nails?" says Horace, his brow furrowed in thought. "Oh," he says, looking down his long skinny nose at Johnny, "that kind of hardware. I was thinking of computers, of course." He glances at Vicki and gives her a look like he's trying to say, why are you even sitting next to this dope? To her credit, Vicki's doing her best to ignore him. Tell you the truth, though, the guy's starting to aggravate even me now. It's all I can do not to give him a slap in the head; not that I could even if I tried. That's just the way things are, but I have other ways of getting my point across when I want to. Pay attention and you'll see later on.

"Yeah," says Johnny, settling back. "Actually, we've got a computer at the shop, but I haven't gotten around to figuring out how to turn the thing on."

"Most of us don't do much better with them," says Emily. "At least not me."

"Well, you can say what you like," says Horace, "but sooner or later we're all going to have to deal with the Internet and the information superhighway."

"Eh, Route Ninety-five's good enough for me," shrugs Johnny. Horace doesn't quite know what to say next, so he just furrows his brow again. Meantime, the others go back to their poetry discussion, all except for Emily, who leans closer and gazes into his eyes.

"Johnny," she says, "I meant it before when I said that you look very familiar. Are you sure we haven't met?"

"I doubt it," he answers. "I don't usually attend poetry readings and you don't look like the type who comes into the shop very often."

"What's the name of your store?" she asks.

"Catini's Hardware."

"*Catini's* Hardware?" she says kind of strangely. She pauses for a moment. "No, I don't think I've ever been there."

"Told ya," says Johnny.

"Johnny's family owns the store," says Vicki. "He's been running it by himself since his father passed away."

"I see," says Emily thoughtfully. "Has it been long, Johnny?"

"A coupla months."

"I'm so sorry."

"Eh, these things happen," says Johnny.

"Yes," says Emily softly. "I suppose they do."

At that the women and Johnny fall silent. The others, though, cackle on unabated until Horace brings the proceedings to a close when he looks at his watch and announces with a yawn that the hour is growing late. Johnny glances at his own watch; he's surprised to see how long they've been there. Soon they're all standing, pulling on their coats and jackets. Before leaving, Emily walks up to Johnny and extends her hand. The strength of her grip catches him off guard, as does the strength of her gaze.

"It was very nice to meet you, Johnny," she tells him. "Will we be seeing you again?" The question is directed more to Vicki than Johnny, but Johnny replies nonetheless.

"Actually, this is my first time out on the poetry circuit, know what I mean?" he says with a smile. "We'll have to see."

"Don't worry," says Emily in a kind voice, "sometimes it takes a while to digest these kinds of events before you really start to enjoy them. Poetry will just start to grow on you if you give it a chance."

"Maybe I'll pick up a copy of your book," Johnny offers. "That'll get me started."

"Well, it won't be out till next spring," says Emily with a laugh, "but they'll probably make me sit through a book signing when it does so you must promise to come and bring lots of friends. We poets need all the support we can get."

"Okay, I promise," says Johnny with a nod to Vicki. "Just let me know when."

Afterward, Vicki and Johnny hoof it back to the car. The rain has let up so that they no longer need to huddle beneath the umbrella. Still, they stay close, now and then brushing up against one another as they make their way through the darkened streets. As they stroll along, Vicki starts to explain to him who each of the people was that he'd met at the café. Horace, she tells him, is the head of Vicki's department. Comes as no surprise to Johnny.

"I figured he was some kind of bigwig," he says, "especially the way everyone was kowtowing to him. No offense, but the guy's kind of a geek, don't you think?"

"Horace is actually very nice," she tells him. "He just tends to have his moments now and then."

"Well, I think he just had one when I told him I sold hardware for a living. He looked at me like I was the skunk who showed up at the picnic. Of course, he didn't mind looking at you, though. That I could see."

"It's not like you're thinking," says Vicki. "Horace has always looked out for me. He's almost been like another father. Sometimes he just gets a little protective, but he's helped me a lot."

"I'll bet."

"It's true," she says. "If I get tenure, it will most likely be because of Horace."

"What's tenure, why's it so important?" says Johnny.

"If nothing else, it means I can teach at Brown for as long as I like," she explains. "Otherwise I'll have to move on to another university. I'd hate to have to do that—I love it here."

"Oh," says Johnny thoughtfully. Up ahead he sees the car. He's almost disappointed. He's tired and still hungry, but he's been enjoying their little chat while they walk. Poetry readings aren't his usual gig, but all in all he's pretty much enjoyed being with her that evening.

"Thank you for coming with me tonight," says Vicki when they're finally back in the car. "I hope it wasn't too boring for you."

"Hey, like you said before, it was somethin' new for me," says Johnny.

"Yes, but did you enjoy Emily's poetry?" she says. "Even just a little?"

"Yeah," says Johnny, "I guess I did—a little. But I probably wasn't concentratin' as hard as I should have. I was a little hungry."

"Oh my God!" Vicki exclaims. "I'm such a jerk. I completely forgot that you hadn't eaten all evening."

Johnny starts the engine and switches on the headlights and windshield wipers. "Don't sweat it," he laughs, "I'll survive. I'll just find myself somethin' to eat after I drop you off at home."

"What do you mean?" says Vicki, sounding a little let down. "I thought we had a deal."

"We did," says Johnny. "I just figured you were probably tired, ya know? I mean, it's late, you probably wanna go to bed or somethin'. I understand." He hesitates. "Maybe we can do it another time."

"No," Vicki says firmly. "I'm coming now. A deal's a deal and I never go back on my word." She gazes for a moment out the window. All the restaurants on Thayer Street have already closed for the night. She turns back and gives him this look of consternation. "There's just one problem," she admits. "I don't know where we can go and get something to eat at this hour."

Johnny chuckles and puts the car in gear. "Don't worry," he tells her. "I know just the place."

Chapter 20

One thing about my son, no matter what the situation, he's always got a plan for where his next meal is coming from. It's like he's got some kind of radar in his stomach that tells him where to go. Right now the radar is pointing him downtown. Johnny drives along until they come to City Hall. He pulls the car over and the two get out.

There's a line of two dozen or more people stretched across the sidewalk up to the back end of a trailer truck parked on the corner. It's a mixed bunch. Some of them look like street dwellers, others are decked out in tuxedos and fancy gowns, while the rest just look like ordinary couples and groups of friends out on a Saturday night.

Johnny takes a deep breath and lets out a contented sigh. For the first time all night he feels like he's back in his own element. "Come on," he says, "let's get in line."

"What is this, a soup kitchen?" says Vicki.

"No," Johnny laughs. "It's Haven Brothers. Don't tell me you've never been here."

"Well . . ." she begins.

Johnny shakes his head. "In that case, your education is sadly lacking, despite hangin' around with all those Ph.D. types."

"But what is everybody ordering?" she asks.

"Effs, what else?"

"What are effs?"

"Oh, God," says Johnny, shaking his head again. "It's worse than I thought. Just pay attention and try not to embarrass me. Okay?"

"Okay," Vicki says softly.

So they take their place in line, but the two don't say much else as they gradually move forward. When they finally step up to the window, Johnny doesn't bother looking over the little menu tacked outside or even stop to ask Vicki what she wants. Instead he just says, "Gimme four effs all the way and two Arizonas."

"Right," answers a gruff voice inside.

"What's an Arizona?" says Vicki.

"Coffee milk. Don't you know anything?"

Vicki shrugs and looks more closely at the menu. "I don't see effs on here," she says.

"Trust me, they've got 'em," says Johnny.

Vicki casts a skeptical gaze around the place. "Are you sure they have a license to serve food?"

"Don't worry," chuckles Johnny, nodding to City Hall, "the mayor himself eats here."

While they wait for their order, Johnny tugs Vicki up to the tin-plated counter and nods for her to take a peek inside. The two of them poke their heads in through the window. Inside there's a tiny kitchen with a sizzling hot griddle and a little fry-olator. Next to the griddle is another counter and the cash register. Farther back is the rest of the trailer's interior, which has been all done over into a small diner with a tin shelf and row of stools lining one wall. A motley cast of characters is assembled there, all munching away, while others come and go through a back door. In the kitchen, there's a little old guy wearing an apron and a Boston Red Sox cap. He's standing in front of the griddle, arranging rows of hot dog rolls with a big spatula. While the rolls get nice and toasted on the griddle, he starts to pull the boiled franks out of the fryolator.

"Those are the effs," Johnny says reverently.

"They look like hot dogs," says Vicki.

"They *are* hot dogs—sort of, but they're the best in town," he says with relish—if you know what I mean.

Anyway, the cook expertly shuffles the effs around and then flips them one by one into rolls. He then lines up all four of them side by side across the palm of his hand and forearm. With his free hand he reaches for a bottle of mustard and squeezes out a healthy amount onto each one. Next comes the relish and then he piles on the diced onions and a shower of celery salt. This little culinary masterpiece completed, he wraps the effs in wax paper and pushes them along with two coffee milks out the window to Johnny.

"Now what?" says Vicki after Johnny finishes paying the man.

"Now we eat."

"Where?"

Johnny pokes his head through the back door to the trailer. He reemerges, shaking his head. "Too many knuckleheads in there," he declares. "Let's go over here."

Johnny touches her arm and leads her up the stairs to the main entrance to City Hall. The stoop of the door is reasonably dry. They deposit themselves there and Johnny unwraps the effs.

"This is what you eat late night in Providence," he says, taking a big bite.

"But they smell," says Vicki.

"Yeah," Johnny laughs. "It's the onions. You won't get the stink of them off your hands for days."

Johnny's right—your hands reek for days after. But me, I could never eat those things. Gave me *agita* every time.

Vicki, meantime, is reluctantly looking over one of the effs, trying to figure out how to bite into it without spilling onions all over herself. She nibbles a little at the fringes and then, after a moment's contemplation, she takes a good-sized chomp.

"See, that wasn't so bad, was it?" says Johnny.

"Well," she says between mouthfuls, "I've had worse things to eat in my life. Why don't you let me have one of those Arizonas."

"Now you're talkin'," says Johnny. He settles back against the door. As he munches away, he gazes down the steps, survey-ing the people coming and going below. "Ya know," he says, "up here is the best view in the city as far as I'm concerned. Saturday nights you see just about everybody come and go. I love watchin' 'em. People who have been out clubbin', guys who just got done workin' second shift, cops on their break, all the motorcycle groupies, actors and singers, you name it. It's dark and cold and late, but all these people flock to the place every Saturday night and get in line for their effs just like they're goin' to communion."

Vicki looks at him and smiles. "You know, Johnny Catini," she says, "in your own way you have a poetic side. You should work on developing it."

"Yeah, right," Johnny chuckles. "Maybe I'll go to college and I can be a teacher like you when I get out."

Vicki takes a sip of her coffee milk. "Did you ever go to col-lege before?" she asks.

"Nah," Johnny replies. "My father wanted me to go, but I just about made it out of high school, know what I mean? I took a few night courses, but I dunno, I never got into it. I guess I just wasn't cut out for it."

"You just didn't give yourself enough of a chance," says Vicki. "It's never too late to go back and start over."

"*Eh,* who needs college?" says Johnny with a wave of his hand. "All I need to do is keep hangin' around you. I mean, I probably learned more about poetry in just this one night than I ever did when I went to school." Johnny's joking, of course, but to his surprise he sees that she's taking him seriously.

"I think maybe we can learn a lot from each other," she says.

"*Hmm,*" Johnny grunts, "maybe." He takes a sip of coffee milk and goes back to watching the people down below.

When they've finished eating, Johnny takes the wrappers and crumples them into balls. Without getting up, he flings the wrappers down the stairs onto the sidewalk.

"Johnny!" Vicki chides him. "That's littering."

"Not here. Just watch."

The words are no sooner out of his mouth than an old street woman appears at the end of the trailer. She shuffles across the sidewalk, picks up the wrappers Johnny threw down, and tosses them into a nearby trash can.

"Thanks, Sally," he calls down. The old woman just nods in reply.

"Do you really know her?" says Vicki.

"That's Sally," Johnny explains. "You see, she hasn't got any-place to go at night, so Haven's lets her hang around inside the truck so long as she keeps the sidewalks clean. If people stop throwing their wrappers on the ground, Sally loses her job. Know what I mean?"

Vicki looks at him for a moment and smiles. She downs the rest of her coffee milk, crumples the paper cup, and tosses it down onto the sidewalk just as Johnny had done. "There," she says smugly, "now I've done my civic duty."

They both laugh and once again their eyes meet and neither looks away. It's one of those Kodak moments and Johnny can feel himself being drawn closer to her when suddenly they hear someone calling.

"Yo, Johnny C!"

Johnny looks across the street and spies a familiar-looking trio approaching. All of a sudden he gets this sinking feeling in his stomach.

"Oh no," he mutters. "Not again."

To his surprise, Vicki takes his hand in hers. "Who are they?" she whispers anxiously.

"The dark side of the Force."

Still cackling like a pack of hyenas, Vinny, Al, and Tony march across the street and up the stairs. Vinny squeezes onto the stoop next to Vicki, who in turn squeezes in closer to Johnny. Al and Tony look on, both wearing skeptical grins like a mother who just caught her son with his hand in the cookie jar.

"Good evening, Mister Catini," says Vinny, flashing that big smile from behind his ever-present sunglasses. "Hello," he says silkily, turning to Vicki, "my name is Vincent."

"It's Vinny," says Johnny, "and why don't you lose those horrendous shades?"

"UV rays, Johnny. They're everywhere, even at night. Didn't you know that?"

"Yeah, right. Why don't you and these other two go home then before you get sunburned?"

Al and Tony crack up. Vinny clicks his tongue. "Johnny, where are your manners? You haven't even introduced your lady friend to us yet."

"I was hopin' I wouldn't have to."

Vicki relaxes her grip on Johnny's hand and reaches it out to Vinny. "Hello," she says. "I'm Vicki."

"Enchanted," Vinny replies. He takes her hand and brings it to his lips. At the last moment, though, he turns it aside and kisses his own hand. Vicki looks perplexed, but Al and Tony are howling.

"Aren't they suave?" says Johnny, taking her hand away from Vinny. "Allow me to introduce you to these hooligans. Vinny you already know. That's Al and he's Tony. I had the misfortune of growin' up with them."

"Nice to meet you," says Vicki.

"Pleasure's all ours," says Al.

"You guys aren't plannin' to stay, are ya?" says Johnny.

"Oh no, of course not," says Vinny. "We were just on our

way back to the Hill. We're goin' to Eddie's for coffee, but Tony had the goolie for some effs, so we stopped here first."

"Which reminds me," says Tony. He hurries back down the steps and falls in line outside the window.

"Anyways," Vinny continues, "when we saw you and Vicki, we figured it would be rude of us not to come up and say hello."

"I would have forgiven you," says Johnny.

"What are friends for?"

"Say, Johnny," Al says. "Why don't you two come with us to Eddie's for coffee?"

"An inspiration," Vinny enthuses. He turns to Vicki. "Please, why don't you join us?"

"*Ayyy,* do you know how much caffeine I've already had tonight?" says Johnny. "I'm gonna be bouncin' off walls pretty soon."

"Don't worry, Johnny, we'll get ya decaf."

"No thanks, guys," he says. "Vicki's a little tired. She wants to get home and I've gotta be up tomorrow to open the shop. But Al, come here for a minute." A light's gone on inside Johnny's head, dense as it is. He stands and walks a few steps down the stairs. "Watch her for a minute," he says, giving Vinny a stern look, "and keep your hands off."

"I'm always a complete gentleman," Vinny assures him.

Johnny takes Al by the arm and leads him farther down the stairs to where Vicki won't hear them. "Listen, Al," he begins. "You start your new job Monday, right?"

"Yeah," says Al with a shrug. "Why, what's the matter, Johnny?"

"Nothin' right now, but I might need you to do a little favor for me. It's a friend of mine who teaches at Brown who's havin' a little trouble with a parkin' ticket. It's not definite, but think you can take care of it for me—that is if he needs it?"

Al's face breaks out in a great grin. "Of course," he says, patting Johnny on the shoulder. "I work for the people now. I'm here to serve."

"Great," says Johnny. "It'll help out Vicki. She needs to get tenure."

"I got two fives in my pocket if it'll help."

Johnny chuckles and shakes his head. "No, just take care of the ticket for me, that'll be enough."

"No sweat. Just call me and give me the name anytime you're ready," says Al as they start back up the stairs. He suddenly stops and tugs on Johnny's jacket. "By the way," he says with a wink, "I don't blame ya for blowin' us off tonight. She's a nice one."

"I know," says Johnny. "I know."

Later, after the Three Musketeers have gone on their way, Johnny drives Vicki home. He parks the car on the street outside her apartment, and for a while they sit in the car, making small talk. They chat about the poetry reading and about Horace and the hardware misunderstanding and then about their stop at Haven Brothers. After a little while, though, there ensues the inevitable awkward silence.

"You know, Johnny," says Vicki after a time, "I remember you mentioning at the café that you didn't know how to use the computer at your store. I'd be happy to teach you how to get started on it sometime—I mean if you ever wanted to learn how."

"Thanks," says Johnny. "I might take you up on that sometime."

There's another awkward silence.

Vicki gazes down at her hands and then looks up at him. "You could start right now," she says softly. "That is—if you wanted to come in for a while. I have a computer inside we could work on together."

"I remember," says Johnny. He stares at the dashboard for

what seems like a very long time. "You sure it's not too late, I mean, you're not too tired?"

"I'll make us some coffee."

"Please," says Johnny, "anything but coffee."

"Whatever you want."

Johnny takes a deep breath. "Okay," he says, opening the door. "I guess it's never too late to learn somethin' new."

Together they leave the car and walk toward the apartment. Vicki opens the front door and steps inside, but Johnny hesitates.

"You know," he says, "all night long I've been tryin' to say goodbye to you, but somehow I never manage to leave. Why is that?"

Vicki doesn't reply, but simply opens the door wider and ushers him inside.

Chapter 21

Face it, you can't fight a tidal wave. No point in even trying. You're better off just trying to cruise in on the crest of the wave for as long as you can and hope that you come out in one piece when it finally breaks. But while you're up there, it's one hell of a ride, let me tell you.

So that's where Vicki and Johnny are now, up on top of the wave, riding it for all it's worth, but they really don't know it. See, they're both in this sort of state of denial about the whole thing, as if they're trying to pretend that it's not really happening. But forces much bigger than the two of them are at work and they both know that there's not much they can do about it.

Let me give you an idea of what I'm talking about. You see, their evenings together will all begin and end pretty much the same in the weeks that follow. This particular night is no different. When Johnny arrives at her apartment, Vicki opens the door before he's even reached the top of the steps. They've got this little routine now that they always go through. Johnny says something about how he was just passing through the neighborhood and decided to stop by to see how she was doing. For her part, Vicki does her best to act surprised at seeing him. Then, as always, she tells him that she's just on her way out, but he's welcome to come along if he likes.

Naturally, Johnny invariably goes. It's all part of this evolving ritual they've got going. Anyway, Vicki never takes him to the same place twice, but it's always something enlightening. One night she makes him sit through a lecture on contemporary art, another night it's a trip to the library, and yet another night she leads him to a piano recital. I mean, think about it, can you see Johnny at a piano recital?

Of course, these little excursions are never formally planned. Just the opposite. The two never make plans to see each other again. Somehow or other, though, Vicki always stands ready to whisk Johnny off to some cultural event at the university or someplace nearby whenever he happens to show up at the door.

Johnny dutifully accompanies her each time without question. Even he's never quite sure why. If you asked him, he'd readily admit that he's never had even the slightest interest in art or literature or classical music. Just the same, he feels compelled to go. It's as if he's a kid again and he's being made to go to school.

"Where are we goin' tonight?" he says as they stroll along the sidewalk.

"You mean, go-*ing?*" says Vicki.

"Huh?"

"I-N-G *ing*," she says good-naturedly. "You know, sounds like *eeen-guh*."

"I don't get it," says Johnny.

"You always say doin', goin', havin', bein'. What is it you have against the letter *g?*"

"Nothin'," he replies.

Vicki lets out a long sigh and smiles. "I think, Johnny Catini," she says, "that you might be incorrigible."

Johnny shrugs. "I thought I was in Providence."

They walk on.

"There's a Fellini movie playing on campus tonight that I've always wanted to see," she tells him.

Johnny doesn't go to the movies much, so the news that she's dragging him to see a foreign film with English subtitles doesn't exactly intrigue him.

"It's a classic!" Vicki exclaims at seeing the look of disinterest on his face. She pauses. "As a matter of fact, so are you." She starts to slip her arm around his, but instead sticks her hands in her jacket pockets. The two continue on toward the theater, never walking more than a few inches apart from one another.

Later, after the movie, they go for coffee, which is something they always do now. Again, it's just part of the ritual. At the café they talk about whatever event they happened to have attended. Actually, it's Vicki who usually does most of the talking; Johnny generally just sits and listens. Surprisingly enough, though, Johnny pays pretty close attention to what she says. He's almost never bored. On this particular evening, he sits there listening to her ramble on about the movie. After a while, he can't stop himself from smiling.

"What is it?" says Vicki, stopping herself in midsentence.

"Nothin'," says Johnny. "I was just thinkin', that's all."

"About what?" she says, sounding a little hurt. "It looked like you were laughing at me."

"No," Johnny tells her, patting her hand. "I wasn't doin' that at all. I was smilin' because I think you're a good teacher."

"Why do you say that?"

Johnny takes a sip of coffee. "I dunno," he says. "I guess maybe it's because I always feel like I'm in class whenever we're together. Know what I mean?"

"No," Vicki replies uneasily.

"It's nothin' to worry about," he reassures her. "I don't mind. It's just that you're always takin' me to all these things that I've never even thought about before, and when you talk about them, you make it all sound interestin'. I mean, you definitely must be good at what you do. It's kind of a privilege for me."

Vicki leans closer. "What do you mean, privilege?"

"Hey, all the students around here have to pay top dollar to hear you teach. I'm gettin' it all gratis."

"I'm just trying to help," she says softly. "I know you haven't been exposed to most of these things before. It's hard to know that they're all happening here when you're not part of the university. But I think it's good that you go to them. You need to take advantage of what's here. It broadens your horizons."

"I appreciate you tryin' to help me," says Johnny.

For a while neither of them speaks. The two just gaze at one another, then go back to drinking their coffee.

Afterward, Johnny walks Vicki back to her apartment. Now it's like there's this ticking time bomb waiting to go off any second. Vicki gets more nervous and talks faster and faster the closer they get to home. It amazes even me that she never seems to run out of topics. Once they reach the doorstep, there's the usual awkward exchange of small talk followed by the inevitable invitation to come inside for another cup of coffee before he goes home. The fact that they've just come from a coffee shop doesn't seem to bother either of them. Vicki might have invited him in for a glass of wine or to watch a television show or to play a game of chess. For some reason, though, it's always for another cup of coffee. Not that it matters, they're not going to be drinking wine or watching television or playing chess. It's all just a pretense for helping Johnny to step over the threshold with her. Coffee's just easy, I guess.

Once inside, Johnny follows her to the living room. Vicki places a CD in the player and, as the music swells, turns to face him.

"I like this music," says Johnny, trying his best to keep his distance. "What is it?"

"Mozart. Symphony Number Twenty-five in G minor," she says breathlessly.

Johnny hesitates, but then takes a tentative step toward her. Every night they see each other, it's a struggle to stay apart, but every night the struggle grows shorter and shorter. As he draws near, Vicki gazes helplessly at him like those deer you see staring into the headlights of an oncoming car.

"I really should be goin'," Johnny says.

"I know," says Vicki.

"I really shouldn't be here at all," he says.

"I know."

"My mother would kill us both if she knew about this."

"I know."

"We've got absolutely nothin' in common."

"I know."

"Your friends all hate me."

"I know, I know," says Vicki.

Then, before Johnny can come up with another reason as to why they shouldn't be together, they fall into one another's arms. That's when that big son of a bitch of a wave comes rolling in and just picks the two of them up and sweeps them away. There's nothing either of them can do, so they don't even bother trying to fight it.

Hey, what do you expect, that's *amore*.

Chapter 22

I don't know what it is about computers, but I could never see the big attraction to them. Everybody makes such a big deal out of all this Internet stuff, but as far as I can see, it's not much different from watching television. The only reason I bought a computer was because one of our suppliers convinced me that I could save some money by using it to keep track of inventory, ordering merchandise, paying bills, the whole nine yards. Made it sound like the best thing since sliced bread. Up till then I pretty much did everything with a paper and pencil. Sure, maybe my bookkeeping wasn't the best, but complete and accurate records aren't necessarily a good thing when you're in business, especially if the IRS comes calling. Besides, I always followed generally accepted accounting principles—if you know what I mean.

Just the same, I figured maybe it was time to give it a shot, you know, bring the shop into the late twentieth century. Trouble is, though, that when I opened the box and set the thing up on the counter, I didn't have the patience to sit there and figure out how it worked. I didn't even know how to turn the damn thing on. So it sat there. Every day I would promise myself that I was going to get the thing up and running, but every day I'd find some excuse not to. Before long I was just using it as a place to hang up Post-it Notes to myself. At least I got something for my money. In the end I just forgot about it and let it become just another piece of clutter. The way I looked at it, I'd done my part in just getting the thing; somebody else would have to come along and learn how to put it to use.

So anyway, Nina walks into the store. She sees Johnny up at the counter and walks over to him.

"What are you doing?" she says.

Johnny doesn't look up from the computer, but continues tapping away at the keyboard. He's trying to put in the numbers from his last inventory check. Now and then he consults the three-inch-thick "getting started" manual next to him on the counter. It's all new and more than a little complicated for him, but Johnny seems to be getting the hang of it. He hums along to the music playing on the cassette player he brought to work that morning.

His sister comes up behind him and leans over his shoulder. "Johnny, what are you doing?" she says again.

"What's it look like I'm doin' here? I'm workin'."

"Since when do you know anything about computers?" she says. "You're always saying that you don't even know how to turn the thing on."

"Well, I'm learnin'," he answers.

Nina steps back. "Pop was supposed to learn how to use that thing before he got sick," she says glumly. "He just never got around to it, he was always too busy. How come you have time to do it?"

"Because I'm not Pop," Johnny replies. "Now you wanna let me get my work done or what?"

"Sure," says Nina, "I just came by to pick up some light-bulbs." She turns and walks down the aisle.

"Let me know how many you take," he calls after her. "I wanna keep the system up to date, know what I mean?"

"Yes, Bill Gates," Nina calls back. She returns a few moments later and places the bulbs on the counter. "Three packs," she says, "all a hundred watts."

"Thanks," says Johnny. He continues working away at the keyboard. Nina comes up alongside, rests her elbows on the counter, and gazes at the computer screen with him.

"You're really getting into this, aren't you," she says.

"*Eh*," shrugs Johnny.

Nina looks over at the cassette player. "What are you listening to?" she asks.

"Mozart."

"*Mozart?*"

"Symphony something or other in G minor. Nice, isn't it?"

Nina looks more closely at her brother, then reaches out and places the palm of her hand on his forehead. She looks at him with concern. "Are you feeling all right?" she says.

Johnny finally turns away from the computer and looks at her. "I'm fine," he says with a laugh. "Why, what's the matter?"

"I'm not sure," she replies. "It's just that you seem—"

"What?"

"I don't know. Different somehow, I guess."

"I'm just busy," he reassures her. "Trust me."

Johnny turns his attention back to the keyboard and resumes working on the computer. Nina stands back and watches him for a time without speaking. Finally she gathers her jacket and purse together and picks up the lightbulbs.

"You know," she says, "Pop always said he'd show the kids how to use the computer once he got it up and running."

"They're a little young, aren't they?" says Johnny without looking up.

"Are you kidding? Now's the time to get them started— otherwise they'll be behind when they get to school. All the kids are using them today."

"*Hmm*, you might be right," says Johnny, trying to concentrate. "I never really thought about it."

"When you get some time, maybe *you* could show them how to use it," she says tentatively.

Johnny spins around in the chair to face her. "Me? Whatta you, kiddin'?"

"Don't make that face," she chides him. "Come on, it'll be fun. The kids all love you. It will be a blast for them."

"But I barely know what I'm doin' here myself, Nina," Johnny grouses. "How can I teach them anythin'?"

"Don't worry," she says. "You'll figure it out."

"Yeah, right. Then you'll be on my case if they get to school someday and still don't know what they're doin'."

"No I won't," she says. "Come on, just say you'll do it."

Johnny replies with a grumble.

"I'll take that as a yes," says Nina, smiling. She pauses and lets her gaze wander around the store for a few moments. A sad look comes over her face.

"What's the matter?" says Johnny. "You okay?"

"Yes," says Nina. "I was just thinking about Pop. It's already two months that he's been gone. I can't believe it."

"Time flies when you're having fun."

"Shut up, Johnny," she says, slapping him across the shoulder, "I'm serious. I feel bad about it."

"I know, I know," he says. "Everybody does. Whatta you gonna do?"

"I guess there's nothing anyone can do, but it helps to talk about it," Nina says. She looks past him to the calendar on the wall. "But it's almost November already. Before you know it, Thanksgiving will be here, then Christmas and New Year's. The holidays won't be the same without Pop."

"We'll make do," says Johnny.

"I guess we'll have to," she says. "Do you think Mommy will be up to having everyone this year?"

"I hope so. Otherwise it'll be World War Three, trying to decide whose house everyone's going to for Thanksgiving."

"I hadn't thought of that."

"Get ready for it."

"Oh well," says Nina, starting to leave, "at least that gives us something to look forward to. I've got to go. Why don't you stop by for dinner tonight. Gina and Jimmy are coming over too."

"Thanks, but I got plans."

"What kind of plans?"

"I'm going to the library."

"The *library?*" says Nina. She looks at him more closely. "Are you sure you're all right?"

"Yes, now will you get outta here and let me finish my work?"

"Anything you say," she says over her shoulder as she walks to the door. "Just let me know when you get your Rhodes Scholarship."

"Right," Johnny mumbles. He might have laughed if he knew what a Rhodes Scholarship was. But he doesn't, so he goes back to work, humming along once more to the music.

Chapter 23

Women love to talk, which is a good thing because, for the most part, men generally go through their lives at a complete loss for words. Without women to fill in the gaps, there'd be little conversation between the sexes. Left to men, all we'd have is long periods of silence occasionally interrupted by, "Pass the salt," or "Would you mind letting me have some of the covers?" Not much else.

But women generally have a lot more on their minds than men, so I guess it stands to reason that they'd have a lot more to say about things in general. I can remember one time at the shop, kind of a slow day, but I was keeping busy by paying a few bills, adding up some receipts, just general stuff. Then the phone rings. It's Teresa. She wants to talk about Thanksgiving or something to do with the holidays, I can't quite remember what. Whatever, I just sort of mumble something unintelligible, doesn't really matter. All that counts is that I offer some acknowledgment that I'm now engaged in an official conversation. This requires no further action on my part other than to occasionally say *"Mm-hmm,"* or *"Uh-huh,"* or an occasional "I know." My job is to listen while Teresa talks, which I do until I realize that my pen's running out of ink and I can't finish doing the bills. So I put the phone down and go looking for a new one. I come back a minute or two later, pick up the phone, and Teresa's still talk-ing away. Hasn't missed a beat.

"Mm-hmm," I say, going back to work on the bills.

Teresa keeps talking. Meantime a customer walks in. I put the phone down again to go help him. He's looking for some paintbrushes or something like that. I find what he's looking for pretty quickly, bring everything back to the counter, ring him up. The guy pays and goes. The whole thing takes what, maybe four or five minutes? I pick up the phone. Teresa hasn't missed me.

"Uh-huh," I say.

Now the next ten or fifteen minutes I'm flipping through some catalogs, just checking to see if there's anything new I should be carrying for when winter rolls in. You have to keep rotating your inventory with the seasons. That's the way it is in most retail businesses. Anyway, I spot a few items that I think might be good to carry and write myself a reminder so I won't forget about them. Teresa still hasn't stopped talking the whole time.

"I know," I say, shoving the catalogs under the counter when I've finished. "So, what's for dinner tonight?"

Don't get me wrong. Much as women love to talk, they're still much better listeners than men. That's why when a woman really has something important on her mind, she'll usually spill it to another woman instead of wasting her time talking to a man about it. That way she's virtually guaranteed to at least get some reasonably intelligent feedback to what she has to say, even if the other woman is a complete stranger. Sometimes I think it's even better that way.

In any case, when a woman needs to talk, she needs to talk, and right now Vicki needs to talk. She's been walking around Brown University day in and day out like she's in some kind of trance, probably because she knows what she's got going on with Johnny is completely off the wall. But just the same, it's like she's got ahold of some kind of forbidden fruit that she can't stop herself from eating.

So, one afternoon while she's cruising across campus after her last class of the day, she sees Emily up ahead and flags her down. It's a brisk day and the wind is just blasting across the campus. Vicki is wearing a heavy sweater, but Emily is bundled up in a big bulky coat, hat, and scarf like it's the middle of winter.

"I'm freezing today!" Emily exclaims.

"I know," says Vicki. "Where are you headed?"

"To my office."

"Mind if I tag along?"

"Of course not. I haven't seen you for a while. We can catch up on what's been happening."

Later, as they're climbing the stairs to the English Department, they meet Horace coming the other way. You remember Horace, the guy I was telling you about that Johnny met that night at the café with Vicki. To tell you the truth, he's not such a bad guy, but he got on my nerves a little bit that night when he got snotty with Johnny, but don't worry, I fixed him. He gives a half smile when he sees Vicki and Emily even though he looks like death warmed over at the moment. He doesn't say much besides a quick hello before going on his way.

"What's up with Horace?" Vicki asks when they finally get settled into Emily's office. "He looks terrible today."

"I don't think it's anything serious," says Emily. "He told me this morning that he's been having a little trouble sleeping lately. Says he keeps having this strange nightmare about a dinosaur chasing him."

"A *dinosaur?*" laughs Vicki. "What's he doing, going to too many horror movies?"

"I think he just drinks too much coffee," chuckles Emily.

"Could be," says Vicki.

Emily starts shuffling papers around on her desk. This is no small task, I can tell you. The top of her desk looks like a paper-recycling bin. It's cluttered with stacks of books, student essays, half-written manuscripts of her own. It's a mess. "So, how have you been?" she says, stuffing some of the excess into one of the desk drawers. "It's been a while since we talked."

"Frenetic," Vicki says, wearily slouching back onto the little couch opposite the desk. She looks up at the wall. Emily's got this picture of a Greco-Roman amphitheater in Taormina. It's in Sicily. Nice place, they tell me. Up on the cliff, overlooking the ocean. I'd like to go there myself someday. Everything in its time.

Anyway, Emily looks at her. "Are you still seeing Johnny?" she asks.

"That's why it's been frenetic," sighs Vicki.

"I see," says Emily. "Do you want to talk about it?"

Does she want to talk about it? What, are you kidding? So Vicki spills it. I mean everything. The works. The whole kit and caboodle. All of it. The whole nine yards. Lock, stock, and barrel. The whole enchilada. The Full Monty. We're talking names, dates, places. I mean, I'm dead and I still can't believe what I'm hearing coming out of her mouth. *Mannagia,* half of the stuff I can't even remember myself! But out it all comes, live and in living color.

So, how does Emily react to all this once Vicki's all done spilling her guts? Well, for a while she just sits there, no doubt appalled because her face has turned just about the same color as this page you're reading. For her part, Vicki's lying back with her arms covering her eyes and head, like she's afraid the ceiling's about to collapse on top of her.

"Don't tell me I need professional help," Vicki laments. "I already know that."

"No," says Emily softly, "you don't need professional help. You just need to spend some time by yourself, trying to understand why it is you fell in love with—*both* of these men."

"Oh, Emily, whatta ya think I been tryin' to do here?" Vicki cries. "That's why I'm in this state."

Emily looks at her. "Say that again, please."

"Wha'?" says Vicki.

"Never mind."

"What's worse," Vicki goes on, "is how guilty I feel."

"You mean about Johnny being Nick's son?"

"No," says Vicki. "I mean about Horace."

"What about him?" Emily says warily. "Don't tell me that you and Horace . . ."

"Oh, for heaven's sake, not that!" Vicki exclaims. "It's something else."

"What then?"

"It's hard to explain."

"You're being vague, Vicki. Just say it."

Vicki throws her hands up. "Horace don't like Johnny," she declares. "There, I've said it."

"Would you mind saying it again, please."

"What?"

"What you just said."

Vicki lets out a sigh. "Horace don't—oh God, listen to me," she says, burying her face in her hands. "What's happening to me?"

Emily laughs softly. "I think you already know,'" she says. "But what is it about Horace not liking Johnny that makes you feel so guilty?"

Vicki lets her hands drop back onto her lap. "Horace has been so good to me ever since I came here. I know it sounds terrible, but deep inside I have this fear that he won't help me get tenure because of Johnny. I feel awful just thinking that, but I can't help it. At the same time, there are days I get angry at Horace for making me feel that way. It makes me want to confront him about it, and the others too, to defend Johnny. I mean, why are all of us such snobs all of a sudden?"

"Horace has always been something of a father figure for you, hasn't he?" says Emily.

"I guess," Vicki admits, "but what does that mean?"

Emily sits back and folds her hands. She gazes at Vicki thoughtfully. "I'm not sure," she begins, "but let me play Freud for a minute and see if we can't figure some of this out."

"Oh God," Vicki groans, "you *do* think I need professional help."

"Bear with me," Emily replies. "Okay, let's start with Nick. Now, your own father died when you were just a little girl, so maybe you fell in love with Nick because he represented part of the unresolved issues you had left over with your father as you grew up."

"What are you saying," cries Vicki, "that I fell in love with Nick because I have some sort of Daddy complex?"

"We're just trying to think this whole thing out," Emily persists. "Now, the way I understand it, the whole purpose of the Electra complex is so that a young woman can move on and form loving relationships with other men. So to do that, she must first get over her attachment to her father. You never got the chance to do that because your father died so early in your life. So, as an adult woman, you still needed to go through that stage of your development. Nick or someone like him was probably bound to come along sooner or later in your life."

"Okay," says Vicki, more than just a little skeptical. "Suppose you're right, that Nick represented my father to me. Are you suggesting that what we had together was just a phase I was going through?"

"Well, we all go and grow through phases, and the people we meet and love along the way are part of those phases. Think about it. Just because you had a crush on a boy when you were in junior high school doesn't mean that he's the only type of person you will ever love, right? How many times have you thought back to someone you dated in college, someone you were really passionate about, and now you wonder, God, what did I ever see in that guy, he was such a loser!"

Vicki can't help laughing now. "Please," she says, "I don't even want to start counting."

"You see what I mean then?"

"Sure, I guess, but there was a lot more to it than you make it sound."

"I understand," says Emily. "While Nick was probably different from the other men you might have dated, you found him attractive because he was established and mature and confident. He knew his way around the world, at least the part of the world he lived in. Whatever the age, those are very sexy qualities in a man."

Who am I to argue?

"It almost sounds as if you knew him too," says Vicki.

"Let's just say I know his type," says Emily. "But getting back to the subject, I would bet that, deep in your heart, you were probably getting ready to call the whole thing off sooner or later, even if Nick hadn't taken ill."

"What makes you so sure?" says Vicki.

"Let me answer a question with a question. Do you think the two of you would have ever married?"

"No," says Vicki with a sigh. "I know it sounds strange coming from me, but Nick was really devoted to his wife and his family. It was just out of the question."

"Mm-hmm," Emily nods thoughtfully. "Let me ask you another one. Did you go many places together?"

Vicki shakes her head. "To tell you the truth, we hardly ever left my apartment when we were together."

"Why not?"

"Well, Nick knew so many people," says Vicki. "He was always worried that we'd run into someone he knew. This is a very small state, Emily."

"I know," she replies.

"And besides that, he was always in a rush to get back to the business. It was always a juggling act for both of us. Sometimes it got on my nerves."

"I can understand that," says Emily, "but that all made for a very comfortable situation for both of you, didn't it? What I mean to say is, knowing full well that your relationship could only go so far made things easier for you, less pressure. Both of you knew that you'd never have to face those really hard questions we ask ourselves when it comes time to decide if we really want to make a commitment to someone."

"Maybe," sighs Vicki. "I've never really thought about it that way before. And what about Horace?"

"Well, I guess with your romance with Nick finally over, Horace now becomes your traditional father, at least psychologically speaking. You don't think of him romantically—at least I hope you don't—but as a person that cares for you, that's keeping watch over you, someone you can turn to for guidance."

"And Johnny?"

"Oh, that's easy," chuckles Emily. "Johnny's the boy you fall madly in love with simply because you know your father can't stand him."

"Oh, God!" laughs Vicki.

Emily laughs in turn. "But can't you see it?" she says. "The more your father disapproves of him, the more attractive you find him. It's an old story."

"So Johnny's Romeo and I'm Juliet, is that it?"

"Sort of," says Emily. "At least that's as far as my thinking takes me."

They both sit quietly for a few moments.

"So what are you going to do?" Emily asks.

"I don't know," Vicki admits. "I'm going home to Maine in a few weeks to spend Thanksgiving with my mother. I think I'll just delay thinking about all of this until I get there, because right at the moment, thinking doesn't seem to help very much."

"C'est l'amour, mon amie."

Vicki takes a deep breath and stands. She glances out the window. The wind is still howling across the Green, scattering the leaves in all these little whirlwinds that look like miniature tornadoes. I've always gotten a kick out of that.

"Thanks for listening, Emily," she says. "It was good to get some of this off my chest. I hope you don't think I'm too much of a crackpot."

"Nonsense," says Emily. "We all need to talk out things like this sometimes. It's what makes us human."

"Thanks," says Vicki, heading for the door.

"Anytime."

After Vicki leaves, Emily goes to the window and watches her cross the campus, straining against the wind. The sun is starting to set now, lighting the sky like a can of orange paint spilling across the horizon. She shakes her head as she turns away and sits back down at the desk.

"Wow," she says to herself, "that girl really needs help."

She could be right, but then again what do poets know?

Chapter 24

Remember what I told you about the plates, you know, the ones God's got spinning up over His head like those performers you see? Well, right about now is when the plates start to wobble a little, so you know it's not going to be too long before some of them hit the pavement. Of course, in Johnny's case, the plates are more likely to hit him right in the head, but he can't see that coming yet. He's got things on his mind.

So there he is, bleary-eyed, reading the letter from American Hardware Stores for about the three-hundredth time since it came in the mail. With a sigh, he lets the letter drop to the top of the desk, rubs his eyes, and lets out a yawn. Overhead, the rays of the rising sun are filtering through the small, grimy window, casting this soft amber glow all about the little office at the back of the shop. The muted light gives everything a surreal quality as if it's all something from a very old photograph. It's actually pretty neat.

Anyhow, Johnny's made it to the shop early this morning, figuring he'd get a head start on the backlog of paperwork he's got piling up. With any luck, he might get a lot done before customers start parading in. Instead of doing his work, however, he's wasted most of the time rereading the stupid letter, particularly the part about receiving the "fairest possible return on his investment." Johnny's no accountant, so he can't help wondering how much "fair" would be. He's tempted to pick up the telephone to find out the answer to that question, but he knows that no one would be there to take his call at that hour. So, like always, he folds the letter and tucks it back into the desk drawer, figuring he'll get around to contacting them one of these days.

"Why would I want to give up this paradise anyways?" he says aloud to no one. He shoves the desk drawer shut and mopes off into the shop.

Johnny's in a little bit of a mood because it's Monday and Johnny has always hated Mondays. As far as he's concerned, there's nothing good about them. No one has ever accused Johnny of being a workaholic so, for him, Monday represents the depressing passage into oblivion of another precious weekend, not to mention the equally depressing prospect of an entire workweek stretching out before him until the next weekend comes along. Worst of all is the fact that this particular Monday is inventory day. Johnny's going to spend the better part of the morning trudging up and down every aisle, counting merchandise so that, later that afternoon, he can order new stock from his suppliers. Tell you the truth, I hated doing inventory myself. It's the pits.

With his clipboard in hand, Johnny reluctantly sets to work. He moves steadily down the first aisle, checking off items as he goes along. It's not rocket science, mind you, but it's pretty tedious because you have to pay attention to what you're doing. Now and then Johnny looks over his shoulder at the computer resting on the counter. Using it has made keeping track of his inventory and ordering new stock a little easier. Trouble is someone still has to physically walk around and check off what's on the shelves, and that's really the worst part. Until they invent a computer that can hop down from the counter and do it for him, the job's all Johnny's. So, for now, the computer just sits there idle, its monitor staring at him like a dark square eye. It kind of irritates him.

But the morning passes and customers trickle in and out, pretty much average for a Monday morning this time of year. Most of the contractors are pushing to finish their outdoor work before the bad weather sets in, so they keep Johnny busy for a while, but then things quiet down. It's getting near noon when Johnny hears the jingling of the bell on the front door. He leans over the counter and peeks down the aisle in time to see Angela step inside. Dolled up as usual in her high heels and painted-on jeans, she prances her way up to the cash register.

Johnny hasn't laid eyes on Angela since the funeral, but in the back of his mind he's figured all along that it was only a matter of time before she showed up. Somehow, though, he'd forgotten all about her, what with all the other craziness going on. His life, he realizes, could get even more complicated in a hurry if he doesn't watch his step. So he takes a deep breath and braces himself.

Angela leans over the counter and kisses his cheek. "Hello, stranger," she says with a sly smile. "Long time no see."

Angela's looking a hundred percent and she's wearing the same perfume she had on when they were last alone together after the wake. Johnny takes one whiff of it and suddenly all the memories of that long night get roused.

"Hi, Angela," he says uneasily. "I've, *uh*—been meanin' to call you."

"I'll bet."

Johnny clears his throat. He knows he's on the spot now. Seems to be a perpetual state of being for him lately. But hey, that's the price of admission, if you catch my meaning.

"Aren't you supposed to be workin' today?" he says.

Angela reaches across the counter and rests her soft, warm hand on his. She lingers there for a few moments, letting her fingers caress his skin.

"I decided to take a day off," she tells him, "so I thought I'd come by and see you."

"That's nice," says Johnny, slowly drawing his hand away. He picks up his pen and clipboard and pretends to scribble some notes on the inventory sheet. He's figuring that maybe if he acts like he's really busy, Angela might just go away on her own. It's not that Johnny's trying to get rid of her or anything, it's just that he's—well—trying to get rid of her. Angela's a good girl, but deep inside, Johnny knows he's way overmatched trying to match wits with her. He's just not foxy enough. Most men aren't when they run up against a woman who knows what she's doing.

Angela, on the other hand, is extremely foxy, in all senses of the word, so she's undaunted by the cool act Johnny's trying to put on. "It's been so long since we last saw each other," she purrs, giving him this knowing look. "I thought you might take me out to lunch so we can talk for a while."

"*Ayyy*, I don't know, Ange," says Johnny with an exaggerated sigh. "I can't leave the store today. There's no one around to watch it for me, and I've got way too much work to catch up on."

Angela gives him a pout, and for a second, Johnny figures he's off the hook. But then she flashes him a smile.

"That's okay," she says sweetly. "Why don't I just go out and pick up some sandwiches for us and we can have lunch right here?"

To his dismay, Johnny can't think of any way to turn down the offer. He stands there, wondering why it seems like women are always able to outsmart him with so little effort. It's something's that really starting to aggravate him—but why should he be any different from the rest of us?

"Yeah," he reluctantly agrees. "I guess that would be okay." Johnny rationalizes that at least in the shop they'd be on neutral ground. How much trouble could they get into? If he'd agreed to go out, there'd be no telling what mischief might have ensued. So he pops open the cash register. "Here," he says, pulling out a few bills. "Just don't get me anything that's gonna give me *agita."*

"Keep that," she tells him with a wink. "This one's on me." Looking quite pleased with herself, Angela turns and sashays back out the door.

When she's out of sight, Johnny buries his face in his hands. "This is trouble," he moans. "I just know it."

It's not long before Angela returns with sandwiches and coffee. While she sets up lunch by the cash register, Johnny pulls two stools up to the counter. He slides the newer of the two over to Angela's side.

"Here," he says, "you take the good one. I'll take the Dennis the Menace chair."

"The what?" laughs Angela.

"The Dennis the Menace chair. I call it that because it's the stool my father used to make me sit on over in the corner when I was a kid."

"Why," she asks, "to punish you?"

"No," Johnny chuckles, "but that's what it felt like. See, my father never made me do too much around the store besides a little sweeping or maybe helping people carry stuff to their cars, but instead he always made me just hang around and watch what was happening. Hour after hour, it seemed sometimes. I'd get bored, so I'd just sit there reading comic books or twiddling my thumbs. Every now and then a customer would come in and he and my father would get to yacking about this or that. I never listened. But later, after the guy left, my father would always turn around and give me that look of his and then he'd say, "Hey, *uaglio,* you payin' attention to any of this over there or what?"

"It's funny," Johnny goes on, "but every now and then I get questions from customers about different things, you know, how to use a certain tool, how to fix a faucet. General stuff like that. What's weird is that nine times out of ten I know the answer, but I can't figure out why. I mean, sometimes they walk away and later on I say to myself, how the hell did I know that?"

"I guess you were paying attention after all," says Angela, smiling. "Your father was a good teacher."

Johnny shrugs and takes a seat. He says little else while they eat other than to comment on the weather or other such small talk. For her part, Angela seems content to just follow along, letting him keep the conversation light. All the while, though, she never takes her eyes off him. It's got Johnny a little worried because he can't quite figure out what she's got up her sleeve.

"Are things always this quiet at lunchtime?" she asks.

"You kiddin'? You should see this place sometimes at lunch, it's nuts. Then other days, like today, it's quiet, but you never know when the lid's gonna come off again. But why, does it being quiet bother you?"

"No, actually I prefer it this way," says Angela. "I was hoping we'd be alone together while we talked."

"How come?" says Johnny.

"Because I have something important that I wanted to tell you."

"Wha'?" says Johnny, taking a bite out of his sandwich.

This is where Johnny's starts to get an inkling of what I've been telling you about those plates, you know, the ones that are up there spinning in the air. He's about to discover how easily they can fly off and smack you in the head.

Angela leans closer and gives him a sweet look. She smiles and takes his hand. "Johnny," she tells him very gently, "I'm pregnant."

Now, Johnny's not sure if the sandwich has gone down the wrong way or if maybe he's having a heart attack, but all of a sudden he gets this feeling like he's choking to death. His eyeballs start popping out of his head and his mouth's hanging wide open. He looks down and realizes that he's just spit a half-chewed piece of *capocol'* onto his lap. I mean, the kid's dumbfounded, so he just sits there staring at her while he tries to get his mouth to say something reasonably coherent. A sort of guttural gurgle is the best he can manage.

Giving him that same sweet look, Angela picks up her cup of coffee. "Just kidding," she says, before taking a sip.

Johnny drops his head onto the counter and finally succeeds in taking a breath. "For Crissakes, Angela," he gasps, "don't ever do anythin' like that again!"

The smile fades from Angela's face. She gazes at him with a sad but understanding expression. "I guess the thought of such a thing is pretty scary to you," she says stoically.

Johnny finally straightens himself up. "Yeah," he says, nodding his head for emphasis, "you might say that it's a little scary."

"I figured that's how you felt."

"So what made you do it?"

"I don't know," Angela shrugs. "I guess I just wanted to see if our little encounter after your father's wake really meant something or if we were both just in the mood for a little . . . recreation."

"I don't know what it was," Johnny admits as he wipes his mouth on his sleeve. He lets out a long sigh. "I'm sorry, Angela, but things have been a little crazy for me lately. So much has happened since my father died that I don't know if I'm comin' or goin' here. I feel like I'm doin' the limbo sometimes."

"You mean you feel like you're *in* limbo, right?" says Angela, smiling again.

"Whatever."

Angela gazes at him more intently than ever. She's known Johnny long enough to know that he's not about to tell her too much, but she's sharp enough to know what the score is. "Is this about another woman?" she says softly.

Johnny rubs the back of his neck and gazes down at the counter. "No, it's not about another woman," he tells her, but his voice isn't very convincing, not even to himself.

Angela gives a bittersweet sigh of her own. "I see," she says in a gentle voice. "Well, why don't you tell me all about it then."

Johnny looks up at her, surprised at her reaction. Tell you the truth, I'm a little surprised myself. I mean, Angela's got a temper on her. I thought for sure that Johnny would have to duck for cover behind the counter so he wouldn't get hit by any flying objects.

"Come on," says Angela, reaching out to tap him under the chin. "We're friends, aren't we? Let me help."

Johnny turns away. "You can't help," he tells her. "Not with this."

"Why not?"

"Trust me," he answers, rolling his eyes. "It's a little too complicated to explain."

"I'm in no hurry."

"Let's put it this way . . ." he begins to say. Just then, though, the front door opens and Teresa comes in. She walks up to them, looking very pleased.

"Hey, Angela," she says with an approving smile, "it's so nice to see you."

"Hi, Mrs. Catini. How are you doing?"

"I'm doing all right," says Teresa. "Better now that I see you two together enjoying yourselves."

"Angela just brought by some sandwiches for lunch," says Johnny, figuring he'd better intervene before his mother gets the wrong idea. It's too late.

"That's nice," says Teresa. "Your father and I ate lunch together on that same counter for thirty years."

Angela smiles and eases herself off the stool. She collects the sandwich wrappers and stuffs them into the paper bag in which she had brought them. Then she tosses the whole load into the trash along with the empty coffee cups.

"I really should get going, Johnny," she says. "Get me a towel so I can wipe the crumbs off the counter."

"Don't you worry about it," says Teresa. "I'll take care of it. Go ahead, Johnny, walk Angela to the door."

Johnny lets Angela take his arm and strolls out with her onto the sidewalk. It's a nice day and the sun feels good on his face. Makes him wish he didn't have to spend the rest of the day inside.

"Thanks for comin', Ange," he says. "I appreciate it."

"Don't mention it," she says, stretching up to give him a quick kiss. "Sorry I gave you a scare."

"Eh, forget it," says Johnny. "I probably deserved it."

"Okay," says Angela. "But don't you forget me. I'm still here if you need me, right?"

"I'll remember," he tells her.

"Good boy. Now go back to work."

With that, Angela turns and glides silkily away. Johnny just stands there for a minute and watches her. It doesn't matter what angle you're looking from, coming or going, Angela always looks pretty good. That's why Johnny can't help smiling.

"Yeah," he sighs, "I'll remember ya, Angela, even if I'm tryin' not to."

Chapter 25

When Johnny returns, Teresa's already got the broom in her hand, sweeping the floor around the cash register. You know, that's just the way it is with her. Long as I've known her, Teresa's always hated the thought that she might be wasting time. She always has to feel like she's doing something useful. Anyway, she barely looks up at Johnny as he approaches.

"That Angela's a good girl," she says. "She'd be a nice one to settle down with."

"Don't start, Ma," mutters Johnny. He picks up his clipboard and goes back to work finishing his inventory list. "How come you came in today anyways?" he says. "What are you doin', checkin' up on me?"

"No," Teresa answers, "not that you don't need checking up on. I was just passing by on my way over to Gina's house so I thought I'd stop in to see how things are going today. That okay with you?"

Johnny doesn't reply, but instead puts the clipboard aside and gazes with a blank stare out the window for a time. As he does so, he listens to his mother as she continues to sweep. Teresa's contentedly humming an old Italian song that she always sang to him at night when he was a kid. Matter of fact, my mother used to sing the same song to me. Brings back memories. Anyhow, Johnny turns and watches her moving steadily across the floor and down the aisle. The gentle scratching of the broom's bristles against the floor seems to keep time with the song's slow melodious strains. It's almost hypnotic. The words go something like:

> *Vananon' angelo mio,*
> *Non tema niente,*
> *Ti guarda Dio.*
> *Luna in alto,*
> *stelle lucenti,*
> *brillar' per te*
> *su Terra dormiente . . .*

It's nice. So Johnny puts his elbows on the counter and rests his chin on his hands. The song is just as soothing to him now as it was when he was a child, and for a while he loses himself in thought. He stays like that for longer than he realizes, and when he finally snaps out of it, he discovers Teresa standing directly in front of him. With one hand on her hip and the other on the broom, she taps her foot patiently, watching him all the while.

"Wha'?" says Johnny, returning to his senses.

"What's the matter with you?" says Teresa. "You in love or something?"

"Whatta you talkin' about?"

"You've been staring out the window with that look on your face for the past fifteen minutes," she tells him.

"What look?" huffs Johnny. It occurs to him then that he's been squirreling up the side of his mouth. He sighs and shakes his head.

"So, are you going to tell me about it?" she says.

"About what?"

"About what's on your mind."

Johnny picks up his clipboard and stares at it for a few moments without speaking. Outside on the street, a long delivery truck rumbles by, rattling the store's windows like an earthquake. But it passes and soon it falls quiet once more. Johnny puts the clipboard aside and faces his mother.

"Let me ask you somethin'," he says at last.

"Go ahead."

"It's about Pop."

"What about him?"

Johnny pauses. "I was just wonderin'," he begins. "I mean, did Pop ever think about getting out of the business?"

"You mean by selling it to someone else?" says Teresa.

"Yeah."

Teresa smiles at him. "Only just about every day of his life," she answers.

"How come he never did it?"

Teresa makes no reply, but leans the broom against the counter and walks past him into the back office. There she opens the desk drawer and pulls out a copy of the yellow pages. She flips open the book and leafs through the pages.

"Come here," she says, beckoning for him. "Look at this."

Johnny goes in and stands by her side. He looks down at the advertisement in the book at which she's pointing.

"Nocelli's Bakery," he says. "So what?"

"Look at what it says underneath," says Teresa.

Johnny looks closer. "Around the corner from Catini's Hardware Store," he reads aloud.

Teresa flips the pages to another section of the book before stopping and pointing at another advertisement. "Now look at this one," she commands.

"Bento Florists," says Johnny.

"Read underneath," says Teresa impatiently.

"Across the street from Catini's Hardware Store," reads Johnny. Maybe it's because he's still getting over the scare Angela threw into him at lunch, but Johnny's a little slow on the uptake.

So he stares at his mother, trying to grasp exactly what her point is.

"Don't you understand, Johnny?" she says. "Your father could never give up the store because Catini's Hardware is a landmark now. When people give directions around here, they don't say, 'Take your first left after the stoplight' or 'Go up two blocks and take a right.' No, what they say is, 'Go left at Catini's Hardware' or 'It's just down the street from Catini's' or 'If you pass Catini's, you've gone too far.' Don't you see? People don't remember the names of the streets around here, but they re-member the name *Catini*. That's because we've been here all these years, through good times and bad. We've sold hardware to generations of families. Our name isn't just attached to this building, it belongs to the earth it's sitting on. That means some-thing to people and it meant a lot to your father. And that's why when all those big-shot chains came waving money in your father's face to try and get him to sell out, he couldn't do it. He couldn't bear the thought of some big faceless corporation's name hanging over the door after all the years of heartache and struggle it took to make this place a success. Why let them have it? Our name is more important than money."

"So what are you sayin'?" says Johnny—predictably.

Teresa slams the telephone book shut. "What do you think I'm saying!" she cries. "I'm saying your father couldn't sell to those sharks because his heart and soul were in this place. So is yours. Those things aren't for sale, not ever."

Johnny shrugs. "Yeah," he says, "well, it was just a thought."

"Good, at least you're thinking about something," says Teresa. "Now start to do some thinking about your life and maybe starting to settle down. You're a man now. It's time. Maybe someday you might even bring this girl you've been seeing every other night to the house so your mother can meet her."

"Right," grunts Johnny. He walks out of the office and picks his clipboard back up. He looks at it and sighs. With all the interruptions, he's doubting he'll ever manage to call in his stock orders by the end of the day.

Teresa follows him out and peeks over his shoulder. "Don't order more than a half dozen of those adjustable wrenches," she advises him. "They don't sell that fast and you'll just be wasting shelf space. And make sure they send you the brand you order."

Johnny looks back over his shoulder at her. "You wanna let me do this, Mom," he says, "or would you rather do it for me and *I'll* go over to Gina's house?"

Experience has taught him a thing or two so, without looking, Johnny knows enough to duck to avoid the open hand whizzing toward the top of his head.

"Don't get smart with me, Mister Know-It-All," says Teresa, annoyed that the slap has missed its mark. "I've been dealing with these suppliers and distributors and all the others since before you were born. Pay attention to what I say and you might learn something."

"Yack, yack, yack."

Teresa sighs and looks up toward the heavens. "God help me," she laments, "but where did he come from?" She gives him another one of her looks, shakes her head, and starts to put on her sweater.

"Let me know if you're going to be eating at home tonight so I don't waste my time cooking for you," she tells him. With that, she turns abruptly and heads for the door. "And sweep the rest of these floors before you close up today," she adds for good measure. "They're a mess!"

Johnny lets out a long sigh of relief when the door finally slams shut behind her. I know he loves his mother, but sometimes she drives him to distraction. If you're a man, though, that's pretty much the general rule for all the women in your life. They take turns making you crazy. It's probably something genetic. Anyway, standing there holding his clipboard, Johnny glances back at the computer before finishing the inventory check. It gazes back at him, dark and silent as ever.

"Whatta you lookin' at?" he mutters before continuing down the aisle.

Chapter 26

You know, sometimes it's kind of funny watching things from this end. If you pay attention, it's amazing to see how often history repeats itself. I'm not talking about the who-discovered-America type of history that you studied in grammar school, but personal histories, the kind you have in families and the people close to you. From what I can see, people keep saying and doing the same things over and over again. It's incredible. It's like life is this big play and everybody's an actor, except there's only a handful of parts to go around so everybody takes turns playing and replaying the same roles. Of course, each of us is different, so we put our own little spin on whatever part we end up playing, and sometimes we borrow a little off of someone's else script just to make things interesting. That's just my theory, but who knows, maybe all the world really is a stage, right?

So Johnny's walking up the front steps to Vicki's apartment after what has understandably been a pretty rough day for him. Between getting the daylights scared out of him by Angela and then getting harangued by his mother, added to the fact that the shop got busy later that afternoon, he'd barely managed to get his stock orders called in before it was time to close. Right about now the kid's feeling wiped out.

Like always, Johnny hasn't bothered calling ahead to let Vicki know he's coming. He's figuring she'll be waiting inside for him, all ready to drag him out on some culturally enlightening excursion. Tell you the truth, he's kind of looking forward to it because he thinks it'll be a good way to clear his head. So he rings the doorbell and waits, wondering what sort of evening Vicki might have planned for them.

"Hello, Johnny," says Vicki when she opens the door. "Come in."

Vicki hasn't got her jacket on and she doesn't seem all that pumped up to head straight out the door as she usually is, so right away Johnny's thinking that something must be up. He's not worried about it, he's figuring she's just decided to try something new, maybe throw a new twist into their routine. Up till now he's pretty much let her direct the show, so he follows her inside, flops down on the couch, and awaits further instructions.

Vicki lets him settle down, stretch his legs out, get comfortable. She stands by the mantel, looking thoughtfully at him. In the corner, the stereo is playing some kind of classical music, one of those tinny old-fashioned piano things Johnny heard a few weeks back at one of the recitals she dragged him to. Surprisingly, he recognizes the tune.

"Don't tell me, 'Well-Tampered Clavicle,' right?" he says, waving his finger in the air as if he's an authority on the subject.

"*Um*—close enough," Vicki replies. She stands there, still looking at him, but not saying anything else.

"So what's up?" says Johnny.

"We need to talk," she says.

"About what?"

"I don't know, anything," says Vicki. "Why don't you tell me about your day?"

Johnny, of course, doesn't realize it yet, but right now he's sitting on that witness stand I told you about a while ago. Why don't you tell me about your day? Just a harmless little question about nothing, right? Little does he know that he's about to be cross-examined, and the prosecutor is inclined to treat the witness as hostile.

"What about my day?" says Johnny, blissfully oblivious to his impending fate.

"I don't know," says Vicki. "Tell me anything—like, how was your lunch?"

Just then it settles in on Johnny that there's something rotten in Denmark and he starts to get that tightening feeling in his throat again.

"My lunch?" he gulps.

"Yes, lunch," says Vicki in this eerily threatening voice. "You know, that little meal between breakfast and supper. How was yours today?"

Does any of this sound familiar?

I hate to admit this, but right about now I can't help laughing. I mean, I know I should probably have a little bit more compassion for my son, given the trials and tribulations he's had to put up with lately, but face it, the kid gets himself into these predicaments. Now, Johnny knows he didn't do anything wrong at lunch. Just the same, he also knows he's on the spot if he says the wrong thing. That being the case, he decides to say nothing.

"Why don't I tell you what *I* did for lunch today," says Vicki. "I decided to take a ride up to Federal Hill."

"R-really," he stammers.

"Mm-hmm," she coos, folding her arms. "I was planning to stop by the store to surprise you, perhaps take you to lunch. Imagine my surprise when I looked in the window and saw that you were *already* having lunch."

"Imagine," says Johnny, clearing his throat.

Vicki's on the prowl now, circling the couch like a leopard. All the while she's staring down at Johnny like he's some kind of wounded animal that she's about to pounce on.

"So is this the reason you're always running off?" she starts before he has a chance to offer any defense. "All those times you said you had to go because you had to get back to the store, all those times I tried to get you to stay a little longer, but you said you couldn't because you had responsibilities to tend to and people who were depending on you. And all those times, when I got left behind, you were really hurrying to see someone else, was that it?"

Vicki's working herself up into a real lather now. I've seen it happen before. Even she and I used to go through these things every now and then. Comes with the territory.

"No, Vicki," he says desperately, "you don't understand. You got the complete wrong idea."

Now, although Johnny's response is perfectly true, it's still pretty much standard issue for most guys caught in this sort of cross fire. So even though he's telling the truth, it comes out sounding like a lie.

"Oh really," she says. "And just what idea is it that you think I have, Mister I-Have-to-Go-So-I-Can-Take-Care-of-the-Store?"

Johnny goes to stand, but bangs his knee on the coffee table, you know, right on the point of the corner. Really hurts. I always hated when things like that happened. So now, in addition to having his head spinning, he's got to hobble around in agony.

"Vicki, you gotta understand," he says, grimacing, "it wasn't what I think you thought. That was just Angela, we're just friends."

"Very *good* friends, it looked like to me."

"We are, I mean we were, but we're not anymore."

My son's starting to babble like an idiot. He obviously realizes it himself because he has the sense to stop and take a deep breath. He limps over to Vicki and takes her by the shoulders.

"Look," he tells her, "I've known Angela since before I can remember. And yes, once upon a time we were—well, you

know what I mean, but that's been all over with since I met you.
Angela decided to stop by today just to make sure it wasn't. The
thing you have to remember is—is—hey, wait a minute." Johnny
stops for a second. "You came to the shop today?"

"Yes," says Vicki. "What's wrong with that?"

"What, are you crazy!" cries Johnny. "My mother came in
today, right after we finished eating. She might have seen you!"

"So what?" she says. "Your mother doesn't know me. What
would have been the big deal?"

Johnny starts squirreling up the side of his mouth for all it's
worth because he figures he's really gone and put himself in the
manure spot now. The problem, you see, is that he still hasn't
gotten around to telling Vicki about that day Teresa spied *me*
sneaking off to lunch up the East Side. Just one of those minor
little details that he figured would be better off swept under the
rug. Now, of course, it looks like the rug is about to get yanked
out from under him.

"Forget it," he finally says. "It was nothin' to worry about.
I'm just always a little on edge about all this when it comes to
my mother. It was no big deal that she showed up today. I'm
sorry. And please, just forget about Angela. We're old friends and
that's all, okay?"

Vicki, her arms still folded, eyes him skeptically for a time,
but little by little, the air starts coming out of the balloon. "I'm
sorry," she sighs, collapsing onto the other end of the couch. "I
shouldn't have jumped to conclusions when I saw you."

Johnny slides closer to her. "Hey, don't be sorry," he tells her.
"It's not your fault."

"Yes it is," she sighs again. "I guess I shouldn't have jumped
to conclusions about anything. It was wrong of me. Besides, I
really have no right to be upset. After all, it's not as if we've made
any kind of commitment to one another. I mean, we haven't
even told each other—what I mean is that I'm not even sure if

both of us are—what I'm trying to say is . . ." She stops and looks at Johnny. "I could use some help here," she says desperately.

Now, you have to understand that, as soon as he hears the word *commitment,* my son starts to hyperventilate. He can see that the conversation is steering its way into very murky waters as far as he's concerned. That being the case, he decides to grab the tiller and change course before he finds himself up on the rocks.

"Maybe we could go catch a movie, have a cup of coffee someplace later, and talk about all this," he offers hopefully. "Anything good playing tonight?"

"La Strada," says Vicki in a tired voice.

"Hey, that's a Fellini film, right?" says Johnny. "I love Fellini films. Come on, let's go."

Vicki just sits there for a few minutes before she resigns herself to the inevitable. She lets out a long sigh, stands up, and goes to get her coat.

Much later, as they lie next to each other in bed, the two of them are just staring at the ceiling. I can tell by the look on Johnny's face that he's starting to feel a little panicked, like he's thinking that maybe now might be a good time to head for the hills while he's still got the chance. To his credit, though, he takes a few deep breaths and manages to calm himself down. By now he knows that, if he stays there long enough, that twisting feeling in his gut that's telling him to escape will go away, at least for the night.

For her part, Vicki looks just about as dazed and confused as Johnny. She lies there, staring wide-eyed into space. You have to understand what Vicki's going through. I mean, some people just bounce from one relationship to the next, never giving too much thought to what they're doing, who they're doing it with, or why. Despite appearances to the contrary, Vicki's not one of them. For her, everything has some cosmic significance. I remem-

ber once when we were together in her living room and a fly
buzzed in through the window. I got up, rolled up a piece of newspaper, and swatted it into next week. Vicki got all upset. Why did
you have to kill it, she wanted to know. She started lecturing me
on her theory that all living creatures are here to learn from one
another, no matter how great or small. She didn't laugh when I
explained that this little creature just learned not to fly in through
open windows. Anyway, all of a sudden, Vicki sits up. She pulls
her knees up to her chest and starts rocking gently back and
forth.

"Tuition-free," she says thoughtfully. "Just like faculty children."

"How's that?" says Johnny.

"Nothing," says Vicki, coming back to herself. "I just had
this really weird thought pop into my head."

"Tell me what it was," says Johnny, sitting up with her.

"No, it's nothing," she says. "I was just thinking about something you said to me one night, about my teaching you for free
and how you were getting it all gratis while all the other students had to pay."

"What's so weird about that?"

"It's not," says Vicki, sounding a little confused. "It's something else."

"Come on," Johnny prods. "Just tell me."

"It's bizarre," she says. "I'm not sure you'll want to hear it."

"Sure I do," he insists. "Tell me."

Vicki winces. "I was thinking," she says at last, "about
Oedipus Rex."

Johnny sinks right back down beneath the covers. "Please,"
he groans. "Let's just leave Mister Oed outta this, can't we?" He
takes a deep breath and closes his eyes. "How does that story
end anyways?" he asks. "Does it have a happy ending?"

"He plucks his eyes out and wanders around blind for the
rest of his life," Vicki replies.

"Great," Johnny mutters.

Vicki sinks down next to him, and for a long time neither of them speaks.

"What's happening, Johnny?" she says in exasperation. "What are we doing here?"

"I dunno," Johnny admits, "but I can't stop doin' it."

Vicki sighs and reaches toward the lamp on the bedside table. "Do-*ing,*" she says with some emphasis and then she turns out the light.

Good night, John-boy.

Chapter 27

Okay, so now it's time for me to go to work. I mean, I've been hanging around here just watching things since I threw a seven, but not doing anything to help. That's one of the things you find out when you're dead. Just because you *are* dead doesn't mean that you can just kick back for the rest of eternity and watch the whole show go by. If you're going to hang around and watch, sooner or later He expects you to do something constructive. But like I said in the beginning, you're not allowed to directly interfere with the living, so you have to get a little creative, but there are still lots of ways you can do your part. It's almost like being a child, growing up and learning how to be useful to the rest of mankind. That's sort of the way it is here. Life is just one big learning experience after the other—even when you're dead.

Anyway, Johnny's having a dream about a dinosaur, one of those Tyrannosaurus rex things he'd seen on television once. But this one's live and in living color—and it's right outside his window.

Johnny sits up, parts the curtain by the bed, and gazes out. There it stands, big as a friggin' house. Jaws dripping blood, its short but savagely powerful arms quivering with rage, the thing begins to roar its lungs out. One look at the monster is all it takes. Johnny jumps back into bed and throws the covers over his head.

Now he's asking himself why he hadn't run away when he had the chance. He'd heard the beast coming for him, stomping and roaring as it smashed its way through the city and down the street. He should have gotten away while there was still time.

But this being a dream, it's too late.

Out on the street, the dinosaur gives this bloodcurdling roar. From deep within, some form of primordial fear wells up in Johnny. He feels it first in the pit of his stomach, then suddenly all over as if he's being wrapped in a million icy tentacles. Then another sensation takes over. Panic. Every part of his being, from his fevered brain and his thumping heart, down to the smallest strand of DNA in his big toe, is screaming in unison:

Run, you stupid son of a bitch!

But he can't. Try as he might to get up, Johnny's frozen in place like a fossil. The dinosaur roars again, so loud it knocks the breath out of him. Johnny knows it's only a matter of moments before it smashes its head through the window and devours him whole. Shivering beyond control, he curls up in a ball beneath the blankets. The roar is deafening now. He squeezes his eyes shut, praying that the end will come fast.

But the end doesn't come, at least not the one he was expecting. Instead, Johnny opens his eyes and strains to listen in the darkness. Nothing—no dinosaur, no shattered window. He drops his head back onto the pillow and stares at the ceiling.

"What a friggin' nightmare," he mutters.

Beside him in the bed, Vicki's chest is rising and falling in rhythmic breaths. She went out like a light long ago. So did Johnny, for that matter, but now he's wide awake. He brushes the back of his hand against his forehead and wipes the beads of sweat from his brow. The skin on the back of his neck is still crawling, and his heart's galloping like a racehorse.

Johnny lies there for a time until he starts to calm back down. Finally, he reaches over and tucks the blanket around Vicki's shoulders. She stirs at the touch of his hand, but settles right back into a sound sleep. He presses up against her and closes his eyes once more. Try as he might, though, he can't seem to fall back asleep.

At least he thinks he can't. He knows that his breathing has fallen in sync with Vicki's, but something else is happening. Johnny suddenly becomes aware of everything around him. The ticking of the clock. Rivulets of rainwater trickling off the roof. The curtains swaying almost imperceptibly from a draft creeping in through the window casing. Matter of fact, I had once noticed that myself and had planned to caulk the window for Vicki. Never got around to it. Anyway, it's then that Johnny gets this odd sensation, as if something's tugging on him, but from the inside. It's a gentle tug, nothing that really bothers him. Actually, it's a nice sort of feeling. So he gives in to it, and next thing he knows, he finds himself sitting up.

He opens his eyes.

There's this soft glow about the room that gradually grows in intensity. Brighter and brighter it becomes, but it doesn't hurt Johnny to look into it. Now Johnny knows that something really weird is definitely going on, but for some reason he doesn't understand, he's not the least bit afraid. So he looks into the center of the light. Way down inside he sees this small, dark form moving away from the center. As it gets closer and closer to him, Johnny suddenly realizes that he's staring down a great tunnel out of which someone is walking toward him. Silhouetted by light, this shadowy person strolls out of the tunnel and stops at the foot of the bed. The light from the tunnel recedes and the person comes into plain view. Now comes the part I love.

"Hello, Johnny," I say.

Johnny's looking at me like he can't believe his eyes.

"Pop? Is that really you?"

"Of course it's me," I tell him. "What, were you expecting someone else's ghost?"

By now the light from the tunnel has disappeared, but I'm still illuminated as if I'm standing beneath a narrow spotlight on an otherwise darkened stage. So I sit on the edge of the bed and gaze at my son.

"I wasn't expectin' anybody's ghost," says Johnny. "What are you doin' here anyways? You're supposed to be dead."

"I am dead, but I felt like stopping by to talk."

"You can do that whenever you want?"

"Of course."

Johnny scratches his side and yawns. He's a real sight right about now, his hair all tousled, dried drool on the side of his mouth. "Then how come dead people don't do it more often?" he says.

"Well, we're busy," I say. "Besides, we can only talk to you when you're asleep, like you are now."

"But I'm wide awake."

"No, you think you are, but really you're just dreaming."

"No, I was dreamin' two minutes ago about a friggin' dinosaur," Johnny grouses. "Scared the crap outta me. Matter of fact, I've been havin' a lot of weird dreams lately."

"Our dreams are what our lives make of them, Johnny," I tell him, trying to sound as philosophical as possible. Not my strong suit. "I was pretty sure that one might get your attention."

"Whoa, wait a minute," says Johnny. "Are you tellin me that . . ."

It's then that Johnny realizes that I'm not looking at him anymore, but at Vicki. His face gets all red like a ripe tomato. "Hey," he says nervously, "this isn't what it looks like."

"It looks exactly like what it is," I tell him, gazing at her. I say it without anger, without the least bit of resentment, as Johnny might well have expected. You know, you get to this side of the fence and you start to see things differently, without so much emotion. Things either are or they aren't; there's no worrying about whether or not they're good or bad because, either way, they exist just the way the Big Guy has in mind. Nothing any of us can do about it, know what I mean?

"Hey, Pop," Johnny starts, "I don't know what to say. This wasn't my fault, you know. If you hadn't made me come over here in the first place to say goodbye for you, none of this would have ever happened."

"*Eh,* don't be so sure," I say with a shrug. "Some things are just meant to happen sooner or later. You can't plan them."

"What are you sayin', that it was destiny or somethin' that Vicki and I were gonna get together."

"*Hmm*—something like that," I say.

"*Ahh,* I don't believe in that stuff," huffs Johnny.

"You have a lot to learn."

"You're startin' to sound like her," he mutters. "No wonder you two got along so well."

I can't help chuckling, but it's time to get down to business. So I put on my father face and give him the look, you know the one I'm talking about. Every father can do it. I remember my own father doing it to me. Never fazed me, no matter how much he screamed whenever I got out of line, but when he gave me that look, forget it, tore me to shreds.

"Have you told her?" I ask.

"Told her what?" answers Johnny.

"You know."

Johnny rubs the back of his neck, a sure sign that I've got him squirming a little. "You mean about Mommy, seeing you guys together, right?"

I just give him a fatherly nod.

"Not yet," he confesses.

I harden my gaze, just to turn the heat up a little on him. "Hey, gimme a break, will ya, Pop. I haven't had a chance, all right? And what's the point anyways? It'll just get her upset. And besides, this is all your fault."

"My fault?" I laugh. "How do you figure?"

"You should have been a little more discreet when you were alive, that's how. If you had, I wouldn't have had anything to worry about."

"Life generally doesn't work that way, Johnny."

"No kiddin'."

Johnny leans closer to get a better look at me. To him I look as fit and full of vim and vigor as he can ever remember. So he reaches out to touch me, just to see what I feel like. His hand, though, can never quite reach me. Just when it looks like he's about to make contact, I move farther away. It's almost like I'm sitting on a big elastic band that keeps stretching back and forth. Tell you the truth, there's nothing I can do about it, just one of the rules.

"Sorry," I tell him. "That's not allowed."

"I was just curious," says Johnny.

"Isn't everybody?"

I can see that Johnny's a little aggravated by this. He wants some confirmation that he and I are really talking to each other, that it isn't all just some weird dream brought on by a bad batch of effs. Of course, it's not like he's going to go blabbing all over town that he spent the night talking to his father's ghost, but he's figuring it would be nice to know just the same.

"I know what you're thinking," I tell him. "But those are just the rules. You can't know for sure. I could be real. Then again maybe I'm just some manifestation of your conscience—your *guilty* conscience."

"Hey, I got no infestations in my conscience," says Johnny. "I'd just like to know for sure."

"Well, you can't."

"Why not?"

"It's the uncertainty of the universe, Johnny," I try to explain. "It rules everything. That's what makes life—life. It's what makes it fun. No one and nothing can know how it all turns out in the end. Everything would be ruined otherwise."

"But what's it like?" says Johnny.

"What?"

"Bein' dead."

I shrug and look around me, surveying a scene I know that Johnny can't see. "It's not bad," I tell him after a moment. "It takes a little getting used to, but I can't complain."

"Yeah, but what's it like when you die. I mean, does it hurt when your life's all over?"

"No, I can't say that it hurt at all. Besides, your life never ends. I can see that now, it's one of the things you learn right away around here. Think of it all like a big hourglass, Johnny. As you get older, the grains of sand trickle down until the top of the glass is empty, but all the while the bottom is getting refilled. Then everything gets turned upside down and the whole thing starts all over again."

"Sounds kind of redundant."

"It is in a way, but we're getting off the subject," I say.

"Which is?"

"When are you going to tell Vicki about your mother?"

"Come on, Pop, what am I supposed to tell her? Oh, Vicki, by the way, make sure you stay outta my mother's way because she'll probably rip your lungs out the second she sets eyes on you."

"Vicki should know what you know," I tell him. "It's important."

"Then you tell her," Johnny grumbles. "Just get her up right now. She's probably not dreamin' about anything special. Besides, what difference does it make? Tonight shouldn't have happened in the first place. And it's not gonna happen again."

Now I can't help smiling. "Yeah right, Johnny," I say. "You've been telling yourself that just about every night for the past month and a half, but still you keep coming back."

"What are you doin'," cries Johnny, "spyin' on me?"

"I'm not spying on you, I'm just looking out for you."

"What, by watchin' everything me and Vicki have been doin' together?"

"Not *everything!*" I exclaim. "What do you think I am, a pervert? I know when I'm supposed to look the other way."

"Yeah, sure."

"Look, Johnny," I say, locking eyes with him, "this is an important time for you. There are some big questions that you need to find the answers to."

"Like what?"

"For starters, do you love her?" I ask, nodding toward Vicki. "I mean, after all, that's what she was trying to ask you tonight, you know."

Johnny gives me one of his own looks. "Pop," he snickers, "I never talked about that kinda stuff with you when you were alive. Why would I do it when you're dead?"

I have to admit it, Johnny's got a point. I mean, we never talked about these kind of things when I was aboveground. How many fathers and sons do? I gave him the standard man-to-man talk one time, but not much else. After that, I figured he was on his own. Besides, it doesn't take very long for guys to figure out what the score is on these things, if you know what I mean.

"It might help to talk about it," I tell him just the same.

"Forget it, Pop."

"Well, at least say you'll think about it."

"Yeah," he shrugs. "I will. But let me ask you somethin'."

"Go ahead."

Johnny starts squirreling up the side of the mouth, so I know he's trying to figure out how to pose a delicate question.

"I know it's none of my business, but—well, what I mean is, I still can't figure out you two bein' together. A guy your age goin' around with someone her age, it doesn't register with me. How could you do it?"

"Wait till you get to be a guy my age," I tell him, "it'll start to register with you. You know, just like they say that women have this biological clock ticking inside, well, men have one too, believe me. Only difference is that with men the alarm is set to go off about twenty years later. Wait till you hear that clock ticking, then come ask me that question again."

"*Eh,* I guess you're right," says Johnny. "But tell me somethin', did you really love her?"

Now it's my turn to snicker. "Hey, Johnny," I tell him, "I never talked with you about this kind of stuff when I was alive, why would I do it now when I'm dead?"

"Ha ha, very funny."

"Sorry," I say. "I'm just trying to get you to think about these things, that's all."

"Well, I have been thinkin' about them."

"That's a good sign," I say. "Speaking of signs, what is it about the one that says Catini's Hardware that's bothering you? Lately, it's all I here you complaining about."

Johnny lets out a groan. "What, it's not enough that you're eavesdroppin' on me and Vicki, now you're watching me at the store?"

I answer him with a shrug.

"*Ah,* it's not just the store, Pop," he says with a sigh, "it's everything lately. I mean, you checked out and all of a sudden it's like everybody expects me to pick up where you left off. They want me to take your place. I feel like I'm gettin' swallowed up, ya know? I just don't know if I wanna do it. Maybe it's like Vicki told me once a while back, that I'm tryin' to find myself."

"If you want to find yourself," I suggest, "why not just go

take a look at yourself in the mirror? You'll save yourself a lot of time and energy."

"Very funny."

"Look, Johnny," I try to explain to him, "you're finding your place in the world, not taking mine. It's up to you to make it all your own."

"But how am I supposed to do that?" he grouses.

Before I have a chance to answer him, they start to pull the plug on me. The room gets that eerie glow and the tunnel of light opens up again. Nothing I can do about it but let them yank me out.

"Hey, where are you goin'?" says Johnny.

"Yeah, yeah, I hear you," I call over my shoulder into the tunnel. Then I turn back to Johnny. "Sorry, but I have to go back," I tell him as I move steadily away. "I'm only allowed to stay for just so long."

"So what am I supposed to do?" says Johnny anxiously. "How am I supposed to work all this out by myself?"

"Just follow your heart, Johnny. It knows the way. Things aren't always what they seem. They're usually just starting when you think they're ending, but they always work themselves out."

I'm getting swallowed up now by the light which, to Johnny, is dazzlingly brilliant. He reaches out to me, but that just makes me recede that much more quickly from his grasp.

"That's it?" he calls after me. "You can't do any better than that for me? Thanks a lot!"

"Just follow your heart," my voice echoes as I fade from sight. Actually, as annoyed as I am to have to leave so soon, I have to admit that the special effects are pretty neat. Anyway, the tunnel of light closes like an eyelid falling across a sleepy eye. The brilliant light shrinks away until all that's left is a tiny orange dot.

Johnny can't remember closing his eyes, but when he re-opens them, he realizes that he's staring into the first fragile rays of the rising sun. He looks around the room as if he's expecting to find me still there. All that's left, though, is the soft glow of the early dawn.

"What a weird dream," he mutters. Then he rolls onto his side and props himself up on his elbow. "But was it a dream?"

Dream or reality, something deep inside must be telling him it's time to come clean because he reaches over and gives Vicki's shoulder a gentle shake. Vicki yawns in protest and tries to wrap the covers around herself.

"Let me sleep," she moans.

"Come on, wake up," he says gently. "There's somethin' we need to talk over before I head to the store."

"Can't it wait?"

"No," says Johnny. "You see, it's about my mother."

Chapter 28

Know what I really miss? Anisette and coffee in the morning. Can't get it here. Nothing like it, especially on a chilly morning late in November when the sky turns that slate gray color and maybe a few snow flurries drift down from the clouds. You're out walking around, looking at the leafless trees and the brown grass and everything looks dead, but you know that really it's all just gone to sleep for a while. It's the end of a long hard year and the earth has earned its rest. If you listen to that little voice inside you, you'll hear it telling you to slow down, that it's just about time to hunker down and get ready for winter. And with me, the little voice would also tell me that it's time to start drinking my anisette and coffee.

Just thinking about the warm, bracing smell of the anisette steaming out of the mug brings back a thousand memories to me. I used to like to make the rounds early in the morning on the weekends, first to Maria's house, because she lived farthest away, then I'd work my way back home, stopping at Nina's then Gina's. I usually brought everybody a copy of the newspaper, maybe some biscuits from the bakery, a loaf of bread. Whatever. I never bothered to call ahead; my daughters always seemed to know when I'd be coming. They'd have the coffee already brewing for me when I came in, but first I'd play with my grandchildren for a bit while they were still in their pajamas. Then, once I was sure I'd caused a big enough commotion for first thing in the morning, I'd sit at the kitchen table and sip my coffee and anisette, dunk my biscuit, chat about the weather, catch up on the latest family gossip. Nothing major, but that's how you keep in touch with your kids when they've grown up and moved out. You've got to go to them; you can't wait around for them to come and visit you. It's not their job. If they're doing what they're supposed to, they're busy at home taking care of their own kids like you used to take care of them. You just have to pop in on them as often as you can, stay for just a little while, and then get out of their hair.

Anyway, it's the kind of morning I was just talking about, day before Thanksgiving and already it's cold and the clouds are threatening snow. Johnny's sitting in the kitchen, sipping a cup of coffee and reading the newspaper when Teresa walks in in her bathrobe and slippers. She crosses the kitchen and looks at the thermostat.

"Who put this up so high?" she says.

"Who else lives here?" says Johnny, not looking up from the paper. "I was cold."

"Then put a sweater on," says Teresa, lowering the heat. "The heat costs money, you know."

Johnny answers with a yawn.

Teresa pours herself a cup of coffee and sits down at the table with him. "You want some anisette in that?" she asks Johnny.

"No thanks."

Teresa pulls a section of the paper over to herself and starts leafing through the pages. "Your father always liked a little anisette in his coffee."

"I'm not Pop," says Johnny.

It's quiet in the kitchen now, save for the whirring of the refrigerator and the clock ticking on the wall. Outside, the wind is picking up a little bit, rattling the windowpanes as it buffets the house. Personally, this time of the morning was always my favorite part of the day, mostly because it was the only time when I had five minutes of peace to myself to sort out what I was doing with my life. Johnny never used to get out of bed this early, but lately he's discovered the same thing for himself. Helps keep your sanity.

Teresa starts humming a tune while she looks at the newspaper. "So, what are your plans for the day?" she says.

"The usual," Johnny answers, still hiding behind the sports section. "But I'm planning on closing up early this afternoon."

"What do you mean early?" says Teresa, giving him one of her looks even though she knows he can't see her from behind the paper.

"And don't gimme that look," says Johnny without showing his face. "I'm not closin' up till three o'clock. Pop used to do the same thing all the time the night before holidays."

"You're not your father."

"That's what I keep tryin' to tell people."

Teresa settles back again to look over the obituaries, just to make sure no one we know has gone to join me. "That's all right," she says. "That will give you time to run some errands for me later. The girls are coming over this afternoon to help me get things ready for tomorrow's dinner. You can do your part by picking up a few things for me."

"Yeah, sure," says Johnny. "Just don't have me runnin' all over creation. I got things of my own to do later, then I'm goin' out with the guys."

Teresa shoots him another one of her looks. "What kind of things do you have to do?" she asks.

"Things," says Johnny. "All right?"

Teresa knows better than to press him any further on the subject. With Johnny, the more you pry him for information, the tighter he clams up. "I'll give you a list before you go," she tells him, then she goes back to reading the paper. She starts humming a tune again.

"You're awful cheerful this morning," says Johnny, getting up to refill his cup.

"I had a good night's rest, that bother you?"

"Nope."

Johnny puts his cup down on the counter and looks out the window. Outside, the bony-looking trees are swaying back and forth in the wind and the few dried leaves that managed to escape the last raking are chasing themselves around the backyard like schoolchildren at recess. Johnny looks up at the gray sky with a shiver and refills his cup.

"I can't believe tomorrow's Thanksgiving," he says. "Already it's gonna be Christmastime. Geez, ever since Pop died, it's like somebody put their foot down on the accelerator."

"It seems that way because you've been busy," says Teresa. "You don't notice the time passing when you're doing things. It's when you're just sitting around *passing* the time that it feels like the clock is crawling. Believe me, I know."

"Since when have you been just passin' the time?" says Johnny.

"*Ay,* it feels that way sometimes," says Teresa.

"How come?"

"Don't even ask," she tells him. "You wouldn't understand."

"Why not?"

"Because you're a man."

"What's that got to do with anything?"

"Everything."

Johnny gives a shrug and sits back down. He's still got a few more minutes before he has to head to the shop, so he picks the paper back up and starts looking over the sports section again.

"So what are your plans?" he says.

Teresa puts down the newspaper and stares off into space for a few moments. "I don't know, but I feel like I need to find something else to do with myself," she finally says. "I need to learn something new. I think that's the only answer. To learn. The way I look at it, when you stop learning, you stop living. Your mind is like a sponge and you have to keep letting it soak up the water—otherwise it dries out. So who knows, maybe I'll go back to school, take a few courses, see what they can show me. Maybe I'll learn how to start a new business. Or maybe I'll take some writing classes and write a book someday. I could write volumes just about you and your sisters and your father. Maybe I'll study a foreign language then do some traveling. Or who knows? The possibilities are endless if I just use the time that God has given me."

Johnny puts down the paper. "What I meant," he says, "is what are your plans for today so that I know what time to bring home whatever it is that you want me to pick up?"

Teresa just stares at him in disbelief. Without a word, she rolls up the section of newspaper she's been reading and rises from the table. As she walks out of the kitchen past Johnny, she lets him have it across the top of the head.

Chapter 29

One of the nice things about holidays, especially the big ones like Thanksgiving, is the way they take on this overblown sense of importance. It's as if ordinary day-to-day life has to be put on hold for a while so that you can run around like a maniac getting ready. Sounds funny, but I always liked that part of the holidays. I mean, your world can be crumbling all around you, everything can be going wrong in your life, but suddenly for a day all you're worried about is making sure you have turkey and stuffing and mashed potatoes and cranberry sauce on the table come Thursday afternoon. It has a way of clearing your head.

Teresa always had me running the day before Thanksgiving. No matter how far in advance she tried to plan, there were always ten thousand things that needed to be done at the last minute. That's why I always closed up the shop early the day before holidays, so that I could run around to the butcher, the baker, and the candlestick maker for Teresa. It was a hassle sometimes, but I never minded. It was the least I could do, especially since the payoff always came the next day when I could lounge around like a king with the rest of the men while the women waited on us.

So now it's my son's turn to do the running around the day before holidays. Three o'clock rolls along and Johnny follows the last customer to the front of the store. As soon as the guy steps out the door, Johnny slams it shut and hangs up the CLOSED sign before anyone else shows up. He stuffs the day's receipts into the deposit pouch, grabs his coat, and scoots out the back to run the errands for his mother. She's given him a whole list, but there's really nothing major, just a few things she needs from the market, some wine and beer from the liquor store, and a few other odds and ends. Now Johnny doesn't mind doing it for his mother, but he's got a face on because he's got other plans, so he goes tearing off to his car like a madman.

When he finally gets back to the house, his sisters are already there in the kitchen. Surrounded by bags of vegetables, the three of them are standing at the counter with knives in their hands—and all of them are in tears.

"Now what?" says Johnny, depositing the grocery bags on the table.

"Nothing," sniffs Maria.

Johnny rolls his eyes and heads back out to the car to bring in the wine and beer. When he comes back in, he's got the wine bottles balanced on top of the case of beer. He barely manages to get into the kitchen without sending any of the bottles crashing to the floor. He puts the load safely down and looks up at his sisters, who are still wiping tears from their eyes.

"What's goin' on?" he says. Nobody answers, so he takes out his wallet and fishes around in it for the list his mother gave him.

Just then Teresa walks in and starts looking through the bags. "Did you get the bottle of vanilla extract like I asked you?"

"Yeah, yeah, yeah. I got everything," he says. "But what's their problem?"

"Don't pay attention to them," says Teresa.

"Fine," says Johnny, rolling his eyes again. "I got things to do." He grabs his car keys and goes tearing out of the house. They all break out in laughter as soon as the door slams shut behind him.

"What's with him?" says Nina.

"Who knows?" Teresa answers. "Probably trouble with one of his girlfriends."

"How many does he have now?" laughs Maria, wiping her eyes with the back of her hand.

"How many does he need is a better question," says Gina, dabbing her own eyes with a paper towel.

"All right, ladies," says Teresa, "enough of chopping the onions. Let's get to work on the other vegetables."

"Thank God," the three sigh in unison. They scrape off their cutting boards, depositing the onions into the same big bowl on the middle of the counter.

"What next?" says Maria.

Teresa puts on an apron and grabs a bunch of carrots from one of the bags. She rinses them under the faucet, then, one by one, starts to peel them, letting the scrapings fall into the sink. "I'll start on these while you three do the potatoes," she says. "We'll need lots of them for the mashed pototates."

So they all get to work. It doesn't take long for them to fin-ish peeling the vegetables and soon they're busy cutting them up. Ordinarily there's never two seconds of silence whenever these four get together. Most times it's an all-out battle with each of them trying to get an extra word in edgewise. For a few moments, though, they all fall quiet, save for the sound of their knives clopping against the cutting boards like hooves against the pavement. Before long Teresa starts humming a cheerful tune to herself. The other three look up at her and smile.

"In a good mood today, Mom?" says Maria.

Teresa slides a pile of sliced carrots into a bowl and grabs another bunch. "I'm in a very good mood today, as a matter of fact," she answers. "I had the first good night's sleep I've had in weeks last night—and the most wonderful dreams."

"What about?" says Gina.

Teresa puts down her knife and stares past them out the

window. "It was the loveliest dream I can ever remember," she begins. "It was a beautiful warm sunny day and I was strolling barefoot through meadow after meadow of all these beautiful flowers. Marigolds and petunias, lilacs and sunflowers, daisies and impatiens. Every color, every type of flower you could imagine. Patch after patch of them spread out like sections of a giant quilt that was thrown across these beautiful rolling hills. I was just walking on and on with all this life bursting out all around me, and I felt happy and peaceful. I felt young again."

"That's nice," says Gina. "What else happened?"

"I woke up," Teresa replies.

The three girls all start laughing, but Teresa holds up her hand.

"But wait, there's more," she tells them. "You see, I only thought that I woke up. The meadow was gone, but I still held on to that wonderful peaceful feeling I had inside. For a while I was just lying in bed all dreamy and sleepy, then I noticed that the scent of the flowers was still in the air. Little by little I realized that it wasn't flowers that I smelled. That's when it dawned on me that it was something else."

"What?" says Nina.

"Cologne," she answers. "Your father's cologne."

The three girls look at one another. *"Pop's* cologne?" they all say.

"That's right," says Teresa, nodding her head. "Your father's cologne, Bombay Rum Number Seven. I'd recognize that scent anywhere."

"But why would you smell Pop's cologne?" says Gina.

"That's what I'm about to tell you," says Teresa with a little smile.

By now, of course, all work cutting the vegetables has come to a complete halt. Teresa, I can tell, is very pleased with herself because she knows that she's got everyone's complete attention. That's no small accomplishment whenever these four get together and start conversing, believe me.

"So tell us!" exclaims Maria.

"Well," she begins, "I sat up, and sure enough, sitting right there on the end of the bed, is your father."

I was going to tell you all about this firsthand, by the way, but then I figured maybe I'd let Teresa give her version of things in her own words. Tell you the truth, sometimes it works out better that way. Besides, hearing her talk about it helps me understand how well I'm coming across, if you know what I mean. But getting back:

"Pop?" says Nina. "What was he doing?"

"He wasn't doing anything but just sitting there watching me with that same smile he always had, the one he gave me the very first time we met."

"But weren't you scared?"

"How could I ever be scared of your father?"

"Well, if I saw Pop right now, I'd probably faint."

"Me too," Maria and Gina chime in.

"Nonsense," says Teresa.

"So what happened next?" says Gina.

"Well, I reached out my hand to touch him and I said, 'Nick, is that really you?'"

"And what did he say?"

"'What, you were expecting someone else?'" Teresa answers.

The girls all giggle. "That sounds just like Pop," says Maria. "Then what happened?"

Teresa picks her knife up and starts cutting some more carrots. "'Of course I wasn't expecting anyone else,' I told him," she says. "'I was just having the most wonderful dream. It was so beautiful and it made me feel so good inside.' Then he looks at me and smiles. 'It was the least I could do,' he tells me. 'I'm glad you liked it.'"

"You mean, *Pop* gave you the dream?" says Gina.

"Well, I was wondering the same thing," Teresa replies. "So I asked him."

"What did he say?"

"He just shrugged and said, 'Sort of. I never got around to sending you flowers very often when I had the chance, so I figured I'd do it this way now. They let us do these kinds of things now and then.'"

"Wow," the three girls say.

"That's just about what I thought," says Teresa. "Then I looked at him and said, 'How are you doing, Nick, they taking care of you there?'

"'Oh yeah,' he says. 'You know how it is.'

"'No I don't,' I tell him. 'I'm still alive, remember?'

"'Oh, right,' he says."

"Then what did you do?" asks Maria.

"Well, I started to get out of bed and I said, 'Why don't you come downstairs, Nick, and I'll make us some coffee. I've got a few things to talk over with you.'"

"And did you go?"

"No," says Teresa. "Your father said it was probably a bad idea."

"Why?"

"He said, 'You're still asleep, Teresa, so stay put. Otherwise you'll just make a mess in the kitchen.'

"'But I feel wide awake,' I told him.

"'Trust me, Teresa,' he says, 'you're out like a light. This is just another dream.'

"And I said, 'Well, it's another nice dream. I'm glad you've come to see me, Nick.'

"'Me too,' he tells me. 'Besides, I thought it might be a good time to drop in. I have a few things to talk over too.'"

"But how did he look?" says Gina. "Did he seem happy?"

"I think so," says Teresa. "But when I looked into his eyes, I could tell something was bothering him. You don't stay married to someone for thirty-seven years and not notice these things."

"What was it, what was bothering him?"

"I asked, and he said it was about Johnny. 'I'm a little worried about him,' he said.

"I waved my hand and said, '*Uff*, don't worry about him. Johnny needs to start worrying about himself and learn how to take care of his responsibilities. Do you know how many times I've had to lock up the store for him so he can go out chasing girls all over town?'

"'Don't be too hard on him,' your father says. 'He's got a lot on his mind right now.'"

"I'll bet," laughs Nina.

"So what else happened?" says Maria. "Did he say anthing about the rest of us?"

Teresa pauses for a moment. "No," she answers. "I don't think so or at least nothing that I can remember."

"Why not?" says Maria, sounding annoyed. "That's not fair."

The others pout in agreement. Amazing, isn't it? No matter how grown up your children are, they still get up in arms when only one of them gets something and the others don't. I mean, even though I'm dead, I still have to make sure that I bring home a little something for everybody. Otherwise there's trouble.

"What do you want from me?" says Teresa at seeing the looks on their faces. "Take it up with your father next time you're praying."

"So, was that it?" says Nina. "Was that all he had to say?"

"Oh, no," says Teresa. "I could tell by the look on his face and the way he was squirreling up the side of his mouth like he used to do whenever he was on the spot that there was something else he wanted to talk about. So I asked him, 'What else is on your mind, Nick?'"

"And what did he say?"

"Well, he starts to hem and haw and finally he says, 'I was just wondering about how you're doing. I mean, I haven't been gone all that long, but life goes on and you have to make decisions.'"

"What kind of decisions was he talking about?" asks Gina.

"That's what I asked him."

"What did he say?"

"He shrugged and said, 'You know what I mean, decisions like what am I going to do with the rest of my life, who am I going to be doing it with?'

"'Nick,' I said, 'are you wondering about whether or not I'm going to get remarried someday?'"

"What did he say?" gasps Gina.

"He starts to hem and haw again," Teresa replies, like it's no big deal. "'Well, no not really,' he says. 'I mean, there's nothing wrong with it, I guess. After all, I am dead. Of course, it's only been a few months, but time marches on. You're still young enough. I understand how it is. Besides, it's your life.'"

"And what did you say?" asks Maria.

"I said, 'So what's the problem?'" she answers. Then, with a wink, she adds, "I always liked making your father squirm now and then, so I figured since I had him on the hook, why waste the opportunity to do it again?"

"You're bad," Gina giggled. "So what did he say to that?"

"'Oh, there's no problem,' he answered, 'no problem at all.' He said, 'I was just bringing it up as a topic of conversation, that's all. I mean, you are entitled to meet new people.'

"'Is there anything wrong with that?' I asked him.

"'No,' he said, 'there's nothing wrong at all, it's just that . . .'

"'It's just that it's different for a woman,' I finished for him, 'is that what you're trying to say?'

"'Well, not that it's any different,' he said, 'it's just that I wouldn't want to see you do anything too fast before you're ready. I don't want you to get hurt, that's all.'

"So I said, 'And you also don't want to see me have too good a time on my own, right Nick?'"

"What did you tell him that for?" says Maria. "You make it

sound like you have been seeing someone. Is there someone new that you're not telling us about?"

"Of course I'm not seeing someone new!" exclaims Teresa.

"Then why would you make Pop think that you might be?"

"Because I have my own reasons, Miss Busybody."

"Forget all that," says Nina. "Just tell us what happened next."

"All right, just be quiet and pay attention," says Teresa. "So your father just looks at me finally and lets out this big sigh. 'It's hard, you know,' he says, 'watching things from this side of the fence, knowing there's nothing you can do about them. You get a little afraid sometimes.'

"'But you're dead,' I told him. 'What on earth do dead people have to be afraid of?'"

"What did he say?"

"He said, 'We're all afraid of just one thing here, that we'll be forgotten.'"

Teresa puts down the knife then and reaches for a dish towel on the counter because her eyes are welling up all of a sudden. "Those onions," she sniffs, dabbing her eyes. "I can still smell them." The other three, though, know that the onions have nothing to do with the tears in her eyes.

"So what did you tell him?" says Gina softly.

Teresa takes a little breath to compose herself and gives them a smile. "I said, 'Don't worry, Nick. No matter what I do with my life, I'll never forget you. You're my husband, remember?'"

"And did that make him feel better?"

"It must have because he smiled and said, 'Yes, I remember, and I wouldn't have had it any other way.' And I told him neither would I. Then he looked back over his shoulder and called, 'I know, I know!'"

"To who?" says Maria. "Was there somebody else's ghost there?"

"No, there was no one there," says Teresa. "So I said, 'Nick, what is it?' And he said, 'Don't worry, they're just calling me because it's time for me to go.'

"'But will I see you again?' I asked him.

"'Of course you will,' he said. "As long as you need to.'

"'I'll always need to,' I said.

"'And I'll always need you to need to,' he answered."

"Then what happened?" says Nina.

"And then I said good night to your father and I fell back asleep, right back into that beautiful dream about the flowers. And when I woke up this morning, I felt refreshed and whole again, almost like I'd been reborn somehow. I still feel that way."

Now my daughters are all in tears again.

"That's so beautiful," sighs Gina.

"I wish Pop would come and visit me," sniffs Maria.

"Me too," adds Nina.

"Visit you?" laughs Teresa. "Two minutes ago you all said you'd faint if you saw your father."

Just then Johnny comes bursting back through the door. He looks desperately around the kitchen table before dashing upstairs.

"Where the hell did I leave my wallet?" he screams.

"It's right here on the counter where you left it," Teresa yells up to him.

Johnny comes tearing back down into the kitchen, grabs his wallet, and is about to go dashing out the door again when he stops and takes a look at the tear-filled eyes of his mother and sisters.

"What is going on with you guys?" he says.

"It's the onions," says Teresa, shooing him toward the door. "Believe me, it's just the onions."

Chapter 30

Let me tell you a little story about me and Vicki. She got it in her head one time that she wanted to see this show up in Boston, some play with Al Pacino in the leading role. I can't remember the name of it. Anyway, she kept talking about it every time we got together. I got sick of hearing about it, so finally I arranged to get tickets, and one night when the coast was clear, I picked her up at her place and we blasted up to Boston.

I was never keen on going out anywhere in Rhode Island with Vicki, for obvious reasons. Everybody knows everybody in this state, and everybody talks to everybody, if you know what I mean. It just wasn't worth the risk. But going up to Boston to a theater at night where you could just blend in with the crowd seemed like a reasonably safe idea.

On the way up, Vicki's all bubbly and happy because this was the first time in weeks, months even, that the two of us had shown our faces together in public. It's a big deal for her, but me, I'm more concerned with keeping a low profile for the night, if you catch my drift.

So we get to the theater, park ourselves in our seats, and watch the show. I like Pacino as an actor, but I thought this particular play was a yawner. I practically nodded out halfway through the first act. Vicki loved it, though. At intermission, as we made our way out to the lobby to get a drink, she was talking a mile a minute about how wonderful it was. Tell you the truth, I probably could have taken her to see reruns of the Three Stooges and she would have been just as excited, anything just to get us away from her apartment for a night out.

Anyway, I'm standing there, sipping a gin and tonic while I pretend to listen to what she's saying. I'm just starting to relax, figuring maybe I can turn the radar system off for the night, when all of a sudden I feel a tap on the shoulder.

"Hey, Nick!" someone says.

It was like getting hit in the back with a blast of Arctic air. The second I hear my name, I'm frozen, completely paralyzed. Vicki too. Very slowly, I turn around and I see that it's none other than Dickie McDougal, a guy from Providence that I've known for ages. Dick the Mick, I used to call him, but Johnny nicknamed him Electric Dick because he's an electrician. Been a customer of ours for as long as I can remember. To make matters worse, Teresa and his wife, Marcia, talk to each other all the time. As it is, Dickie's a motormouth himself. Suddenly I've got this massive headache that's so bad I can barely see. It's like someone buried a pickax in the middle of my forehead.

"Hey, Dickie," I say, pretending to be pleasantly surprised. "What are you doing here?"

"Are you kidding?" says Dickie. "I love Pacino. I've been dyin' to see this show. You know, I tried for two weeks to get tickets for this thing, but it was sold out every night that I wanted to come up. I should have called you, you're gonna say, right?"

I just give a little shrug and I can feel the side of my mouth squirreling up for all it's worth. Both Vicki and I have gone pale, but there's not much point in acting as though she and I aren't together.

"Dickie," I say, with a nervous little cough, "this is Vicki . . . a . . . uh . . . friend of mine."

"Hey, how do you do," says Dickie, as if it's no big deal that he's run into me while I'm with another woman. "Say, that's a great dress you're wearing," he tells her.

"Thank you," says Vicki, blushing.

Suddenly Dickie lets out a big laugh. "Hey, Dickie, Nicky, and Vicki," he says. "What a great name for a band! I betcha we could get a record contract overnight just with the name. We'd be millionaires! Whatta ya think?"

"I think I should go use the ladies' room before the next act starts," says Vicki. "I'll see you back inside, Nick. Nice to meet you." With that, she makes tracks and disappears in the crowd.

"Hey, pretty girl," says Dickie with a nod of approval.

"Listen, Dickie," I tell him. "You can't let Marcia know that you saw me—"

Before I can finish the sentence, this sharp little blonde steps out of the crowd, slinks right over to us, and takes Dickie by the arm. "What are you doin', Dickie," she says, snapping a wad of bubble gum. "I been sittin' all by myself, waitin' for you to come back."

"Hey, lighten up," laughs Dickie. "I was just talkin' to a friend of mine. Nick, say hello to Vanessa."

"How do you do, Vanessa," I say.

"How do I do what?" she answers between snaps.

At that, Dickie lets loose with another laugh. "Don't pay any attention to her, Nick," he tells me. Then he leans closer to me and says in a voice just loud enough for her to hear, "I call her Vanessa the Undresser—just for fun."

"Dickie!" she cries, giving him a playful punch in the shoulder. "You're such a jerk."

Just then the lights flicker, letting everyone know that the second act is about to begin.

"Woops, time to go," says Dickie. "See ya around, Nick."

As Vanessa drags him away, Dickie looks back over his shoulder and pulls his thumb and forefinger across his mouth like he's zippering his lips shut. Then he gives me a wink and a smile just before the two of them duck back into the theater.

By now the rest of the herd is moving back inside to catch the start of the next act, but not me. First thing I do is down the rest of my drink and head straight back to the bar for another. Feeling like every ounce of energy has just been sucked out of my body, I stagger up to the bartender and order a double.

Neither Vicki nor I enjoyed the rest of the show very much. Honestly, I think we were both happy just to get out of there when it was all over. On the ride home, Vicki just stared out the window with this gloomy look on her face. The whole night had gone flat for her, like a great bottle of champagne that had been left uncorked for too long.

Finally, after we'd been on the road for a while, she turned to me and sighed. "I guess this is just how it really is for us," she said sadly, "how it's always going to be." Then she went back to staring out the window, and neither of us spoke for the rest of the way. Tell you the truth, things were just never the same after that.

I bring this story up only because right now Vicki's staring out of the window of Johnny's car with that same sad look as that night on the way back from Boston. Actually, she's been wearing that face just about every day since Johnny told her about his mother seeing me at lunch that afternoon up the East Side. Things haven't been so hunky-dory for them since then, if you know what I mean.

In any case, Vicki's been having car trouble, so giving her a lift to the bus station was one of the "things" that Johnny had to do that day before Thanksgiving that he didn't want to tell Teresa about—for obvious reasons. Trouble is, after running all those errands for his mother, and then forgetting his wallet at the house, Johnny's running way behind schedule and it's a sure bet that he's not going to get Vicki to the station in time to catch the last bus home to Kennebunkport. That being the case, Johnny starts driving like a maniac to get there.

"Don't worry," he tells Vicki, "we'll make it."

Johnny couldn't have timed the words any better if he

wanted to because, right at that moment, he looks up and sees the flashing lights in his rearview mirror. He lets out a groan and pulls the car over. Vicki doesn't say a word, but just sits there rubbing her forehead. The clock, meantime, is ticking.

One thing that I've never understood is why it takes so long when the police pull you over for speeding. For some reason they always leave you sitting there like a dope for everyone to see while they go back to the cruiser for what seems like hours and do whatever it is they do back there. All you can do is sit there and stew. So now, by the time the officer comes back to the car with the ticket, the steam is coming out of Johnny's ears. There's nothing he can do about it, though, so he just takes the ticket and tosses it over his shoulder onto the backseat. Then he looks with dismay at the clock.

"Come on," he says, putting the car in gear, "those buses almost never run on time. I betcha we'll make it."

Naturally, by the time they pull into the Bonanza parking lot, the last bus for Maine is long gone. Nonetheless, Johnny runs inside to the ticket window just to make sure there's not a later bus. There isn't, of course, and he trudges back to the car to give Vicki the bad news.

"Sorry," he says, slouching into his seat.

"It's not your fault," Vicki sighs. "That's just the way things are with us now—the way they'll always be, I guess."

"What do you mean?"

"I mean I'm always going to be second to your family and the business," she says, looking all dejected. "I understand. There's nothing either of us can do about that."

For a while they both just sit there, watching the other buses come and go.

"Wait a minute!" Johnny suddenly exclaims. "Your bus has to stop in Attleboro. It'll only take us five minutes to get there. I know right where it stops. Maybe we can catch it there."

Before Vicki can offer an opinion of the plan, the car goes

screeching out of the parking lot and up onto Route Ninety-five North. When they get to Attleboro, there's no bus in sight.

"It left fifteen minutes ago," the ticket agent tells Johnny.

"Argh!" Johnny grimaces. "Where does it go next?"

"Braintree."

So, back in the car he gets and the two of them blast off for Braintree, Massachusetts. Johnny's doing ninety the whole way, so he figures he's got a pretty good shot at making it there in time to catch the bus. Of course, he's got an equally good shot at getting another speeding ticket. And there's one other little problem: Johnny was in such a hurry to get back in the car when they were in Attleboro that he forgot to ask where the bus stops in Braintree. So they make it to Braintree in record time, but Johnny's clueless as to where they go once they get off the highway. He goes tearing all over town trying to guess where the bus station might be, but it's no use. Finally he pulls the car over and drops his forehead onto the steering wheel.

"You have no idea where you're going, do you?" says Vicki with icy calmness.

Johnny just shakes his head.

"There's a Burger King up ahead," she sighs. "Maybe someone in there can give us directions."

Johnny drives over to the Burger King and goes inside while Vicki waits in the car. He comes back out a few minutes later, carrying two cups of coffee.

"Do you know which way to go now?" says Vicki when he gets back in the car.

Johnny hands her one of the coffees and takes a sip of his own.

"Yup," he answers, starting the car. They drive back the way they came and up onto the on-ramp to Route Ninety-five.

"But Johnny, you're getting back on the highway," says Vicki. "Where are you going?"

"Where do you think we're goin'?" he says as he steps on the gas. "We're going to Maine."

Chapter 31

I only went to Maine once in my life. It was one summer, I don't know, maybe ten years ago. Teresa had been talking to one of her girlfriends, who told her all about this little area along the coast of Maine where they supposedly had all these great factory outlets and all sorts of interesting little shops and wonderful little hotels and quaint little bed-and-breakfasts and lots of great restaurants. In other words, a real nightmare of a place for the average guy. How I let Teresa talk me into taking a ride up there, I still don't know. I mean, like most men, the thought of going on a shopping trip with my wife in the middle of the summer was about as appealing as having my teeth drilled. But somehow or other I went.

The plan had been to drive up, stroll around, let Teresa do some shopping, find a nice little place somewhere to stay overnight, maybe have a nice dinner, and come back the next morning. Sounded reasonably painless, all things considered.

Forget about it.

First of all, it's about a hundred degrees in the shade and the area is just jammed with tourists, so right away I'm hot and miserable the minute we hit town. So is Teresa because we end up sitting in traffic most of the day, trying to find our way around, instead of shopping. When we finally get around to looking for a hotel, every place is booked, not a room anywhere this side of Mount Washington. On top of that, come dinnertime the restaurants are all jammed, hour-and-a-half wait minimum everywhere you go.

So now it's the end of the day and we're sitting in the car, both of us hot and tired and hungry and cranky and no place in sight to hang our hats. It finally sinks in that there's nowhere else to go but home. That's when Teresa turns to me and screams, "Why did I ever let you talk me into coming up here in the first place!"

Times being what they were, I gladly shouldered the blame. I turned us right around and drove straight home to Providence in time to catch a late-night plate of pasta up the Hill. And that, my friends, was the end of my shopping career.

Anyhow, by the time Vicki and Johnny pull into Kennebunkport, it's well after nine o'clock. Turns out that Kennebunkport, coincidentally, is right up the pike from where Teresa and I went that summer. Unlike in the summer, though, the roads through the area this time of year are practically deserted at night. Some guys have all the luck. So Johnny drives through the center of town and back out onto a darkened road that winds its way along the ocean. Down below them, jutting out into the bay, is a little strip of land. Johnny can just make out the silhouette of the stately home resting on it.

"That's the Bush house," Vicki tells him as they pass the gate at the top of its long driveway.

"What, the beer people?"

"No, silly," says Vicki, smiling for the first time since she got in the car. "The president people."

"Oh," Johnny shrugs.

Farther along Vicki tells him to turn off onto a side road that leads away from the ocean. They drive a little ways before a house comes into view up ahead. It's a nice old house, with a wraparound porch and big windows looking out toward the bay.

"That's it," says Vicki.

Johnny turns in and drives up the stone-covered driveway leading to the house. He pulls up to the garage, an old converted barn, and turns the car off while Vicki gathers her things together.

"My God, we flew up here," she says. "I don't think I've ever made it here this fast."

"Please remain seated until the plane has come to a complete halt," says Johnny. "And remember to take all your carry-on belongings with you."

Vicki turns to him and takes him gently by the arm. "You know, Johnny, you really didn't have to do this," she tells him for about the fifteenth time since they left Braintree.

"Hey, I aim to please," he says with a shrug. "Come on, lemme go grab your bag out of the trunk."

It's a chilly night, made colder by a light wind coming in off the ocean. As he gets out of the car and stretches his arms over his head, Johnny blows out a little puff of steam. Arching his back and rolling his neck to shake off the long ride, he casts a glance around to take in what he can of the place. The lights are all on inside the house and there's a smell of burning wood in the air. He looks up and sees the little curl of smoke rising out of the chimney. He pauses for a second and looks out toward the bay.

"What's the matter?" says Vicki.

"Nothin'," he says. "I just realized that you can hear the ocean from here. I like that sound."

"We spent all our summers here when I was growing up. I love that sound too."

Before they make it up the steps to the porch, the front door swings open and Vicki's mother comes out. She's all smiles and she gives her daughter a big hug.

"I was just starting to get worried about you," her mother tells her. "When you didn't call from Portland, I began to get afraid that something might have happened to the bus."

"Sorry, but we had a little change of plans," says Vicki, giving Johnny a nod. "I missed the bus, so we ended up driving."

"Well, come on inside, both of you, and get warm so you can tell me all about it."

Once inside the light of the front hall, Johnny gets a better look at Vicki's mother. She's an attractive lady with shoulder-length silver hair and deep blue eyes like her daughter's. Judging by her apron and rolled-up sleeves, she's been busy in the kitchen.

Vicki turns to Johnny and takes her overnight bag from him. "Mom, this is Johnny," she says, "a friend of mine from Providence."

"Well, it's a pleasure to meet you, Johnny," says her mother, extending her hand. "Thank you for bringing my daughter home safely to me."

"*Eh,* it was no big deal, Mrs. Sanders," he says, shaking her hand. "I was happy to do it."

"Please," she tells him, "you can call me Elizabeth or Sandy, if you prefer."

"*Sandy?*"

"Of course, don't be shy. All my friends call me Sandy, it's my nickname."

"Okay," says Johnny, giving a little cough. "Sandy it is." He shoots a look at Vicki, who's doing her best to look the other way.

"Whatcha got cookin', Mom?" she says to change the subject.

"Come along," says her mother, heading toward the kitchen. "You can get to work helping me."

Johnny takes a look around as he follows them through the house. It's a great old place with nice high ceilings and hardwood floors throughout. They pass the living room and Johnny takes a peek in. It's a cozy room with comfortable-looking furniture and a nice little fire burning in the fireplace. What strikes him most, though, are the books. There are books cramming just about every inch of the shelves that line the walls; there are books on the coffee table next to the couch; there are books piled on top of the little upright piano in the corner; there are books just about everywhere. Johnny can't help smiling.

"Now I know where you get it from," he says to Vicki.

"What's that?" she says over her shoulder.

"Never mind."

"Have a seat, Johnny," says Vicki's mother when they enter the kitchen. "I'll get you a cup of coffee."

"Don't go to any trouble, Mrs.—I mean, Eliz—I mean . . ."

"It's already made," she says before he has a chance to stammer any further. "Go on, have a seat at the table and I'll cut you a piece of pie to go with it. You must be hungry after such a long ride."

"You sound just like my mother," chuckles Johnny.

"Well, we're all cut out of the same cloth, dear."

Johnny obeys and takes a seat at the table. Before he knows it, there's a plate of apple pie in front of him along with a steaming mug of coffee. This, by the way, is a classic example of what I call the dating double-team. Just about all mothers do it whenever their daughters finally drag home a boy that they like. That's when it becomes two against one. You see, women make up their minds about men within a nanosecond of the time they first lay eyes on them, and their initial assessment is usually pretty accurate. Don't ask me how they do it. It's an innate skill that men just don't possess. Now, if a mother likes what she sees when the kid walks in the door, she inevitably figures that the first thing to do is get him to sit down at the kitchen table and give him something good to eat. She knows that the wiring of the typical male is much less complex than that of a woman. Males are driven by a handful of basic instincts, the first of which is the desire to eat. They almost never forget where they've had a good meal, so all you have to do is feed 'em once and they're sure to keep coming back for more. And it doesn't change much when the boys turn into men.

Anyway, while Vicki puts on an apron, her mother starts to pull out vegetables from the grocery bags on the floor.

"So, Vicki says you're from Providence, Johnny," she says, piling everything on the counter. "Do you work at the university too?"

"Oh no," Johnny chuckles. "I'm not what you'd call academically inclined, if you know what I mean. I sell hardware."

"Johnny runs his own store," says Vicki as she helps her mother sort out the groceries.

"*Ah,* you're an entrepreneur," says her mother, smiling. "I always dreamed of running a little business of my own back when I was a teacher."

"You were a teacher too?" says Johnny.

"Second-grade elementary for thirty-two years," she answers. "And I enjoyed every single one of them. The money was never very good, of course, which is why I always tried to get Vicki interested in some other profession when she was growing up, but she insisted on going into teaching herself. My daughter's very stubborn, you know, especially once she gets an idea in her head. She inherited that from her father."

"Thank you for that interesting tidbit, Mother," says Vicki.

"*Eh,* she's doin' okay," says Johnny, giving Vicki a wink.

"You know, I've always thought that it must be nice to run your own business," her mother goes on, "being your own boss, not having to answer to anyone else."

"Hey, believe me, you have to answer to plenty of people when you run your own business," says Johnny, "mostly your customers. Sometimes it feels like you got ten thousand bosses instead of one."

"I never thought of it that way," she says. "I guess we all have to answer to someone no matter what we do, Johnny."

"Seems that way."

"So tell me," she says innocently, "how did you two meet?"

That question produces what can only be described as a pregnant pause. Johnny looks at Vicki and Vicki looks at Johnny and then there's this quiet moment of desperation. Johnny starts to open his mouth even though it's obvious that he has no clue as to what he's about to say.

"We had a mutual friend who introduced us," says Vicki, coming to the rescue. "Then we happened to see each other a few weeks later when I was on my way to a poetry reading and Johnny decided to come along."

"I see, how nice," says her mother. She's sharp as a tack, I can tell, so she knows that something's up between the two of them, but she's also sharp enough not to make too much of it. "Do you enjoy poetry readings, Johnny?" she asks.

"*Eh,* sometimes more than others," he answers. "It depends."

"So who's coming tomorrow, Mom?" says Vicki, trying to steer the conversation to something less poetic.

"Well, let's see," she replies. "Your brother and Jocelyn and the kids are coming. Aunt Sarah and Uncle Charlie. Your cousin David and his wife are spending the weekend in town, so I invited them. Mildred at the library was going to be home all alone tomorrow so I invited her too. Then there's you, of course—and I hope you'll be joining us, Johnny."

"Me?" says Johnny. "Oh no, I can't, Mrs . . . San . . . ma'am. Thank you for askin', but I have to head back to Providence tonight."

"All the way back to Providence after my daughter made you drive all the way up here? Nonsense. You can spend the night right here. We have plenty of room."

"I already told Johnny on the way up that he could stay, Mom," says Vicki, "but he just wants to have Thanksgiving dinner with his own family."

"I understand," says her mother with a little sigh. "I just feel bad that he's come all this way and now he has to turn right around and go back. It's getting late, you know."

"I'll be okay," says Johnny. "Really, don't worry about it."

So with that issue settled, Vicki and her mother get to yacking about this and that while Johnny sips his coffee and eats his pie. He doesn't pay much attention to them. Having grown up with three sisters, girl talk has become little more than background noise to him. He should try having three daughters and a wife—but that's another story. So he just munches away on his pie and looks around. The air is full of the warm smell of pies baking in the oven. There's something simmering as well in the frying pan on the front of the stove. On the back burners sit two big pots, the steam from them rising and condensing on the panes of the back window. Over on the counter where Vicki goes to work helping her mother are bunches of carrots and beats and celery as well as a bag of potatoes, butternut squash, and other vegetables. All in all, the scene's not too different from the one he left in Providence a few hours earlier.

When he finishes his pie and coffee, Johnny stands and picks up the plate and mug. "That was great pie, Mrs. Sanders," he says, starting toward the sink.

"Thank you, Johnny," she answers. "I don't get around to cooking very often, so I try to do the best I can whenever I do cook."

"Here, let me take all of that," says Vicki. She snatches the plate and mug from Johnny's hands and brings them to the sink. After rinsing them off, she turns off the faucet, but a trickle of water keeps running out no matter how much she tightens it.

"What's wrong with this faucet?"

"Oh, it's been like that for weeks," says her mother. "I just haven't gotten around to calling a plumber to fix it."

Johnny walks over to take a quick look at it. He fiddles with the faucet for a minute then, without a word, turns around and heads out of the kitchen.

"Where are you going?" Vicki calls after him.

"Be right back."

Johnny returns shortly, carrying the toolbox he keeps in the trunk of his car. He sets the box on the counter by the sink, opens it, and fishes out a wrench and screwdriver. "This should only take a minute," he says. So he reaches under the sink to turn off the water, then he unscrews the top of the faucet. "I think all it needs is a new washer."

Before long, Johnny's got the top of the faucet apart with the pieces laid out on the counter. He rummages through his toolbox and pulls out a washer. It fits and a few minutes later, the faucet is reassembled and running properly again. Feeling quite satisfied with himself, Johnny tosses his tools back in the box and closes the lid. Actually, I'm kind of pleased myself. The kid at least learned something from hanging around me all those years.

"Wonderful," says Vicki's mother, trying the faucet. "How much do you charge for house calls?"

"A piece of pie and a cup of coffee usually covers it."

"In that case, I'll be sure to call you the next time the hot water heater needs fixing," she says with a big smile.

"Glad to do it."

Later, when it's time to go, Vicki walks to the door with Johnny. While he's standing in the hallway pulling his coat on, Vicki's mother stays in the kitchen, filling a thermos full of coffee for him. She covers it securely and puts it on the counter. From the drawer underneath she pulls out a lunch bag and tosses in a handful of cookies along with an apple and some paper napkins. She places everything in a plastic grocery bag and hurries out to the hall before Johnny leaves.

"Well, it was a pleasure to meet you, Johnny," she says. "Will we be seeing you again?" This question is directed more at Vicki than Johnny. She makes no reply other than to give her mother an irritated stare.

"Eh, stranger things have happened," says Johnny with a shrug.

"Well, I hope we do," her mother says, handing him the bag. "Here, take this with you. Make sure you at least drink some of the coffee on the ride. It will help you stay awake."

"Thanks," says Johnny. "You didn't have to do that."

"And call us when you get home. Otherwise we'll be worried."

"Okay," Johnny chuckles.

"Come on, Johnny," says Vicki, opening the door. "I'll walk to the car with you."

"Good night, Johnny," Mrs. Sanders calls after them as they descend the steps on the porch. "Have a safe ride home and a happy Thanksgiving tomorrow."

Johnny waves goodbye as they walk across the front lawn to the driveway. When he gets to the car, he slides in, stows the coffee and cookies beside him on the passenger's seat, and rolls the window down to say goodbye to Vicki. Shivering in the pale moonlight beaming down from the cloudless night sky, she leans in and kisses him on the cheek.

"Thank you," she says, "you know you didn't—"

"I know, I know," says Johnny. "I didn't have to drive you all the way up here. Don't worry about it, I just decided I wanted to, okay?"

"Okay," she answers. She pauses for a moment and gazes out toward the bay, where the moonlight is shimmering across the top of the water. "You know," she says, "it might have been nice if things were different and you and I could have spent the day together with one of our families tomorrow."

"What can you do?" sighs Johnny. "You just play the game with the cards you get dealt. As it is, I think we've bent a bunch of the rules."

"But whose rules are we playing by?"

"God's, I guess," says Johnny. "He's the one we all answer to, right? So I guess you can blame the whole thing on Him—not that it'll do you much good."

With that, he starts the car and flips on the headlights. "Gimme a call if you need a lift home from the bus station Sunday," he says before backing out.

"I already arranged for a ride," she replies. "but thank you."

"Well, I guess I'll see ya then."

"Goodbye, Johnny."

Back in the house, Vicki and her mother stand at the front door and watch Johnny drive away. When he's out of sight, her mother turns and heads back to the kitchen.

"What a nice fellow," she says over her shoulder. "Handy around the house, has his own business. A little rough around the edges, maybe, but those can be smoothed off without too much trouble. You could do a lot worse."

"Don't start, Mom," grumbles Vicki. She stares sullenly out into the distance for a time before closing the door. Then she follows her mother back into the kitchen to finish preparing the vegetables.

Chapter 32

Let me tell you, of all the holidays in the year, I always figured that Thanksgiving's the best. Christmas and Easter and all the others are nice too, but how can you beat a day that's devoted to nothing else but rejoicing in God's abundance by stuffing yourself senseless with good food and then lying around the rest of the day on the living room couch, watching football games till you nod off? It's the most relaxed holiday of the year, at least for the men. Now for the women, that's a different question. Nine times out of ten, the cooking chores fall on them, so the day isn't quite as restful as it is for the men. But listen, that's how the Pilgrims did things, right? Tradition is tradition.

One of the great holiday traditions in the Catini household has always been the sound of screaming coming from the kitchen while Teresa and the girls try to get everything prepared and out onto the dining room table before the natives get restless. This Thanksgiving is no different. All four women take turns airing out their lungs. Standing outside the kitchen with your ear to the door, you'd think that they were all at each other's throats in there. In reality, though, it's all harmless blather because no one pays much attention to what the others are saying. It's all just a way of relieving tension.

"Get out of my way!" screams Teresa, squeezing her way over to the sink to strain a steaming pot of boiled potatoes.

"I'm not mashing those!" cries Maria. "Let someone else do it, I hate mashing potatoes."

"You hate doing everything," snips Nina. "You're so lazy sometimes."

"Will you all please just shut up!" adds Gina. "Who can even think straight in this kitchen with you three?"

"Us three? And what about you . . ."

And on and on it goes. It looks and sounds like sheer chaos, but they have their own order for doing things and the meal always ends up on the table one way or the other as planned. By then the nerves aren't so frayed and civility returns among the women so that everyone can eat their turkey without getting *agita*.

All the men and the children are seated at their respective tables when Teresa and Maria start the proceedings by bringing out the antipastos, two platters of lettuce lined with little rolls of sweet *prosciutt'* and slices of provolone. The center of each is covered with piles of marinated mushrooms, olives, roasted peppers and pepperoncini, artichoke hearts, and anchovies and all sorts of other good stuff that you can't get around here. The antipasto is just the opening salvo. Once the ravenous hordes have devoured it, Teresa will serve the escarole and meatball soup, which I always loved, followed by some macaroni in just a light marinara sauce so that there'll be enough room left over for the turkey and the stuffing and the vegetables.

Teresa holds her hand up to bring order before everyone starts to dig in. "Quiet, everyone," she says. "Isabella has started her first communion classes at catechism so she wants to be the one to say grace before we eat."

All eyes turn to the little table in the corner that Teresa set for the children. Isabella looks up shyly, even though she's obviously basking in all the sudden attention.

"Go on, honey," says Maria. "Say it just like you did for me and Daddy last night."

Isabella folds her hands reverently and bites her lip. "Let us be thankful to God for all this wonderful food we are about to eat," she begins softly. "And let us be thankful for all our family here with us today. God bless Mommy and Daddy and Rosie and Mikey, and Auntie Nina and Uncle Ralph and cousin Tommy and Joanna, and Auntie Gina and Uncle Jimmy, and Uncle Johnny and Great-Uncle Victor, and Nonna Teresa." She pauses and looks around. "Did I forget anybody? Oh yes, and most of all, God bless Papa Nick. We miss you and we hope you have a nice Thanksgiving up in heaven. In the name of the Father and the Son and the Holy Ghost . . ."

"Amen," they all say together.

There's a little moment of silence before Nina cries outs, "Oh my God, that was so sweet, Isabella!"

Everyone else agrees, naturally, and before you know it, it becomes bedlam once more at the table. Nobody's screaming at each other anymore like they were in the kitchen, but everyone's talking at once, everyone except for Johnny, that is. He's sitting there at the end of the table, gazing off into space like he doesn't hear a sound.

"Hey, space cadet," says Gina, giving him an elbow in the ribs, "you want some antipasto or what?"

"Yeah, sure," says Johnny, coming back to earth.

"What's the matter with you, you feeling all right?" his sister asks.

"I'm fine," yawns Johnny, "just a little tired. I got in late last night."

"What else is new?" says Teresa from the other end of the table. "He comes home at three o'clock in the morning every other night of the week."

"Out with the guys last night?" says Gina as she fixes him a plate of antipasto. Johnny doesn't answer, but just reaches over and grabs himself a couple of slices of bread.

"You want some mushrooms?" she says.

"Why not?"

"How about the anchovies?"

Johnny shakes his head; he's never liked anchovies much. Then he pauses for a moment when he catches the mischievous sparkle in his sister's eyes. That look usually means that she's about to share a really good secret with him.

"Whatta you got goin'?" he says. "Somethin' goin' on?"

Gina just smiles. "Here," she says, setting the plate in front of him, "just start eating and don't be a mope all day."

"Uh-huh," he says, eyeing her suspiciously.

A little while later, after the antipasto has been cleared away and Teresa has ladled out the escarole and meatball soup, Gina gives her husband Jimmy a nod. On cue he gets up from the table and leaves the room. He returns shortly with two bottles of champagne in hand.

"Before the main course is served," he says aloud as he pops open the first bottle, "Gina and I thought it would be nice if we had some champagne because we'd like to make a little announcement."

"A very little announcement," Gina adds with a smile.

Everyone, including myself, is all ears while Jimmy walks around the table with the bottle, filling the glasses. When he finally completes the circle, he stands behind Gina with one hand on her shoulder and the other around his raised glass. He pauses for dramatic effect.

"Well, you gonna tell us or what?" says Johnny impatiently.

"Come on," the others join in, "out with it!"

Jimmy holds up his hand for quiet. "We thought you'd all like to know," he begins, "that after careful consideration and planning, and many, many weeks of, shall we say, practice, Gina and I have decided to do our part in expanding the gene pool of our two families."

"What's he talkin' about?" Johnny says to Gina.

Gina smiles. "What he's saying, Johnny, is that I'm pregnant."

There's a very brief moment of silence before a communal scream of joy goes up. As you can imagine, the level of noise in the dining room suddenly goes up exponentially. Everybody's happy; I even feel like doing a tap dance myself.

Teresa jumps up and rushes over to Gina. "That's so wonderful!" she cries above the hubbub. "I'm so happy for both of you." She gives Gina a big hug and pinches Jimmy's cheek. "And it's about time!" she screams.

"Really," says Maria. "What took you guys so long?"

"Hey, it wasn't like we weren't trying," laughs Gina.

"Hey, what's all the racket about over there!" cries little Tommy from the kids' table.

"Auntie Gina's going to have a baby," Nina tells them.

The kids all look at one another. *"Right now?"* they all gasp.

"No, not right now, you sillies," she laughs, "in a few months."

"But when?"

"That's right," says Teresa, "when's the baby due?"

"April twentieth," Gina replies.

"So you're already four months along!" exclaims Teresa. "When were you going to tell us?"

"We just thought it would be a nice surprise to tell everyone on Thanksgiving," replies Gina.

"Hey, the middle of April, it'll be spring," says Uncle Victor, throwing his two cents in. "That's a nice time to have a baby."

"But look at her!" screams Teresa. "Four months pregnant and she hasn't put on an ounce. There's a baby growing inside you, you know. Eat something!"

"All right, all right," laughs Gina. "Let's all eat."

When things finally settle down a bit and everyone gets back to finishing their soup, Johnny nudges Gina with his elbow.

"Nice goin'," he says softly, giving her a wink.

"Thanks," says Gina, beaming.

"Hey, Johnny," calls Uncle Victor. "Everybody's havin' babies around here. When are you gonna get married and start having some of your own?"

"*Ayy,* don't start, Uncle Vic," says Johnny.

"Don't worry," says Gina, giving her brother a nudge of her own, "it will happen one day."

"Yeah, well, don't hold your breath," he replies. He tries to say it with some bravado, but for once there's a hint of uncertainty in his voice. It's very slight, probably something only a father would pick up on, but it's there nonetheless. The others are getting ready to needle Johnny a little more, but then Teresa brings out the macaroni and the next round of feasting begins.

Afterward, when everyone's certain that if he has one more bite of turkey or stuffing or mashed potato or cranberry sauce that he'll spontaneously combust, the forks drop to the table and the men stagger off to the living room to digest and watch football while the women clear the table for coffee and dessert. As usual, Teresa has the mandatory selection of pies: pumpkin, apple, mince, coconut custard. Added to that are the carrot cake Maria baked, the cookies Nina picked up at the bakery, and the wandies, the puffs of dough sprinkled with sugar, that Gina tried making for the first time.

Naturally, it will be a while before the men (or the women, for that matter) can even look at the desserts. For now it's enough to just collapse into a comfortable chair and doze off for a bit in front of the television. Johnny's the last one in, so the best seats are all taken by the time he gets there. At the moment there's a commercial showing on the television, one of those beer ads with the frogs and lizards talking to one another. Not for nothing, by the way, I was never any advertising genius, but do talking reptiles and amphibians really help people sell more beer? But what do I know?

Anyway, Johnny takes a seat on the carpet next to the couch and stretches out his legs. "Who's playing today?" he says.

"Detroit," answers his brother-in-law David. "Who else?"

"Good game?"

"They're gettin' shellacked by Indy," says Victor with a yawn. He's looking pretty shellacked himself. By the looks of it, he'll be down for the ten-count in about two minutes. He loosens his belt and settles back into his chair.

It's not long before Isabella and Michael and Tommy and Joanna come parading in. Ordinarily they like to take turns crawling all over their Uncle Johnny. Today, though, they're all stuffed to the gills too, so instead of hanging on Johnny, they all go and squirm up onto their fathers' laps. Rosalina, Maria's middle child, wanders in last.

"Hey," she cries at seeing that all the room on her father's lap has been taken, "what about me?" With a pout, she plops onto the floor next to Johnny.

"Come on, Rosie," says Johnny, lifting her over onto his lap. "You can sit with me."

The ball game comes back on and everyone focuses their attention on the television. Johnny, though, looks around at the others. Victor is already long gone, his head back and mouth wide open. Isabella and Michael are all snuggled up against David, who's doing his best to keep his own eyes open. Tommy is dangling off Ralph's knees, trying to untie his father's shoe, while Joanna fidgets with his ear and the hair on the side of his head. Ralph does his best to ignore them while he chats with Jimmy about the first time Nina had a baby and what it's like being a father. Johnny looks a little blue, if you asked me, as he just sits there and listens to them talk and laugh. Looking at him, I'd say that maybe it's sinking in on him for the first time that there might be a few things in life that he's been missing out on. Before he can ponder that profound thought for very long, Rosalina looks up at him with her big brown eyes and tugs on his shirt collar.

"Uncle Johnny, Uncle Johnny," she calls to get his attention. "I have to ask you something."

"What is it, honey?"

"Well, when I stick my finger in my belly button," she says very seriously, "and then I sniff it, it stinks. Why is that?"

Johnny cracks up. The other guys laugh along with him. "You know something, Rosie," he says, hugging his niece, "your Nonnie Teresa is always saying that I got an answer for everything. But on that one, I think maybe you've got me stumped."

"But I want to know!"

"*Hmm,*" grunts her uncle, rubbing his chin thoughtfully. "Well, I can't be sure, of course," he says, "but maybe when God made you, He said to Himself, 'I'm gonna make a beautiful little girl who looks just like an angel and I'm gonna call her Rosalina 'cause she's pretty as a rose. But I can't make her completely perfect because then she wouldn't be real, so I'm gonna put just this little tiny bit of stink in her belly button that no one can smell but her.' Know what I mean?"

That explanation seems to satisfy my granddaughter because right away she squirms off Johnny's lap, gives him a kiss on the cheek, and runs off to the kitchen.

"Mommy," she calls in delight, "Uncle Johnny says God made my belly button stink!"

"See that, Johnny?" laughs Ralph. "You've got the touch with kids. You'd make a great father."

"*Eh,* who knows, maybe someday, Ralphie," says Johnny, settling back against the couch, "maybe someday." Then he closes his eyes and listens to the ball game until his mother calls them all back for dessert.

Chapter 33

December can be a funny month in New England. It's the deepest, darkest time of the year, but you can never be sure of what kind of weather to expect. Some years it's cold right from the start. The winds roar down out of Canada like a locomotive, and you know right away that you're in for a long, bitter winter with a lot of snow. Other years, the breeze puffs gently out of the South, and you can get a stretch of days with the temperatures well into the sixties—it's almost balmy. Those years you can forget about a white Christmas and that ski trip up north you were planning. Better to start thinking about taking a trip to Florida or one of the islands after the holidays, know what I mean?

Anyhow, this year's one of those cold years. The week after Thanksgiving the bottom drops out of the thermometer, and the mercury struggles to pull itself up to twenty degrees during the warmest part of the day. The skies are crystal clear, so there's no snow in sight, but the winds just howl all day long and the frigid air nips at you like an angry dog whenever you step outside. Sounds strange, but deep in their hearts, people around here prefer it that way. Warm Decembers just feel contrary to the natural order of things; it's like they throw everyone's biorhythms out of kilter.

Business-wise, the week can't possibly start any better for Johnny. People just go crazy at the mention of winter weather around here, and by midweek just about everything to do with cold weather and snow has been snatched up. It's nuts. Rock salt? Gone. There's maybe one or two small bags left on the shelves. Car brushes and scrapers? Forget about it, they were the first things to go. Snow shovels? What, are you kiddin'? Those things were all gone yesterday. Even the two snowblowers Johnny decided to carry that season are already sold. All this despite the fact that barely a flake of snow has hit the pavement yet. The cash register doesn't stop singing and ringing for a minute. You ask me, it's the most wonderful time of the year, right?

Come Wednesday, Johnny's already scrambling to reorder stock and get it in before the weekend. The way the cash has been coming in, you'd think that he'd be whistling Christmas carols all day long. But he hasn't. All week long he's slouched around, just going through the motions, counting the money as it rolls in, but not getting any joy out of it. Even over the past weekend, when his sisters and the kids helped him put up the Christmas decorations around the store, he was about as cheerful as Scrooge. He just wasn't in the holiday spirit. And he still isn't now. The kid's got things on his mind, and he knows that he won't feel any better until he deals with them. When closing time comes that dark afternoon, he knows just what he has to do.

When Johnny shows up at the door, Vicki doesn't look at all surprised to see him. At the same time, she's not standing with her coat and hat, ready to whisk him off to a piano recital or a poetry reading or any other intellectually stimulating affair for that matter. She just opens the door and lets him in.

Johnny says nothing, but heads straight for the living room and flops onto the couch. For her part, Vicki disappears into the kitchen while Johnny stretches out his legs and tries to relax. He looks around and notices for the first time how low the lights are turned. In the corner, the dark strains of Mozart's "Requiem Mass" swell from the CD player. All in all, the place doesn't have what you'd call a happy feel to it at the moment. So, he takes a deep breath to calm himself and catches the aroma of coffee brewing in the kitchen. Sure enough, Vicki appears a few moments later with two steaming mugs in hand. She sets one on the table in front of Johnny and sits down with her own in the chair opposite him. She takes a sip from her mug and just gazes at him for a time.

"We need to talk," she finally says.

"I know," Johnny answers. He picks up his mug to take a sip, but then it occurs to him that he's squirreling up the side of his mouth, so he puts his hand to his face to make himself stop doing it.

"Too late," says Vicki. She puts her mug on the table and stares down at her hands for a moment before looking up again. "Why don't you go first and tell me what's on your mind."

"No," says Johnny, squirming a little. "Ladies before gentlemen, that's the way it should always be, right?"

"Okay," she says.

"So what's on *your* mind?"

Vicki looks him square in the eye. "Johnny, I'm pregnant," she says straight out.

Johnny doesn't say anything, but his jaw just about hits the floor and he spills a few drops of hot coffee onto his trousers. Despite the pain, he doesn't move. He's too paralyzed.

"No I'm not," says Vicki with a sad sort of smile. "It was a bad joke. I just wanted to see what you'd say."

The color gradually comes back to Johnny's cheek. "Why is it," he says once he manages to get his breath back, "that lately everybody's tellin' me they're pregnant? What is this, some kind of conspiracy?"

"Sorry," says Vicki, "it's a pretty scary thought, I guess, isn't it?"

"Yeah, you might say that," says Johnny.

"I shouldn't have done it. Forgive me."

"Forget it—I guess," he says irritably. "So was there something that you really wanted to talk about?"

"It can wait," she says. "Please tell me what's on *your* mind."

Johnny looks away for what seems a very long time. That's to be expected. Long as I've known my son, saying what's really on his mind, especially to women, has never been his strong suit. "I don't know how to say this," he begins slowly, "but . . . but—"

"Yes?"

Johnny takes a deep breath. "Well, we can't do this anymore," he finally blurts out. "We gotta stop seeing each other." Then he sits back, cringing because he figures the fur's about to start flying.

Vicki, though, just lets out a long sigh of her own. "Is that what you want?" she says softly.

Johnny throws up his hands in exasperation. "I'm not sayin' that that's what I want," he laments. "It's just that I don't know what else to do here." He collapses back into the cushions and covers his face in the palms of his hands. "It might be a good idea, at least for a while," he goes on, "you know, to give it a break, maybe clear our heads a little."

"Why now?"

"I dunno," he replies. "It's just that ever since my sister told me that she's gonna have a baby—"

"Your sister's going to have a baby?" says Vicki. "That's nice."

"Yeah," Johnny continues, "anyway, I don't know what it was about it when she told me, but it's like somethin' clicked in my head. All of a sudden I'm thinkin' that I'm not gettin' any younger and maybe it's time to start thinkin' about where I'm goin' in my life."

"And who you're going there with?" Vicki adds.

"Maybe, I dunno," says Johnny, shaking his head. "I mean, I'm not sayin' that I'm ready to get married and start havin' kids and mortgage payments and all of that."

"Yes," says Vicki with a nod, "I could guess that by the look of terror on your face when you thought *I* was having a baby."

"Yeah," he sighs, "but maybe I'm figurin' that it's time to at least start thinkin' about these things. And . . ."

"And?"

"And . . . well, I just don't know how I'm ever gonna work this thing out with my mother and you. I mean, I just can't see any way for it to happen. This whole thing is too bizarre for me. It's way outta control. You must have thought about this yourself."

"Yes," agrees Vicki. "I've thought about it a great deal. And I think you're right."

"You *do?*" says Johnny, sounding like he's not sure if he's surprised or relieved or a combination of both.

Vicki stands and walks over to the mantel, where she keeps some of her family photographs. One of them is a picture of her and her father when she was just a baby. She picks up the picture and gazes at it for a few moments before gently placing it back.

"You know," she begins, barely above a whisper, "inside I always knew that what your father and I were doing was wrong—and I felt guilty about it, but at the same time I believed that nobody else knew about it but us—and somehow that made everything okay. You know? But when you told me that your mother knew, that she had seen us, then it sank into me for the first time how wrong I really was. Now I have this ache inside me that won't go away, which is probably only right since it's exactly what I must have caused her."

"Listen," says Johnny. "It's old news now. Don't beat yourself up about all that stuff. Things like this just happen sometimes.

But it's in the past now and there's nothin' anybody can do about it, so forget about it."

"But the past always comes back to haunt you, doesn't it?" she says. "You can see that too, can't you?"

"No," says Johnny, shaking his head. "I don't."

"Look at us," she sighs. "I mean, if things were different, if we had met differently, I think maybe that we could have had . . ."

"What?" says Johnny, leaning closer.

Vicki shrugs. "Something," she says. "I don't know, something special. But we'll never have the chance to find out because of what I did. It's like God's punishment for my sinning with your father."

"*Eh,* I don't know about all that," says Johnny. "You'll have to take that up with God. But you're right, we're both right. Besides, I'm all wrong for you."

Vicki gapes at him. "My God," she says, "you sounded just like your father. He was always saying things like that."

"It's true," Johnny goes on. "Look, I appreciate all these things you've been showin' me and tryin' to teach me, but bottom line is, how much do you think you can change me?"

"You've got it wrong, Johnny," she says. "I don't want to change you at all. I've only tried to show you these things to help you see beyond the problems with the business and your family, to understand that there's more to life than just what you've seen. You don't need me to help you change; you can become whatever you want, whenever you want."

"Well, right now I'm a palook' named Johnny Catini and I sell hardware. That's what I am and I don't know how to change that, especially with my family lookin' over my shoulder. It's like everything in my life is tied up with them and the business. I mean, God forbid I sell out or screw up and let the name *Catini* come off the building, I'll have all of them at my throat."

"Then don't take the name off the building," says Vicki.

"Huh?"

"Who says that it has to be Catini's Hardware? Ever since we met, you've been telling me that you hate the hardware business. If that's the case, why not make it Catini's Restaurant or Catini's Gift Shop or Catini's Bookstore or whatever you want it to be? Why not take what your family has given you and turn it into something all your own, but something that they can all still be proud of. I think that's all they want. You've been given a great gift, Johnny. All I wanted was to help you make the most of it."

Johnny sits there in silence. All of a sudden his face brightens, like a lightbulb just snapped on in his head. That's the way it goes sometimes in life. You feel like you're stumbling around in the dark until somebody lights a match and shows you how simple the way can be. You think you're at a dead end, but suddenly you realize all the wonderful possibilities.

"But where does that leave us?" he says, his face clouding over again.

"I need more," says Vicki. "You do too—even if you don't think you're ready for it. We both need to move forward in our lives. Just going on like we have without a chance for something more isn't fair to either of us."

Johnny lets out a long sigh. "So, whatta we do next?"

Vicki gazes down once more at her hands. "I guess," she says, "that we just say goodbye."

Later, when Johnny's walking to the door, he pauses and takes a look around at everything for what he figures is the last time. By now the music has stopped playing, and it's quiet save for the humming of the refrigerator in the kitchen. Vicki comes up alongside and leans against the wall as he pulls his coat on.

"You know," she says wistfully, "I would give anything to be able to start all over again, to have a clean slate, to do things right this time."

"I think that way myself sometimes," says Johnny. "Probably everybody does." He opens the door and peers out into the darkness. "But then, of course, I realize that if I could start over again, I'd probably just find some new way to screw things up—so I don't worry about it."

"Goodbye, Johnny," she says, fighting back the tears.

"Goodbye, Vicki."

And then my son goes on his way, wherever that way might lead him. If I had to guess, I'd say the first place he'll end up at is a bar. Vicki, of course, has other plans . . .

When she walks into the church later that evening, the pews are all empty, save for the front row, where an old woman is saying the rosary. Vicki finds a seat close by to the confessional, kneels down, and begins to pray. It's not long before the little light at the top of the confessional goes off and another woman emerges from behind the curtain. The woman pulls a scarf around her head and makes her way out of the church.

Vicki takes a deep breath, makes the sign of the cross, and rises. She pauses outside the confessional, then parts the curtain and steps inside. Kneeling within the darkened cubicle, she waits for her turn, listening to the sound of her own breathing and the low murmur of the priest's voice and the person confessing on the opposite side. The little window to the priest suddenly slides open, startling her, and for a moment she doesn't know what to say.

"I'm here," says the priest in a kind voice.

"Bless me, Father," Vicki begins, "for I have sinned."

"How long has it been since your last confession, my child?"

"A lifetime, Father," she answers wearily, "a lifetime."

"In that case you come to God at the end of one lifetime and start afresh a new one. Welcome back to the world. Now tell me what's on your mind . . ."

Chapter 34

Let's face facts: The sum total of what the average man truly understands about women could be easily written on an area roughly the size of the fingernail on his pinky. It's not much, trust me. So I'm not going to pretend for you that I understand how the female mind operates any better than the next guy. I have learned one thing, though, which might have been helpful if I'd ever given it a try when I was topside. That is, if you can ever manage to hang around a hairdresser's shop, even for just a little while now and then, there's a good chance you'll pick up a few insights as to what's going on between their ears, and that can only help matters.

You can't believe the things women yack about while they're getting their hair done. Myself, I never had any idea, not that it's any of my business, but sometimes I can't help being curious, so I drop in and eavesdrop for a while. It's good for a laugh now and then, which breaks up the monotony when I'm occupied with other things, if you know what I mean.

Things can get pretty raucous in there, believe me, but it's when they get to talking about men that the lid really comes off. Like this day, for instance, a typical Saturday morning, and it all starts when one woman is saying, "My husband thinks he's *so* tough until he gets a little tummy ache. Then he's on the couch all day and can't lift a finger to help himself."

"They're all like that, honey," laughs another. "Men are such babies when they get sick. I wish just once that they all could get their periods and see what real cramps are all about."

"Why stop there?" a third chimes in. "Let them all try having a baby."

"Oh *puh-leassse!*" all the mothers cry out in a unanimous uproar. "Could you *see* it?"

That's it, they're off to the races. Nothing gets them going like talking about how different men would act if they knew what it was like to have a baby, to know what pain really is. Personally, until you know what it's like to take a good swift kick in the aggots, don't talk to me about what pain is.

Enough said.

But anyways, the place is bedlam now. Why *are* men such babies, they all want to know. Everyone's got an opinion, everyone except for these two ladies sitting beneath the hair dryers. One of them is my Teresa. It's the week before Christmas and she's in to get her head tuned up before the holidays. The other woman, young and very attractive, sits under the little plastic dome, her head covered in a plastic bag. By the way, I still have no clue what the bag's for, but I'll let you know soon as I do. Anyway, she's not paying much attention to the others. Instead she keeps her nose buried between the covers of a tattered paperback edition of *Barchester Towers.*

Teresa leafs uninterestedly through an old copy of *The New Yorker,* occasionally looking up with a smile at the others in the salon as they cackle away. Now and then she steals a glance at the younger woman seated across from her. I know the two have seen each other plenty of times before in the salon, but have never really spoken to one another.

You'd only have to be there for a minute to figure out that the younger woman is different from the others. Though pleasant enough, she rarely speaks, and when she does, she reveals next to nothing about herself. Based on my own observations, this trait alone immediately sets her apart from everyone else. I mean, these women tell their hairdressers things they'd never divulge in the confessional. But not this one—she likes to keep quiet.

Now, Teresa would be the first to tell you that in general it's better not to let on too much to others about yourself or what you have; someone might put the *malocchio* on you. Just the same, I can see that the temptation to try to prod *something* out of the girl is almost overwhelming. She can't help it; it's just part of the female psyche. Anyway, the young woman looks up unexpectedly and notices Teresa staring at her.

"That must be a good book you're reading," says Teresa amiably.

The younger woman closes her book and leans out from beneath the dryer. "I'm sorry," she answers, "I couldn't hear you from under this thing. What did you say?"

"I said, that must be a good book," Teresa replies, "to hold your attention with all these *chiacchieressas* making so much noise."

"All these who?"

"Chiacchieressas," Teresa repeats.

The woman makes a queer expression as if she hasn't understood.

"Chatterboxes," Teresa explains, nodding toward the other women. "They like to talk a lot."

"Oh," says the young woman, her face breaking out in a smile. "That's a word I hadn't heard before. How do you say it—*cackeraser?*"

"No," says Teresa. "Like this. KEE-ACK-KYEER-AYSA."

"Chiacchieressa," says the woman with near-perfect pronunciation.

"Now you have it."

"And that means someone who talks a lot?"

"That's right," says Teresa.

The young woman smiles once more. "See that, you learn something new every day."

"That's what every day is for," replies Teresa, obviously pleased with herself that she's managed to pry a few words out of the girl's mouth. "It looks as though you had something different done to your hair," she continues before the woman has a chance to return to her book. "Going someplace special tonight?"

"Sort of," she replies, uneasily. She gazes down at her book, and for a moment it looks like she's about to clam up again. To Teresa's surprise, though, she puts the book aside and looks up once more. "Actually," she admits, "I'm not going anyplace at all tonight, certainly no place special. I just decided that I needed a change. I want a new look—for the new year, I guess."

"Just broke up with your boyfriend, eh?" says Teresa.

The young woman gapes at her for a moment. "How on earth did you guess that?" she asks in disbelief.

"Listen, honey," Teresa tells her, "you get to be my age, you know how to read the signs."

"My God, I guess so," she says, shaking her head. "I didn't think it was so obvious."

Now, something about being in a salon turns everybody into a busybody. Teresa's no different, so she can't possibly stop there. Predictably, she tries to see how much more she can weasel out of her.

"What's the matter," she asks her, "things not working out the way you wanted?"

"Well," the young woman answers, "actually it's been over for a couple of weeks now. It's just one of those things. I guess it just wasn't meant to be, that's all. It's not that we were fighting or anything like that. If anything, it was just the opposite. But you see, we're very different from one another. Maybe it doesn't matter right now, but it will eventually."

"So, you decided that it would be better to stop it now before it goes too far," says Teresa. "If you ask me, from the sound of your voice, it seems like you rushed into a decision you weren't sure you wanted to make."

The woman herself seems unconvinced by what she has just told Teresa. She pauses and for a moment looks past her with a faraway gaze. "Plus there are other things," she goes on in a hesitant voice.

"What kinds of things?" says Teresa.

"Well, let's just say that there are things that both of us agree we'll never be able to overcome."

"If two people love each other, they can overcome anything," says Teresa.

"Life never seems to be that simple."

"It is if you let it," says Teresa. She ducks out from beneath the dryer and leans toward the woman. "So, do you love him?" she says in a hushed tone.

The woman doesn't reply, but gives a shrug and sighs.

"And what about him?" Teresa presses on. "Does he love you?"

The woman's eyes are welling up now. Again she doesn't reply, but bites her lip and shrugs.

"I think what you two need is a good talking-to," says Teresa with some authority. Not surprising for her.

The woman smiles and laughs. "Maybe you're right," she says with a sniffle.

Teresa settles back under the hair dryer and opens her magazine. "There now," she says, "go back to your book. I've pried enough secrets out of you for today. Next time in I'll let you pry a few out of me."

"It's a deal," says the woman.

"By the way," adds Teresa, "what do you think, why *are* men such babies sometimes?"

The young woman thinks about it for a second before her

face lights up in that really beautiful smile again. "I think," she answers, "it's because they just like to be taken care of sometimes."

"Hah!" laughs Teresa. "It's more like *all* the time." Then she leans closer and gives her a wink. "But would we want them any other way?"

"Probably not," she answers with a chuckle and the two share a good laugh together.

"My name is Teresa, by the way."

"Mine's Vicki," the young woman answers.

"Nice to meet you, Vicki."

"Same here," she replies.

Then Teresa goes back to reading her magazine and Vicki goes back to reading her book and the other women keep on cackling away and the world keeps on turning, just like it does every Saturday morning.

Go figure.

Chapter 35

One of the funny things about living in Rhode Island is that it's practically impossible to go anywhere in the state without bumping into someone you know or someone who knows someone you know. It's incredible. Stop virtually any stranger on the street, and if he or she's from Rhode Island, you'll either have friends in common or you'll discover that the two of you are distantly related. Guaranteed. That's because we're a little state and the train tracks cross in an awful lot of places around here, if you catch my meaning.

So it's no big surprise for the average Rhode Islander to bump into someone he knows no matter where he happens to find himself on any given day. Out-of-towners, though, are usually amazed at how often it happens, which I guess is why Horace looks so surprised to see Johnny at the Motor Vehicles Registry one afternoon a couple of days before Christmas. Horace has been teaching at Brown for ages, but he's from out of state originally and he rarely gets off campus. The guy's in his own little world up there.

Anyway, Johnny's on his way to see his buddy Al to take care of the speeding ticket he got tagged with the night before Thanksgiving. He'd almost completely forgotten about the thing until he happened to find it when he was cleaning out the backseat of his car. A phone call to Al would have been enough to take care of it, but Johnny likes to do things in person whenever he can. Got that from me. Besides, it's a chance to get out of the store for a while and maybe grab lunch downtown.

When he walks into the lobby, Johnny catches sight of Horace standing there in the middle of the floor. Horace looks a little dazed and confused as he tries to figure out where he's supposed to go. I tell you, the guy might be a bigwig on campus, but off it he's like a fish out of water.

"Hey, Horace," calls Johnny. "Whatta you doin' here?"

Horace whirls around. When he sees Johnny, he turns about six different shades of red. "Well, hello, Johnny," he says in that same nasally voice of his, except it's even worse because now he's got a cold. "What a . . . surprise to see you."

"Yeah, well, I got a little business to take care of," says Johnny. "Whatta you got goin'?"

Horace holds up a manila folder. "My parking tickets," he admits with a pained expression. "I completely forgot about them, so on top of the increased fines, now they're threatening to suspend my driver's license. It's quite a mess, I'm afraid. I thought perhaps there might be someone here I could talk with to clear this whole thing up."

"They still hasslin' you over those?" says Johnny. "Here, lemme see 'em."

"I don't think there's much that anyone can do about them at this point," says Horace, handing him the folder. "I suppose I'll just have to pay the fines and be done with it."

"Not so fast," says Johnny. He looks over the tickets in the folder for a moment. "Tell you what," he finally says, nodding to a bench against the far wall of the lobby. "Go have a seat over there and wait for me."

Not knowing what else to do, Horace obeys orders while Johnny heads upstairs to Al's office. So he sits down and waits. Ten minutes go by. Fifteen. Twenty. Horace is just about ready to give up and head home when Johnny emerges from the crowd and gives him a grin.

"You're all set," says Johnny.

"What do you mean?"

"I mean you can go. It's all taken care of."

"I don't understand," says Horace.

Johnny walks him toward the exit. "Come on," he says, putting his arm around his shoulder. "I'll explain it to you outside."

It's a dark, cold day outdoors, and the gray clouds are hanging low in the sky over the city. Been that way for a couple of days, and you can almost smell the snow in the air. But it just stays up there, teasing everybody the way it does sometimes. As they make their way to the parking lot, Johnny tries to bring Horace up to speed on the facts of life without telling him too much. Naturally he doesn't want to take a chance on getting Al into any hot water, especially since he only just started working at the Registry.

"But what did you mean, that it's all taken care of?" Horace asks again.

"I mean it's no longer on your driving record," Johnny tries to explain to him.

"Why not?"

Johnny clears his throat. "Let's just say there was some kind of computer glitch that accidentally deleted all your parking tickets."

Horace gives him a skeptical look. "A hardware problem, I suppose?" he says.

"Hey, I'm a hardware kinda guy," chuckles Johnny. "You know that."

"Yes, indeed," nods Horace. "Well, thank you very much. But I would love to know how this—hardware problem arose."

"Look at it this way," says Johnny. "Let's just say that it pays to have friends and leave it at that. *Capisc'?*"

Up ahead, a sandwich vendor stands outside his truck, stamping his feet and blowing on his hands to keep warm. It's almost noon and it won't be long before all the state workers come piling out to get their lunch.

"Got time for a coffee?" Johnny offers.

"Yes," says Horace, "but please, allow me. It's the least I can do."

So the two get their coffees and stand off to the side as workers from inside the Registry and the other state office buildings file out and start lining up. I tell you, it's amazing how much business this guy does, even in winter. I once heard he made a good sausage-and-pepper sandwich, but I'd never wait in the cold to get one. Though I guess it's convenient—people get their sandwiches practically right outside the door, then scurry back inside to eat them before they get frostbite. Anyway, Johnny and Horace stand there for a while, just sipping their coffees, chatting about the weather.

"We—um, haven't seen you much lately," Horace finally says.

"*Ay,* I've been busy," says Johnny, none too convincingly. "You know how it is."

"Yes, I suppose," says Horace. He takes a sip of coffee and looks across the parking lot to the Registry building. "You know," he says, "I don't know how to repay you for helping me today."

"Oh, that's easy," says Johnny. "Just help Vicki get that tenure thing."

Horace smiles. "Oh, there's never been any question about that, Johnny," he says. "Vicki is one of our best professors. She's more than earned her place at Brown—with or without my help."

"That's good," says Johnny, smiling himself. "That'll make her happy."

"Yes, I'm sure it will," says Horace, looking pensively at him.

He hesitates for a moment. "You know," he says, "when I first met you, I really didn't think . . ."

"What?" says Johnny.

"Never mind," says Horace, shaking his head. "It's really not important."

Johnny shrugs and takes a look up at the sky. "I dunno, Horace," he says, "but I think it wants to snow up there. God's just not lettin' it come down. Hard to believe tomorrow's Christmas Eve already."

"It is indeed."

"I take it everybody on campus is blowin' town for the holidays," says Johnny.

"Yes," says Horace. "Most of the students will have already left by this afternoon and the rest along with the faculty by to-morrow morning. There's always a last-minute mad exodus at the end of the semester."

"Yeah, I can imagine," says Johnny. He looks up again at the dark clouds overhead. "Well, I should probably get rollin' back to work. I got my sister watchin' the store for me, and she gets bent if she's there too long by herself. But it was nice seein' ya, Horace."

Now it's Horace's turn to stare up at the clouds. "It was good to see you, Johnny," he says. "Will we be seeing more of you around campus next semester?"

"I wouldn't count on it," says Johnny with a shrug.

"I see," says Horace, extending his hand. "In that case, I'll just thank you again for your help today."

"Don't mention it," says Johnny, shaking his hand. "Have a merry Christmas." Then he turns and starts off for his car.

"Good luck to you, Johnny Catini," Horace calls after him. "You're a good man."

Johnny doesn't look back, but just waves over his shoulder. When he gets back to the car, he climbs in and starts the engine just as the first few snow flurries start floating to the ground.

Instead of heading straight back to the shop, however, he decides to make a quick detour to pick up some flowers to drop by Vicki's place before she takes off for Maine. It's just a spur-of-the-moment thing, just a little Christmas gesture, he figures. No harm in it. Of course, as he blasts over to the East Side, there's no way for him to know that, right at that same moment, Vicki's on her way over to the store to drop a present off for *him* before she gets on the highway to head home for the holidays.

If I could, I'd let one or the other know what's up, but what can I say, rules is rules. These two are on their own now. They have to figure things out for themselves, know what I mean?

Chapter 36

Let me tell you something—inspiration is a strange thing. The more you search for it, the less likely you are of finding it. It's kind of like a Chinese finger trap; the harder you pull, the harder it is to get out. But if you just relax and go easy, your fingers slide right out, no problem. That's the way it is in life when you're searching for the answer to a really hard problem. You try and try and try to work it out, but it doesn't help. Then, sometime later when you're doing nothing of consequence, when you're not even thinking about it, the answer sneaks up on you and wakes you up like a *schiaff'* across the top of the head. And then your jaw drops and you say to yourself, but that was so obvious, why didn't I think of it sooner! But you know, God can be funny about stuff like that. He has His own timing for just about everything, and He's not going to breathe that idea you need into your head until He figures that He's good and ready to do it. Hey, rank has its privileges, right?

Anyway, it's Christmas Eve, and like every year, Teresa's got half the Atlantic Ocean set up buffet style on the dining room table. She's got the squid (both fried and stuffed, of course), a bowl of snail salad, some nice *baccala,* a tray of broiled shrimp on skewers, a platter of fried smelts, a bowl of little necks, a tray of stuffed quahogs, some oysters on the half shell, and a big baked stuffed lobster set up in the middle of everything. Added to that, she's boiling a big batch of linguine on the stove to go with the red and white clam sauces she made.

Johnny's contribution to the whole thing is the very nice bouquet of flowers adorning the center of the table that he happened to bring home after work the day before. They actually look quite nice, even though the dinner table wasn't their intended destination—but things have a way of working out for the best sometimes, know what I mean? In the living room, Teresa's got a Christmas tape playing on the stereo. Elvis is singing "Blue Christmas." It's perfect because, at the moment, Johnny's leaning against the kitchen counter, staring out the back window with this forlorn look on his face that he's been wearing all day.

Teresa comes into kitchen, tests a strand of linguine to see if it's done, and turns off the gas. "Hey, *uaglio*, wake up!" she says to Johnny. "Everybody's going to be here in two minutes. Help me strain this linguine."

Johnny walks over and lifts the pot off the stove for his mother. She positions the strainer in the sink, then lets him pour the steaming water out. The linguine plops down into the strainer like the head of a mop.

"And try putting a smile on that face of yours," she chides him. "It's Christmas Eve, you know."

"Yeah, yeah, yeah," mutters Johnny.

Teresa shakes her head and rolls her eyes. "And they say women are moody."

As predicted, the rest of the crew shows up a few minutes later. Everyone's starving and stressed out from all the last-minute running around, so they all descend on the food like a swarm of locusts. The kids, however, are too wired to eat, so they just run around the house like demons while the adults chow down. It's the same every year.

"Hey, nice arrangement," says Maria, pointing out the flowers on the table.

"Really," agrees Nina. "Where did you get them, Mom?"

"Believe it or not, your brother brought them home yesterday."

"Johnny?" says Gina. "Wow, I'm impressed."

"Very funny," mumbles her brother.

"Nice going, Johnny," says Maria. "Hey, David, how come you never bring me home flowers like that."

"Because you're not my mother," her husband answers before biting into a piece of shrimp.

"You're so romantic."

"My God, I'm starving," says Gina, loading up her plate with some linguine.

"What do you expect?" says Teresa. "You're eating for two, remember."

"It feels like I'm eating for six."

Johnny takes a dish and serves himself a spoonful of snail salad. He sprinkles a few drops of Tabasco sauce on top, grabs a piece of bread, and heads off for the living room.

"What's with him tonight?" says Nina.

"Who knows?" says Teresa.

Johnny walks into the living room and sits down at the end of the sofa near the tree. The kids are all crawling around on the floor, checking the tags on the gift-wrapped packages piled underneath its branches. Isabella's the only one who can read, so she's the leader of the pack.

"This one's for Tommy!" she cries out gleefully. "And this one's for Rosie! And this one's for Michael! There's one for everybody! Merry Christmas!"

Johnny smiles for the first time all night and goes to stick a forkful of snail salad into his mouth. Just then he notices one of the lightbulbs on the tree is flickering like it's getting ready to burn out. He pauses for a second and sits there staring at the little blue light.

That's when it hits him.

From out of nowhere, Johnny suddenly gets this incredible idea for the business. It seems so simple that he tries to dismiss it at first because he figures it'll never work. Like all really good ideas, though, this one refuses to go away. So Johnny sits there, staring into the light of the tree, as he turns the whole thing over and over in his head. The whole time, of course, he's got his fork full of snail salad suspended in the air in front of his mouth.

"Hardware," he says to himself. "I'm a hardware kinda guy. Hardware is hardware, right?"

"Hey, what are you looking at, Uncle Johnny?" says little Joanna.

Johnny puts his plate and fork down and takes his niece in his arms. He continues to look into the tree, his face all lit up from its warm glow. "The future, Joanna," he says, giving her a big hug, "I'm looking at the future." Then he lets her go and gets down on the floor with the rest of the kids.

"Who's comin' tonight!" he asks them all.

"Santa Claus!" they answer in unison.

"You got that right," laughs Johnny. "You got that right."

And then the whole lot of them break out in a chorus of "Jingle Bells" with Johnny singing the loudest. Two seconds ago he was Mister Lonely, but now all of a sudden there's at least a little bit of joy back in Mudville.

Chapter 37

I hate to have to admit this, but deep down I used to worry that Johnny didn't have it between the ears to take over the business after me. I know, I was no Einstein either, but Johnny was always so bored and distracted with the whole thing that I was afraid he'd screw it all up first chance he got.

Looking back, I can see now that I made some mistakes with my son. I probably should have given him a freer hand in things, let him try out some of his own ideas, make his own mistakes in the business, and let him build on them. But it's hard for a father to understand sometimes that kids don't learn much from lectures, they learn a lot more by living. You just have to learn how to let go of the leash and give them a chance to run. If you've set them any kind of an example, they'll probably end up doing things your way on their own—at least in the beginning. Before you know it, though, they figure out how to do it all way better than you could have ever imagined because that's what kids are put on this earth for.

Anyway, if you had asked me before he did it, I would have told you that Johnny's idea of selling computers out of the store along with the regular hardware we carry was crazy. No chance in a million years that it would ever work. But I have to hand it to him, it turned out to be a great little gimmick.

Come the New Year, Johnny's out there hustling. It's turned into one of those brutal, cold and snowy winters and the postholidays gloom has set in on just about everybody else, but Johnny's like a live wire. He spends a month learning everything he can about personal computers, reading all the books, talking to distributors, crunching the numbers. He's into it up to his earlobes and loving it because for the first time, maybe in his life, he figures he's latched on to a good idea, and it's his *own* idea, nobody else's. He's seen the prize and he knows exactly what he has to do to get it. The kid's pumped, know what I mean? It's good to see.

By the middle of February, Johnny figures that he's got the situation about as scoped as possible. The time has come to make his move. So he clears out the back corner of the store, puts in some new shelves, reconfigures the whole friggin' place, and then moves in the merchandise.

It all looks beautiful, these nice shiny computers and monitors and scanners and printers. All the latest stuff. Only one problem: Nobody buys them, not a single unit. You see, in business it's not like *Field of Dreams*. If you build it, people don't just show up at your door like magic. You have to get out there and tell them about it. You've got to tell them your story, tell them what you've got, get them to like you, make them want to come and buy what you're selling. It takes a couple of weeks of seeing all that sparkling inventory sitting there on those shelves, collecting all that dust, before Johnny realizes that if he wants to move any of those things, he'd better do some heavy duty advertising pronto. That's when he gets his next big inspiration.

The night the commercial's set to air for the first time, Gina has everybody over to her house. They're all gathered around the television, eating popcorn and candy like they're at a movie premiere. Teresa and the girls and the kids are all squeezed in together on the couch while Johnny hangs around with the guys in the kitchen, trying to act like he's not nervous.

"So what's the deal, Johnny?" says Jimmy. "How many times are they going to air the commercial?"

"Three times a day for a month," answers Johnny. "Then we'll see how things go."

"What I want to know is how much this whole thing is costing," calls Teresa from the den.

"Money, money, money," Johnny calls back to her. "You're just like your husband, always worrying about how much money you're spending. You know, if Pop had spent less time worrying about money, he probably never would have got sick. Sound familiar?"

"Let me off this couch," says Teresa.

"What for?" says little Tommy.

"Because I want to go in and give your uncle a slap across the head."

"Come on," says Maria. "Everybody be quiet. I don't want to miss it."

When the moment of truth finally comes, the guys all pile into the den and Johnny plops himself center aisle on the floor in front of the television. "All right everybody, shut up," he says. "It should be on any second."

"Here it is!" cries Nina.

"There's the store!" adds Gina.

The ad's pure poetry—by that I mean it's pure Johnny. The shot fades from the front of the store to the interior, where my son's standing next to a shelf full of hand tools. With him is his buddy Al, who's pretending to be a customer. Johnny's making it look like he's helping him pick out a skill saw. Al nods thoughtfully, as if Johnny's the ultimate authority on the whole thing. Meanwhile, in the background, Vinny and Tony are prowling around the aisles pretending to peruse the merchandise.

Anyway, Johnny turns to the camera.

*"Hi, I'm Johnny Catini—it starts—my family's been selling hardware to the good people of Providence since before I was born. But you know, after nearly forty years in the business, we decided that it's time for a change. So now, instead of selling just hardware we sell—*and the shot shifts to the back of the store with Johnny standing in front of all the computer stuff—*hardware. That's right, we sell the latest personal computers, complete with monitors, printers, scanners, and just about anything else you need, all at the best prices in town. So, if you're lookin' for hardware, come to Catini's Hardware on Federal Hill in Providence, and if you're lookin' for hardware—*gesturing to the computers—*yeah, we've got that too."*

And that's it, thirty seconds of glory. Everybody breaks out in applause. They're all patting Johnny on the back, and his sisters are mussing up his hair. "Careful, careful!" he laughs. "I'm a star now, you know."

"That's it?" says Teresa. "That's all you get to say?"

"What did you expect in thirty seconds?" says Johnny. "I'm supposed to get up there and read *War and Peace?*"

"Well, I expected a little more for all the money you must have spent!"

"Trust me," Johnny assures her, "the money is gonna start comin' back to us. You'll see."

"And what about the rest of us?" says Maria. "When do we get to be in a commercial?"

"Really," agrees Nina, "how come Vinny and Tony and Al got to be in the first one?"

"I just hope you checked their pockets before they left the store," says Gina. "That crew probably walked out with half your stock."

"Don't worry," Johnny laughs. "I made them all walk through a metal detector before they went home. And I promise, if this works out the way I think it will, anybody who wants to can be in the next commercial. All right?"

"Hooray!" all the grandkids cheer. The big kids are pretty happy about it too.

Well, I tell you what, things don't work out exactly the way Johnny figured they would—they work out way better. Big-time. Here's how it starts: The commercial's been airing for two or three weeks, but still there's been no action. The regular hammer and nail customers come and go, barely looking at the computer stuff. One day, finally, the door opens up and in walks Angela, dolled up to the max as usual. She struts up to the counter, looking like she just stepped off a fashion show runway.

"Hello stranger," she purrs. "Long time no see."

"Hey, Angela, how you doin'?" says Johnny, leaning over the counter to receive a kiss on the cheek. "Say, you're lookin' pretty sharp today."

"Thank you," she says, arching her neck ever so slightly, obviously pleased that he's taken notice.

"So, whatta you doin' here first thing in the mornin'?"

"Well, my boss is planning to buy all new computers for our office pretty soon," she tells him. "When I saw your commercial and found out that you were selling them now, I told him we were old friends and that I'd stop by before work this morning to see what you're carrying, maybe see if you can work out a deal for us." She pauses for effect. "Besides, it was a chance to stop in and say hello. It's been a while."

"Yeah, well, I'm glad you came by, Angela," says Johnny. "Come on, I'll show you what I got."

So Johnny leads Angela to the back of the store and starts giving her the whole spiel on disk drives and chips and memory boards and megahertz and all that crap. It's all Chinese to me, but Johnny's spitting it all out like he wrote the book on it.

"Slow down," laughs Angela. "I have to tell you the truth. For me, using the computer is like driving the car. I can start it up and get it to go, but don't ask me about what's going on under the hood. I have no clue."

"It's like this . . ." Johnny starts to explain. Just then the little bell on the front door jingles. He looks over Angela's shoulder and sees another attractive young woman enter the store. Like Angela, she's dressed smartly, probably on her way to work too. She walks in slowly, looking the store over, before she notices them in the back.

"Be with you in a minute," calls Johnny.

"No hurry," she says.

"Okay," says Johnny, beginning again. "You gotta think of your personal computer as an office. Your disk space is all the filing cabinets you have around you. The more filing cabinets you have, the more files you can hold. It's the same with the computer. The more disk space you have, the more files you hold."

"But is that the same as memory?" says Angela, batting her eyes.

By now, the other young lady has drifted over to the computer section and is listening to what Johnny's saying. Angela casts a quick look her way, just long enough to give her daggers. The other girl gives them right back. Johnny, meantime, is oblivious to this vicious little exchange.

"No," he continues, "your memory is like the top of your desk in the office. The bigger the desktop, the bigger the files you can open up and work on, and the more files you can work on at the same time. If you have too small a desktop, files start slippin' off the edge and fallin' on the floor and it's a big mess. Well, that's sort of what happens with the computer. You want as much memory as possible so that you'll have a nice big desk to work on. Get it?"

"I think so," says Angela uncertainly.

He reaches over and grabs some product literature and a price list. "Here," he says, handing it to her. "Take a look at this stuff for a minute." He turns to the other young woman. "Can I help you with something?"

"Yes," she says pleasantly with a sideways glance at Angela, "I'm looking into buying a personal computer, but I don't really know much about them. I couldn't help overhearing some of your explanation about how everything works. Would you mind going over it again?"

"Yeah sure," says Johnny. "You see, it's like this . . ."

And that's how it all begins. Every day, the women are coming in, checking out the computers, checking out Johnny. Thing is, even when they don't buy a computer, they almost never leave without buying some lightbulbs or gardening gloves or any little thing, just to make a purchase. So besides selling the computers, lots of other stuff is starting to move.

Now, it doesn't take long for all the carpenters and electricians and all the other guys who are regular customers to notice the new clientele coming into the store. And believe me, they don't object, not one bit. What was once a fairly mundane part of their day has turned into a very pleasant little excursion. Before you know it, guys are coming in just to check out the chicks who are checking out Johnny while they check out the computers. I'm thinking maybe it's time to hang up the shiny ball and start playing disco music. The best part of the whole thing is that, just like the women, the guys always buy something before they leave too, just to save face.

To Johnny's credit, he ignores all the newfound female attention he's getting. He's too busy trying to keep up with all the new business that's pouring in. He's doing all he can to keep that cash register singing and ringing. It's such a beautiful sound. You see, Johnny's finally got his first real taste of it, not just the money, but the juice. And like I told you before, when the juice is flowing, life is good. Know what I mean?

Chapter 38

Take it from me, when the juice is flowing, life really *can* be good. Everything seems brighter; the wind feels like it's always at your back; the rain falls soft upon your fields; the sun shines warm upon your face; God holds you in the palm of His hand. You get the picture. I think I got that whole bit from Dickie McDougal. But it's really true. What's more is that you get this kind of aura about you and suddenly everybody wants to be near you. It's almost as if they figure that if they just get close enough, some of the juice will flow their way too. It's strange, and a little intoxicating if you don't know how to handle it.

But even during the best of times the juice doesn't flow non-stop. You still have those little periods when things drag. Everything slows down for a while and finally you get two seconds to yourself to relax and catch your breath. It's during those brief quiet moments, when he's wandering around the store by himself, that Johnny stops now and then at the front window and gazes glumly up the street toward the East Side. He pauses there, day after day, watching the snow gradually shrink away from the sidewalks as winter melts into spring. You see, the juice is great, but it just doesn't taste as sweet when you don't have someone there to share it with. Johnny's discovering that for himself.

Anyway, it's one of those quiet moments I was just talking

about, a Monday morning, and Johnny's pushing a broom down the aisle. It's early April and just starting to warm up a little. The last of the snow is gone, but people still traipse in with salt and sand all over their shoes from the streets and sidewalks. It can be a mess. At any rate, the front door opens up and two men dressed in jackets and ties step inside. Johnny doesn't recognize either of the two, but judging by their attire, he figures they must be looking for computers. Both of them, however, just stand near the door, surveying the store. They talk in hushed voices while one of them jots down notes on a clipboard. Johnny tucks the broom away in the back and walks out to see what they're up to.

"Can I help you?" he says.

"Good morning," says one of them, a burly, bald-headed guy in his forties, I would guess. He whips out a business card as Johnny approaches. "Ned Featherstone, American Hardware Stores. May I assume that you're Mister Catini?"

"Last time I checked," says Johnny, taking the card.

"Sorry to drop in on you like this without an appointment, but we happened to be in the area," says Featherstone. He nods to his sidekick, who's holding the clipboard. "This is my assistant."

"Lester Potts," says the other man, extending his hand. "Nice to meet you." Potts is a skinny little guy with an unruly mop of hair and big Coke-bottle eyeglasses.

Johnny shakes his hand and gives them both a shrug. "So," he says, "what can I do for you guys today?"

Featherstone clears his throat. "You might recall our previous correspondence with you. American is looking to expand into this region. Yours is one of the locations on the top of our list that we are, quite frankly, very interested in."

The light finally goes on in Johnny's head. "Oh, geez, American Hardware Stores," he says, nodding his head. "Sure, I remember you guys now."

Lester looks up from his clipboard. "We're very impressed with what you've done with your operation, Mister Catini. Hardware and hardware, it's a super concept."

"Thanks," shrugs Johnny.

"A great little gimmick," adds Featherstone.

"Yeah, well, it seems to be working out pretty good," says Johnny.

"Things are going well, are they?" says Featherstone with great interest.

"I can't complain," says Johnny. "My biggest problem is keepin' up with it. I'm thinkin' that I might need to hire some help pretty soon."

"Perhaps we could relieve you of that trouble," says Featherstone, smiling broadly.

Johnny eyes the two skeptically. "What did you have in mind?"

Featherstone puts his fat paw around Johnny's shoulder. "Perhaps," he says confidently, giving his assistant a wink, "there's someplace quiet where the three of us might be able to sit and talk for a short while."

"Ten times net income?" says Johnny, looking up from the American Hardware Stores literature that Featherstone has laid out on the desk in the back office.

"The average net for the past three years," Potts hastens to add. "That's pretty much standard for what we pay for a typical acquisition."

"*Uh-huh,*" grunts Johnny. He's trying hard to play it cool, but you can tell by the look on his face that he's got the calculator running full throttle in his head. He's thinking about a new car. He's thinking about maybe getting a house of his own. He's thinking about a vacation place in Florida for all the family to go to in the winters. He's thinking about never having to sweat out a buck again. I know all this because not too long ago I was the guy behind that same desk Johnny's sitting at right now. You can't help it—that money gets waved in front of your face and the wheels just start to turn in your head.

"Naturally we would have to see your audited tax returns for those years," says Featherstone.

"Naturally."

It all sounds too good to be true, but you can see Johnny warming up to the idea. Just then, though, the bell on the front door jingles and a customer walks in. Johnny excuses himself and goes out to help him. While he's away, the two hardware executives nod knowingly to one another.

"I think we've got this one in the bag," says Potts.

"I think you might be right," replies Featherstone, smiling with satisfaction.

Johnny returns a short while later and deposits himself behind the desk. "So," he says, picking up one of the American Hardware brochures, "where were we?"

"We were discussing the future," says Featherstone. "Your future, to be more precise."

Johnny settles back in his chair and lets out a little sigh. For a moment he falls quiet and just gazes at the top of the desk. "Yeah," he finally says softly to himself, "my future. I guess that's what this is all about, isn't it? I don't think I was ready for that this morning."

"You never know when opportunity is going to knock on your door," says Feathersone reassuringly. "But when it does show up at your door, you should let it in."

"With open arms," adds Potts.

"Lemme ask you a question," says Johnny. "Suppose I was to sell the business to you guys. What happens then?"

"Catini's Hardware becomes American Hardware Store," says Featherstone. "Aside from that, not much will change but the name on the building. We take over all the headaches and you get to sail off into the sunset."

"I guess that sounds nice," says Johnny thoughtfully.

"Then can I assume that this is something you would like to pursue further?" says Featherstone.

Johnny looks at Featherstone. Then he looks at Potts. Then he looks at the top of the desk. And then my son does what he always does when he can't make up his mind. He shrugs.

Later, Johnny walks Featherstone and Potts to the door just as Gina is walking in. It's perfect timing because the store has suddenly become busy again. Gina's due to have the baby in a couple of weeks, but just the same she waddles straight to the cash register to keep an eye on things while Johnny finishes up talking with the two hardware execs. Johnny gets rid of them as quickly as he can and hurries back in. Right away he starts darting about, trying to help people select their merchandise. It's one of those crazy times you get now and then. Let me tell you, that's when running the store becomes more like running a three-ring circus. But things settle down again after a little while so that Johnny can take a breather. When the last of the customers meanders out the door, he trudges up to the cash register and rests his head on the counter.

"Thanks, Gina," he says wearily. "You saved my life there."

"Don't mention it," she answers, smiling. "But who were those two guys you were walking out before?"

Johnny looks up and rolls his head around to stretch his neck. "Featherstone and Potts," he replies.

"Who?" laughs Gina.

"They're from some big hardware chain. They wanna buy the store."

"Oh, my God," gasps Gina. "I hope you told them no."

"I didn't tell them anything," says Johnny.

"Why not? You should have told them you weren't interested."

"Why, what difference does it make, I'm the only one stuck here runnin' things," says Johnny.

"That doesn't matter," says Gina, shaking her head. "Don't you see? Even if you own the place by yourself someday, it will still belong to all of us. You *can't* sell it. It's part of our family, an important part."

Johnny groans and drops his head back down onto the counter. "Please don't harangue me about all that today. All I did was talk to the guys."

"Sorry," says Gina. "I didn't mean to harangue you about anything. I just stopped by because I needed to pick up a couple of things for the house."

"Help yourself."

Gina gets off the stool and starts to walk around from the back of the counter. Being nearly nine months pregnant, she's not moving too quickly. Johnny takes one look at her round belly and holds up his hand.

"Stop," he orders her. "Sit back down on the stool. What am I doin' here, makin' you work the register and everything. You shouldn't be on your feet, you should be restin'. I'll get whatever you need. You want anythin' in the meantime, a glass of water or somethin'?"

"Johnny, I'm not sick, I'm pregnant," laughs Gina. "There is a difference."

"Why take chances," he replies.

"You're as bad as Jimmy," says his sister. "He's been so excited lately, he won't let me lift a finger."

"He's a good husband," says Johnny. "Now go sit back down and tell me what you need."

"You're the boss."

So Johnny walks around the store, collecting the rubber gloves, new mop heads, and other household cleaning items his sister wants. I have to laugh because it's the same thing I had to do every time Teresa was about to have a baby. Without fail, two or three weeks before the baby was due, she'd call me at the store and give me a list of cleaning supplies to bring home. It didn't matter that the house was already immaculate. Anyway, Johnny brings everything up to the counter and starts rummaging around for a box to put it all in.

"Looks like you're plannin' a big spring cleaning," he says.

"It's the baby," says Gina. "It will be here in two weeks, God willing. I think I'm just starting to get my nesting instinct."

Johnny finds an empty computer box and starts to pack everything into it. "What's the deal, anyway," he asks, "you havin' a boy or girl?"

"We won't know that until it's born."

"Why not?" says Johnny. "I thought they could tell if it was a girl or boy by doin' one of those phonogram things."

"*Sono*-grams, dopey," laughs Gina. "And yes, we could have found out if we wanted, but we'd rather it be a surprise."

"How surprised you gonna be?" says Johnny. "It's gotta be one or the other, know what I mean?"

"As far as I know, they haven't come up with a third yet," Gina agrees. She pokes around inside the box to make sure she has everything.

"Satisfied?" says Johnny. "Got everything you need to get ready for the baby?"

"It looks that way," says Gina. "Now all I need to get are some more baby clothes."

"Sorry," says Johnny, gesturing about the store, "but we're all out of baby clothes today. Why do you want to buy more baby clothes anyways—didn't you get enough at the shower?"

"*Ayy,* you know how Mommy is," says Gina. "She wants to buy something special just in case the baby is born on Easter."

Johnny scratches his head. "Wow," he says, "that's right. This weekend it's already Palm Sunday."

"Right," says Gina. "So Mommy made plans with Nina and Maria to go shopping for clothes Saturday at Jean Pierre's."

"Where?"

"It's a new store up the East Side on Thayer Street, right

across from the bookstore. I heard they have some really adorable stuff, but *really* expensive."

"Sounds exciting," says Johnny, faking a yawn.

"It is, smarty," says Gina. "Just wait until you're married someday and your wife is going to have a baby."

"I'm just kiddin'," says Johnny. "I just wish we didn't have to be in suspense for another two weeks to see if we got another ballplayer in the family."

"*Ayy*, so long as the baby's healthy, God willing, that's all we care about at this point. Besides, I'd rather not know what we're having until the baby is born. It's more fun this way."

"Yeah, I suppose I can see that," says Johnny thoughtfully. "It's part of the uncertainty of life, I guess."

"The what?"

"Nothin'," says Johnny. "I was just thinkin' about somethin' Pop once told me."

Suddenly the smile fades from Gina's face. She stands and begins to pull her jacket on.

"What is it?" says Johnny. "Did I say somethin' wrong?"

"No, it's not you," says Gina with a sniffle. She takes a deep breath. "I was thinking about Pop this morning, that's all," she says, her eyes welling up. "I was wishing that he could have been here to see the baby when it's born."

Johnny picks up the box with one arm, puts the other around his sister's shoulder, and the two walk toward the door. "Hey, don't worry about it," he comforts her. "Pop'll be there when the time comes."

"What do you mean?"

"I've got this whole theory," he explains. "You see, I think maybe people hang around after they die, you know, just to look after the people they cared about. We can't see or hear them, but they're there just the same."

"Do you really believe that?" says Gina.

"No question about it."

Gina stops and casts a worried look about the store. "You're not really planning on selling the store, are you?" she says.

"I'm not plannin' on doin' anythin' at this point," he tells her. "I'm just linin' up my options, that's all."

"There's so much of us here in this place, Johnny," says Gina. "I want it to still be here for my children when they grow up. We all feel that way."

"Don't worry," sighs Johnny. "I won't let anyone down."

Gina smiles and kisses him on the cheek. Johnny walks her out to the car, stows the box in the trunk for her, and sends her on her way. He heads back into the store and stops for a moment. Standing alone in the aisle, he gazes upward.

"Hey, *uaglio!*" he calls up to the heavens. "Are *you* payin' attention to any of this?"

Johnny pauses, as if he truly expects some sort of reply. None is forthcoming, however, so he shakes his head, trudges into the back office, and throws away all the brochures from American Hardware Stores.

Chapter 39

You know, Ned Featherstone and his sidekick Lester were right about one thing. When opportunity lands on your doorstep, you really *should* let it in with open arms. From what I can see, very little in life happens by accident. The powers that be are always up there conniving for our benefit and tossing these little context clues in our path to try to show us the way. Of course, they can't come right out and tell us what we should do with our lives because what fun would life be then? Only problem is that generally we're all too dense to pick up on the little hints they try to throw our way, so we just keep stumbling along in the dark from day to day. But when the chance to change your life does show up, and you finally manage to recognize it, you gotta take your shot. It's like that with everything, not just money and business, but life and love too.

So opportunity lands at Johnny's doorstep in the form of the daily newspaper that following Saturday morning. The sun's just peeking over the horizon when Johnny slouches downstairs and opens the front door to pick it up. The birds are chirping, and from the looks of it, there's not a cloud in the sky. The fact that it'll probably turn out to be a beautiful day is no big deal to Johnny since he'll be spending just about all of it cooped up in the store. Comes with the territory. So he yawns and heads back inside to make his coffee.

Later, with his coffee mug in hand, he takes a seat at the kitchen table and opens up the paper. Most mornings Johnny scans the front page to catch up on the latest catastrophes before turning to the sports page. This particular morning, however, something makes him decide to first take a look at the entertainment section instead. He opens it up and peruses the listings of what's going on in and around the city that weekend, just to see what he'll be missing. April's not the most exciting month of the year around here, so there's not a whole lot to attract his interest. Johnny's just about to toss the section aside and turn his attention to the sports page when one small item catches his eye. It's the announcement of a book-signing event to take place that very afternoon at the Brown Bookstore on Thayer Street up the East Side. And who do you suppose is the featured author? Come on, you know. It's Emily, Johnny's favorite poetess. You remember Emily, right? Well, it seems that her latest book of rhymes is finally ready to hit the stands, so the university wants to do it up big.

Johnny puts the paper aside and stares off into space. Now, you don't have to be a psychic to figure out that my son doesn't have the slightest interest in buying a book of poetry. Hell, who knows when the last time the kid even set foot in a bookstore? What he's really interested in is the other people who are likely to be in attendance at the big event. You know who I'm talking about. Literary types, poetry aficionados—and in particular, comparative literature professors. Catch my drift?

So Johnny sits there mulling it over and he gets this vague recollection about making a promise to Emily one time that he would go to the book signing when the book came out in the spring—this is way back in the fall we're talking about. In any case, he starts wondering what harm there could possibly be in his taking a swing by the bookstore that afternoon—just to say hello to his old friends. But then, of course, he hears his mother moving about upstairs and common sense promptly returns.

"Just leave it alone," he mutters before downing the rest of his coffee. Then he marches upstairs to get ready for work.

So Johnny heads off to the store and all morning long he's trying to leave *it* alone, like he told himself to do. Only trouble is that *it* won't leave *him* alone. The thought of going to the book signing keeps buzzing around in his head like a pesky fly. The more he tries to shoo it away, the more it returns to pester him. It doesn't help that business is slow that morning, so there's not much for Johnny to do to keep his mind occupied.

Around lunchtime the front door swings open and Johnny's friend Vinny steps in. "Yo, Johnny C, my handy hardware man!" he calls jovially as he struts up to the counter.

"Just when I thought my day couldn't get any worse," moans Johnny.

"Johnny, what's the matter?" he chuckles. "Tell your ole pal Vinny."

"*Eh,* I'm just havin' one of those days," says Johnny.

Vinny stops and looks at him for a minute. "Let me tell you somethin', my friend," he says, dead serious for one of the few times I've ever seen. "You're gonna have a lot more of those days if you don't start gettin' your ass outta this store more often."

"Whatta you talkin' about?" huffs Johnny.

Vinny walks behind the counter and deposits himself on the stool. He pushes it back against the wall and props his feet up on the counter. "What I'm tellin' you," he says, wagging his finger for emphasis, "is that I know that this business is goin' gang-busters for you these days, but you need to get a life. All you do is sweat it out in this store practically seven days a week. Every time I see you now, it's like you got a puss on. And it's because you're hagged out. You're burnt and you're turnin' into a mope. And don't gimme that look, 'cause you know I'm right."

Johnny just stands there, scowling at his friend. But then he can't help himself and he cracks up laughing.

"I'm not kiddin'," says Vinny. "This is serious."

"So what do you suggest I do, Mister Serious?" says Johnny.

"I want you to get outta here," orders Vinny. "That's what I suggest you do. Get outside. Get some sun on your face. Go find something to do for a couple of hours."

"Yeah, right," laughs Johnny. "I'll just close up right now and go to the park."

"Nope," says Vinny smugly, "you don't have to close up the store. I'm gonna stay here myself while you're gone and watch things for you."

"Please," groans Johnny. "I can't afford to have you watch things."

"Johnny, relax, this is totally gratis," his buddy assures him. "And I won't palm anything. Scouts honor. Now go take a long lunch and don't come back until you have a clear head. And then tonight you're goin' out with the boys, no questions asked. *Capisc'?*"

Johnny scratches his head for a second. "Well," he says, "come to think of it, I did have a little errand I was thinkin' about runnin' this afternoon—that is, if I had the chance today."

"Well, now's your chance," says his friend, "so take it while you can 'cause you may not get another one anytime soon."

So Johnny takes his shot. He gets in the car and makes a beeline for the East Side. He cruises Thayer Street, trying to score a parking spot near the bookstore, but there's not one to be found anywhere. Both sides of the one-way street are lined with cars and the sidewalks are bustling with people. Typical Saturday afternoon. Johnny comes around for a second pass by the bookstore, hoping someone might have left, but no one has so he gives up and turns off onto a side street. He drives along, and a few blocks later, he finally comes across a free space.

The bookstore is packed when Johnny finally steps inside. Like I said, it's been a while since my son last set foot in a bookstore, so he stands there for a minute, surveying the place, trying to get his bearings. In the center of the store there's a line of people leading up to a table. Emily is sitting there surrounded by stacks of her new book that rise above her like miniature skyscrapers. Behind Emily, a young girl is getting ready to cut open another boxful with a big pair of scissors. Emily's all smiles, and why not? She signs copy after copy as the procession to the table goes on nonstop. You ask me, this is how a poet gets the juice, know what I mean?

Anyway, Johnny's not in the mood for just standing in line like a dope, so he decides to take a stroll around and check out the rest of the store until the line thins out. First stop is a small stack of calendars. No surprise in that. I mean, where else did you think my son would start? This being April, all the calendars are on sale. To Johnny's disappointment, though, there are no swimsuit numbers in the mix. Instead he finds the works of several great artists. Monet, Renoir, the usual suspects. As he sifts through the pile, Johnny picks up one with pictures of desert scenes featuring snakes and cattle skulls. He holds it up and flips through the pages, shaking his head. Unimpressed, he tosses it back on the pile, but somehow in the process he manages to knock the dozen or so others onto the floor.

Johnny's cover is totally blown now since just about everybody in the place is looking his way to see what all the commotion's about by the calendar pile. He turns about ten different shades of red and kneels down to pick up the mess he's made. The kid's got his head down as he scrambles around collecting all the calendars, so at first he doesn't notice the young woman kneeling right beside him, trying to help.

"So," she says to him, "do you come here often?"

Johnny stops and looks at her because he recognizes the voice right away. It's Vicki kneeling beside him. She's smiling from ear to ear as she holds out the calendar with the pictures of snakes and cattle skulls that caused all the trouble in the first place.

"Taking up an interest in Southwestern art?" she says, handing it to him.

"Nah," says Johnny, trying his best to act nonchalant. "Dead cows—they're not my thing."

"Not mine either," she laughs.

There's a long pause and the two of them just stay there, kneeling on the floor next to one another like they're getting ready to take their vows. Believe me, the sparks are still flying between the two of them—anyone with eyes can see it. Finally Johnny reaches out his hand to help her up and the two of them stand.

"I'm so surprised to see you," Vicki says at last as they get up. "Pleasantly surprised, that is," she adds.

"Yeah, well," Johnny says with a shrug, "I'd sort of promised Emily way back that I'd come to this, so . . . so . . ."

"So here you are," she says.

"Right," Johnny nods. "But I gotta tell ya, the parkin' on Thayer Street is brutal today."

Vicki gives him a sly grin. "You just gotta know somebody," she says, doing her best Johnny Catini imitation. Johnny, though, is a little slow on the uptake.

"Huh?" he grunts.

Vicki gives this exaggerated shrug of her shoulders and squirrels up the side of her mouth. "I know somebody down here with a lot that lets me park for the bubble," she goes on. "But I still duke him a coupla bucks, know what I mean?"

"I think you've been hangin' around me for too long,"

chuckles Johnny. He looks at her more closely. "By the way," he says, "what did you do to your hair? It's so short now."

"Actually, I'm letting it grow out again," she answers, passing her hand through her hair. "You should have seen how short it was this winter."

"Well, don't get me wrong," Johnny adds hastily, "it still looks good—you look great as a matter of fact."

"Thank you," she says softly. "You look great too. I've seen you on television, by the way. Your commercial is really cute."

"Yeah, that's been workin' out pretty good for us," he says. "But how 'bout you, how you doin'?"

"I'm okay," she answers. "It's almost the end of the semester, so I've been keeping busy."

"How's the tenure thing goin'?" he asks.

Vicki winces and looks up to the heavens with fingers crossed. "I'm afraid to think about it," she admits, "but I'm hopeful, really hopeful."

"Hey, just get your boy Horace workin' for ya, know what I mean?" says Johnny with a smile. "I mean, we wanna keep all the good professors we can around here."

"I'm doing my best," she says. "Speaking of Horace, he's over on the other side of the store. I need to talk with him for just a few minutes. Will you be here for a little while longer?"

"Oh yeah," says Johnny with a wave of his hand. "Go ahead. I still gotta get in line to get my autographed copy of Emily's book. I'll be here."

"Great," she says and then she starts to walk away.

"Hey, Vicki," Johnny calls after her.

"Yes?"

Johnny rubs the back of his neck. "Listen," he starts awkwardly, "I was thinkin' maybe later on, that is if you're not busy, I dunno, maybe we could get together or somethin'. Maybe grab a cup of coffee."

Vicki beams a smile at him. "Sure," she says, "coffee sounds great."

So off she goes to see Horace and off Johnny goes to see Emily and now it won't be long before the coffee really starts to percolate, if you know what I mean.

Chapter 40

Ever read one of those astrology columns in the newspaper? Every now and then they'll tell you that all these weird things are going to happen today because of the alignment of the planets and stars. Venus is in conjunction with Mars, or Saturn is rising in Scorpio, or Pluto is in opposition to Hoboken. You know what I'm talking about. Well, on this particular Saturday, it's like the Earth and Moon and Sun and all the planets are all aligned together at the same time, and they're all pointing directly at the East Side of Providence. It's like conjunction city. You just know there's gonna be a big tremor in the Force anytime now.

So here's the deal. Teresa and the girls are just stepping out of the restaurant into the bright sunshine. It's a gorgeous day, like I told you before. Warm, breezy, as nice as it gets in April. The four of them start strolling down the sidewalk along Thayer Street, gabbing all the way as they head toward Jean Pierre's to buy clothes for Gina's baby.

"Have you and Jimmy talked about names yet?" says Maria.

"Not really," Gina admits.

"Don't wait too long," Nina warns her. "Before you know it, the baby will be born and you won't know what to call it."

"Nonsense," says Teresa. "I didn't name any of you until the moment I held you. All you have to do is look at a child the first time it's in your arms and the name comes to you."

"Come on," says Maria, "you're telling us that Pop didn't have any say about names when we were born?"

"Hey, I was the one that had to do all the work bringing you kids into the world," Teresa replies. "All your father had to do was stand around in the waiting room and hand out cigars. When he finally came in, I told him what to call you and he did what he was told."

At that, all four of them break out in laughter. Gina, though, suddenly stops and places her hand on her tummy. *"Ooh,* that was a big one," she says, smiling.

"The baby give you a kick?" says Maria.

"Actually, he feels like he's swinging from my rib cage," Gina laughs.

"What made you say he?" says Nina, all excited. "Do you think it's a boy?"

"It must be, the way it's bouncing around inside of me."

"Don't be too sure," says Teresa. "Maria kicked me every day for almost the whole nine months. I was so sure I was having a boy that I had your father paint the nursery blue."

"Poor Pop."

So on they go, ambling along toward Jean Pierre's. Now and then they stop for a moment to take a peek into the shop windows as they pass. Before too long, the bookstore comes into view up ahead. They stop there at the crosswalk and wait for the light to change so they can cross the street.

"What's going on in there today?" says Gina, nodding toward the bookstore.

"I don't know," says Maria, glancing over her shoulder at the steady stream of people coming and going through its doors. "But it looks jammed inside."

"Sure does," Nina agrees.

Teresa takes a look of her own at the bookstore and notices

the little poster on the front door. It's an announcement for the book signing going on inside. On it is a picture of Emily along with some complimentary blurbs from her fellow poets. Teresa's eyes open wide and she walks closer to get a better look. All of a sudden her shoulders get all hunched and you can almost see the hair on the back of her neck stand up. She looks like a big cat getting ready to do battle.

"Come on, Mom!" calls Maria. "The light's changed."

"You girls go ahead," she calls after them. "I just want to make a quick stop here."

"What for?"

"I want to see if they have any get well cards."

"Who's sick?" says Nina.

"None of your business!" snaps Teresa. "Just go and I'll see you there."

The girls know better than to argue when they hear that tone of voice from their mother, so off the three go across the street. Meantime Teresa steps up to the bookstore's front window. She leans close and gazes inside. Emily is still at the table, signing away to her heart's content. There's a sizable line leading up to her while a bunch of other people mill around the store. Teresa just stands there for a moment, not moving until her gaze happens to fall upon a young man near the back of the store. Unable to contain her surprise, she raps her knuckles on the window.

"Johnny!" she cries.

Chapter 41

I remember watching PBS one time when they had this show on about birth and childhood. It was interesting. They did all these scientific studies and they discovered that, even at the earliest moments of cognizant life in the womb, the sound of a mother's voice sets off a ton of emotional and physiological responses in her child. It's unreal. The heartbeat of the fetus, for instance, quickens measurably whenever the mother speaks, and the child becomes more active. And in a newborn, the kid starts drooling right away in anticipation of getting nursed, just by hearing her voice. Even throughout life, a mother's voice can stimulate in her children feelings of joy and comfort and security, an overall sense of well-being. Wonderful, right?

Well, a mother's voice can also stimulate feelings on the opposite end of the spectrum. It's more in that range where Johnny's physiological and emotional responses at that moment might be measured. A chilling numbness, like he's touched a live wire, races through his body. There's something vaguely familiar about the sensation, something that joggles a distant memory somewhere in the dusty far reaches of his brain. Then, all at once, he understands. It's panic, just like in his nightmare about the dinosaur. So now, when Johnny turns toward the voice and gazes up at its source, it's not the sweet face of Mama Teresa he perceives, it's the Tyrannosaurus rex!

Johnny freezes. He wants to run, but there's no place to hide. He wants to pull the covers over his head, but he's painfully awake and far from the warm safety of his bed. The nightmare, as he's feared all along, is finally coming true. The kid stands there trembling, watching his mother turn to walk toward the store's front door, and he knows that it's just a matter of moments before the T. rex smashes its head through the window and devours him whole.

"I'm back," says Vicki, suddenly appearing behind him. *"Heyyyy!"* Johnny's got her by the arm, yanking her down behind the row of bookshelves. "What are you doing?" she says testily.

"Shhh," Johnny whispers. "Sorry about that, but you gotta get outta here—right now."

"Get out of here? Why?"

"Because my mother's comin'. She's right outside the door."

"Your *mother?* What on earth is she doing here?"

Johnny buries his face in his hands. "I completely forgot," he moans. "That friggin' baby clothes place is right across the street. She and my sisters were all goin' there today."

"Oh my God," Vicki gasps. "What do we do?"

Johnny stretches up and peeks over the books on one of the middle shelves. From this vantage point he can see his mother making her way through the door. "I don't know," he finally says. "Just find a back door somewhere and run for your life. I'll figure out somethin' to tell her, and you and I can meet up later."

Vicki decides to hazard a peek of her own at the front door. She turns back to him with this puzzled look on her face.

"Is *that* your mother, the woman standing in the door right now?" she says.

"That's her," says Johnny. "Stay down."

"Johnny—" she begins to say.

"Don't talk, just get outta here," he tells her.

"But Johnny, you don't understand—"

"Go!"

With that, Johnny slips away from her and marches to the front of the store to face his mother. All the way over he's making buttons wondering if she's seen Vicki, or worse, if she's seen the two of them together. He braces himself for either possibility as he approaches her and tries to force a smile.

"What are you doin' here, Ma?" he says, taking the offensive.

"Me, what are you doing here?" says Teresa.

"I just came in to check on the computer books," Johnny fibs, "you know, maybe find some we can carry in the store."

"Well, you'd better get out of here, Johnny," she says in this ominous voice. "There's gonna be trouble."

"Trouble? Whatta you talkin' about?" he asks, but of course he knows all too well what she's talking about.

Teresa pulls him aside. "It's *her*," she says in a low growl as she advances toward the center of the store.

Johnny gets this terrible sinking feeling in his gut. This is the moment he has dreaded. It's like the T. rex is breathing right down his back now.

"Who?" he says with a gulp, doing his best to slow his mother's progress. "Who's here?"

"That tramp I saw with your father that day, that's who. She's right in this very store!"

Despite his efforts to slow her down, Teresa backs Johnny all the way up to the line of people waiting to see Emily. Johnny takes a look over his shoulder. Emily's still there, still smiling away, still autographing book after book while the young girl assisting her opens another box with the big pair of scissors. She plops a stack of books next to Emily and lays the scissors on the table. Johnny looks past them to the back of the store. Vicki's nowhere in sight. When he looks back at his mother, he sees the wild, dangerous look in her eyes. I'd seen that look on my wife's face on more than one occasion myself. Put the fear of the Almighty into me every time.

"Get out of my way, Johnny," says Teresa in this quiet, malevolent voice.

Johnny reaches out and grips her by the shoulders. Right about now, Teresa's like a powerful spring that's straining to uncoil. He can feel the tension in her body.

"Don't do anythin' crazy here, Ma," he tells her. "There's all these people around. Just get yourself under control."

"You're right," she says, to his surprise. Suddenly she relaxes and an icy calm comes over her. "I'll just wait in line like the others," she says in a faraway voice.

"That's a good idea, Ma," says Johnny. "Stay here for a minute while I go check things out."

Johnny leaves her side and pushes through the crowd to the back of the store. He hurries about, hoping desperately that he doesn't find Vicki cowering behind some bookcase. It's then that he notices a side entrance to the store. With any luck, Vicki escaped through it to safety. A little relieved, he returns to Teresa's side. By then there's only one or two people remaining in front of her before she reaches Emily.

"Why don't we go, Ma, and you can tell me all about this whole thing later," says Johnny. "I gotta get back to the shop."

"You go ahead," she replies with that same icy calmness. "I'll just be a minute."

Johnny takes another look around the store just to be sure Vicki's gone. To his relief she's nowhere to be seen. He turns and gazes out the window, but there's no sign of her out on the busy sidewalk, so he figures that she must have hightailed it home. Outside, the university students are coming and going, not a care in the world. Watching them go by, Johnny zones out for a second, wishing maybe that he could be out there with them.

While he's staring into space, he doesn't notice that, behind him, Teresa's finally standing before Emily. Gradually, though, the sound of his mother's voice brings him back to attention. He hears her talking to Emily, saying something about wanting her to sign the book with best wishes to Teresa Catini. Johnny's jolted completely back to reality by a sudden commotion behind him.

"Oh my God, she's got the scissors!" someone screams.

Johnny whirls about in time to see Teresa looming over Emily, the scissors clenched in her upraised arm. For her part, Emily's just looking up in helpless terror, unable to move. Johnny looks at his mother like a dope, wondering just what the hell she's doing. It's not till he sees her arm swooping down at the terrified poetess like a guillotine to its victim, that it dawns on my son that she's probably trying to kill her.

"*Putanna!*" cries Teresa as the blades flash through the air.

There's this sickening thud and the whole place goes dead silent. Johnny races to the table, fully prepared to find Emily with the scissors buried in her heart. The impact, he sees, has caused the little woman to topple over backward. So now she's just lying there, motionless. To Johnny's astonishment, however, there's no blood anywhere. That's because the scissors, he discovers, aren't buried in Emily's heart, but in the pages of the book that Teresa had asked her to autograph. The blades have pierced right through to the table. There's still this eerie, stunned silence over the place. Teresa turns around with a sinister smile that makes the others all back away.

"I wasn't really gonna kill her," she says with a contented sigh. "I just wanted to see the look on the little tramp's face." She rubs her hands together like she's wiping them clean, dusting the whole little incident off them. *"Now* all's forgiven," she says with satisfaction.

Johnny gapes at his mother. "Wait a minute," he says, the side of his mouth squirreling up into a knot. "Are you tellin' me that *she's* the one you told me about, the one you saw with Pop in the restaurant that time?"

"Of course," answers Teresa. "Who did you think it was?"

Before Johnny can answer, he hears someone groaning. He turns and sees that Emily is starting to come back around. People are all rushing to her now, helping her to her feet.

"We'll be across the street," says Teresa, starting to leave. "Stop by and see us after you buy your computer book. And by the way, who's running the store?"

"Vinny," Johnny admits with a sheepish grin.

Teresa clicks her tongue and shakes her head in disgust. She says nothing, though, but heads straight for the door. As if in awe, the crowd parts to let her pass. The moment she's out the door, the whole place comes to life, abuzz with loud talk.

Johnny stands in the midst of it all, still trying to sort things out. He looks back at Emily, who's been reinstalled in her seat. Sipping a glass of water, she looks even paler than normal, but it's obvious she's going to survive.

"Wait a minute," Johnny says to her. "You mean to tell me that you and my father were . . . that you two used to . . ."

Emily gazes up at him forlornly. "I always said you looked familiar to me," she says with a shrug. She leans closer and, in a whisper, adds, "There's really no need to tell Vicki about this—is there?"

"Rhode Island," he mutters, shaking his head. "This state is just way too small."

Johnny looks at the table, where the scissors still stand upright in the book like a sword rising out of a stone. The others seem reluctant to even go near them, but Johnny calmly reaches out and plucks the scissors free. He holds the scissors up, brandishing them to get a better look at them. To his amazement (and mine), the scissors' blades weren't damaged at all by the collision with the table. Not a scratch on them.

"Not bad," he says to himself, tossing the scissors back onto the table. "I oughta start carryin' that brand in the store."

Later, Johnny walks across the street to Jean Pierre's. The kid's feeling like a wet rag, but he figures the worst is over, at least for this particular day. When he steps inside the baby store, he finds his mother and sisters huddled together, *oohing* and *ahhing* over some cute little outfit they found. Johnny's about to make a smart remark when Vicki suddenly emerges from behind a rack of clothes. To his utter astonishment, she walks straight over to his mother and sisters, holding up another outfit.

"Have you seen this one?" she says to the others.

"Isn't that adorable!" Gina cries. The rest of them join in.

"What's goin' on here?" says Johnny, now even more confused than he was in the bookstore.

"We're looking at baby clothes," says Gina. "What did you think was going on?"

Johnny finds that he can only mumble in response. Then Teresa beckons for him to come closer.

"Johnny," she says, "don't just stand there like a *mammalucc'*. Come over and introduce yourself to a friend of mine from the salon."

Johnny doesn't budge, but his eyes dart about, scanning the room as if he's waiting for the guys from *Candid Camera* to come out. The cameramen don't show, though. Vicki puts the outfit she's holding aside and reaches out her hand to him.

"Hi," she says, beaming him a smile. "My name's Vicki."

"She teaches at the university," says Teresa.

"Hi, Vicki, I'm Johnny," he replies, taking her hand. "I sell hardware . . . and hardware."

"So I've heard."

Chapter 42

Okay, so here's how it is. You're thinking it's time to turn over a new leaf, clean the slate and start your life all over again? Well, if you want to do it right, the first thing you do is go square up things with the Big Guy, know what I mean? Once you're clear with Him, the rest's easy. That's what Johnny's hoping, at least, as he stands on the rectory's doorsteps, gazing at the doorbell. It's Wednesday night and things have been rattling around in his head since the weekend's escapades at the bookstore. He figures it's time to do something about it, but he's not sure what. This seems as good a place as any to start.

Johnny takes a deep breath and shakes out his arms like he's a basketball player getting ready to shoot a free throw. Feeling more composed, he reaches out and presses the button. A few moments later the door opens and an old lady appears on the threshold. She's a tiny woman with a sweet, serene face, but penetrating blue eyes. Her name's Maggie. I used to see her all the time whenever I stopped by. She's your typical church lady, likes to help out at the rectory whenever she can.

"Good evening," she says in this perfectly tranquil voice.

"Hi, I'm here to see Father Giuliano," says Johnny. "I need to talk with him."

Maggie nods and opens the door wider to let him step in.

Johnny follows her down a darkened hall to a small waiting room. The lights within are dimmed to a somber glow. It's a sparsely furnished room with four straight-back chairs and a small table upon which rests a copy of the Bible and the latest issue of the *Providence Visitor,* our local Catholic newspaper. The dark-paneled walls are undecorated save for a picture of Christ and a small crucifix presiding over the doorway leading to another room.

Two other people are waiting in the room. One's an attractive, stylishly dressed woman, probably in her mid-thirties; the other's a younger man of Johnny's age. Though the woman's hands are folded primly on her lap, she sits with her legs crossed in such a way as to lift the hem of her dress just enough to reveal the sleek line of her calves and just a hint of her thigh. The young man sitting next to her is rubbing his chin thoughtfully as if he's doing his best not to appear to be staring at her. Maggie gestures for Johnny to take a seat and then she beckons to the woman.

"Father will see you now," she says in the same quiet voice.

Johnny can't help himself now. As the woman stands and steps toward the door to where Father Giuliano is waiting, his eyes automatically roam up the back of her legs and across the curve of her hips as she glides away. Johnny glances at the other man, who's also admiring the view. The two of them look at one another and exchange a little nod of approval. The door closes behind the woman and the two settle back once more. Johnny slouches down and stretches his legs out straight to relax. He's not in the mood for reading the Bible or the *Visitor,* so he passes the time by staring at the floor.

"I know you," the other man says after a time.

Johnny looks up.

"How's that?"

"You're Nick Catini's son Johnny, aren't you?" says the man.

"That's right," replies Johnny. "How do you know me?"

"I've seen you around. You run the hardware place, right?"

"Yeah. Who are you?"

"Eddie Carlone."

"Eddie Carlone," says Johnny. "You related to the plaster-board man?"

"Yeah, that's *my* father. I'm Eddie Junior."

"You're Little Eddie!" laughs Johnny. "I always hear your father talking about you whenever he comes in."

"That's funny," says Eddie, "'cause your father used to always talk about *you* whenever he stopped by our place. All good stuff, of course," he adds with a smile.

"Oh yeah," snickers Johnny. "I'll bet."

"Yeah," Eddie goes on, "your old man and mine go way back. Your father was a nice guy. He used to stop by our place all the time whenever he needed tickets."

"Tickets?" says Johnny.

Eddie shrugs. "My father knows a few people around town that he scores tickets to the Civic Center from. The ones he gets that he don't want for himself, he sells." Eddie pauses and gives another shrug. "Actually, he sells just about all of them. It's a little hobby of his, if you catch my meaning."

"Geez, you know somethin'?" chuckles Johnny. "All these years, I never had any clue how my father managed to always get tickets for shows downtown whenever he wanted."

"Well, it's not exactly something that we like to advertise," says Eddie. "Know what I'm sayin'? We need to make sure that the people we sell to are—let's say, discreet. You see, when we get the tickets from—"

Johnny holds up his hand. "Stop," he says, "don't tell me where you get the tickets from. I don't wanna know."

"Okay," laughs Eddie. "No problem."

"So, your father still doin' it?" asks Johnny.

"Well—yes and no," says Eddie. "Tell you the truth, he's

plannin' on retirin' soon, so I'm kinda pickin' up the slack for him. You might say I'm keepin' the family business goin'. You know what that's all about."

"Sure do," says Johnny with a nod.

Eddie reaches into his jacket pocket and pulls out a pen and a scrap of paper. He scribbles something on the paper and hands it to Johnny. "Here's my number," he tells him. "You ever need tickets to anythin' downtown, just give me a call, I'll find you somethin'."

Johnny takes the number and tucks it in his pocket. "Thanks," he says. "I'll remember."

Eddie eases back onto the chair and folds his arms. "So, what brings you to the pain room?" he says.

"The what?"

Eddie smiles. "Obviously, you don't come here very often, do you?"

"My first time," Johnny admits. "Why do you call it the pain room?"

"That's what Father G calls it," Eddie explains. "People go in there and tell him all about what's on their minds, what's botherin' them, where they're goin' wrong in their lives, and he tries to straighten them out. You talk about this and that and all the rest and he tries to get you to stop doin' the things that are hurtin' you, you know? Like he says, you share your pain with him. It's kinda like goin' to confession, but without the box."

"Ay, I haven't been to confession since Auticott' was king," says Johnny.

"So what brings you now?"

"I dunno," sighs Johnny. "I've just had a lotta strange stuff goin' on since my father died. Things have gotten kinda weird, know what I mean? I figured talkin' to a priest might be a good idea before it gets too outta hand. What about you, what's your story?"

"Eh," grunts Eddie, "mine's not too different from yours, I figure. I stop by every now and then to see the padre. We talk for a while, I tell him what's been goin' on, he tries to straighten me out and tells me to say a few prayers, I duke him a few bucks to say a few prayers for me, and I go away. I feel better. He feels better. Then, of course, I go right out and start doin' all the same crazy shit I was doin' before. A few weeks later, I'm back in the pain room."

"Sounds kinda redundant."

"It is, when you think about it," says Eddie. "So I don't think about it. Besides, we can't all be saints. Hell, what fun would that be for God if we were, right? And think about priests like Father G. If it weren't for sinners like you and me, they'd all be out on the streets, hustlin' for a job like the rest of us, know what I mean?"

"I never thought of it that way," laughs Johnny.

Just then the door to the pain room opens and the stylishly dressed woman reappears. With her gaze averted from them, she pauses for a moment, self-consciously tugging her skirt and blouse into place before hurrying out. Eddie looks at Johnny, his eyebrows raised.

"Makes you wonder, doesn't it?" he says.

Maggie comes back into the room. "Father will see you now," she says to Eddie.

Eddie stands and gives Johnny a nod. "I'll see ya around," he says. "Gotta go talk to the man." With that, he steps into the pain room and closes the door behind him.

Alone now in the room, Johnny eases back and looks over at the picture of Jesus Christ on the opposite wall. It's that same picture of Christ's face that you always see, the one that stares at you with those haunting, haunted eyes that send shivers down your spine every time. Johnny knows that, even if he changes seats, those eyes will be following him. So he tries staring at the floor, but still he can't help looking up. Finally he lets out an exasperated sigh and stands. He walks across the room and stops in front of the picture.

"So, whatta you think?" he says to it. "Should I tell the priest everything or just keep my mouth shut? Or how 'bout this: I'll tell him what I think he needs to know and the rest we keep just between You and me for a while. That way we can figure it all out as we go along. Deal?"

No response is forthcoming, naturally, so Johnny goes back to his chair. He sits down, stretches out his legs again, and scratches his chin while he tries to decide just how much of his pain he really wants to share.

Later that night, Johnny catches up to Vinny, Al, and Tony at Haven Brothers. There's a line of people stretched out across the litter-strewn sidewalk, waiting to get up to the window to order their effs. Wrapped in her usual rags, Sally traipses about, picking up the wrappers and cups as she goes. Around the corner, leather-clad bikers sit on their motorcycles, munching away while cars roll by with stereos blasting. Johnny and the rest of his crew sit on the steps of City Hall, devouring their effs and Arizonas. They're all talking and laughing, everyone except for Tony.

"What's with you tonight?" Johnny asks him. "You've had a face on since I got here."

"Don't pay any attention to him," says Al. "He's bummin' because he can't get tickets to the show."

"What show?"

"Tony Bennett," snickers Vinny. "Can you believe it?"

"Hey, what's wrong with Tony Bennett?" grouses Tony.

"Nothin'," says Vinny, "I just happen to like music that was written before the Ice Age."

"*Ay,* whatta you know," says Tony with a wave of his hand.

"When's the show?" asks Johnny.

"Saturday night," Tony replies gloomily. "All the best seats are long gone."

Johnny rubs his chin for a second and gives him a shrug. "You know, I might know somebody who can get you some good seats."

"You serious?" says Tony, his face suddenly beaming.

"Eh, I think so," says Johnny. "No guarantees, but let me see what I can do."

Tony reaches up and gives Johnny a high five. "You duh man, J.C.," he says, all happy again, "no questions asked."

Johnny just smiles and looks up at the moon beaming down on him like a spotlight. It's a warm, breezy night, that perfect kind of spring night that lets you know that the cold weather is finally gone for good and the hard part of the year is over. Johnny settles back and drinks it all in.

After, when Johnny finally hits the sack and falls fast asleep, I decide to pay him a little visit. Johnny opens his eyes to find me sitting on the end of his bed. Behind me he sees my father and behind him another man who looks remarkably like Johnny. It suddenly dawns on him that he's looking at his great-grandfather. And behind *him* is another man, my own great-grandfather who resembles myself. The pattern's repeated in different combinations, over and over again, the line of men stretching back into infinity like a mirror reflected in a mirror.

"Come with me," I tell him, extending my hand. "Let me show you how things could be."

So the scene changes and Johnny sees himself seated at the head of the dining room table. Everyone's there at the table, all the family, and Vicki too. Around the table, children Johnny's never seen before are gleefully running about. At the far end of the table, Teresa is filling their plates, one by one, with pasta while behind her my portrait keeps watch over them all. Suddenly the whole family turns its eyes to Johnny as if they're waiting for some signal from him.

Johnny shrugs and raises his wineglass. *"Salute,"* he says simply. "Let's eat."

As he watches them happily dig into their plates, Johnny becomes aware that I'm at his side once more, even though he knows the others can't see me. I reach over to the simple arrangement of flowers adorning the center of the table.

"I appreciate these a lot more than I used to," I say, holding the flowers out to him. "You should too."

Then my son closes his eyes once more, breathing deep, letting the flowers' sweet fragrance fill him with optimism. He drifts back to sleep, happy because he knows in his heart that it's spring and things are going to be all right. Soon there'll be flowers everywhere again. Life's returning to the world, and you know, where there's life, anything is possible.

Trust me.

Epilogue

So that, my friend, is all there is to tell for now. What, you want to know more? You want all the loose ends tied up in a nice neat package? Forget it, things just don't work like that except in the movies. Besides, what fun would it be if they did? All I can tell you is to get out there and enjoy this crazy ride we call life. Hold tight to the people you love, even if it's only in your thoughts. Do that and they'll always be there for you.

You know, maybe God does have a master plan or maybe He just makes it up as He goes along. I don't know. One life's not enough to figure it all out. Who knows, maybe He lets *us* make it up as *we* go along. Either way, it doesn't really matter much, so long as He keeps all those plates spinning up there over His head. Sure, every now and then one or two of them fly off and get smashed, but there's nothing any of us can do about it, so don't worry about anything. As long as you have life and love and family and friends, you're gonna be all right.

Know what I mean?